W9-BFD-388

Praise for
the Southern Beauty Shop Mysteries

**"A CHARMING NEW SERIES."**
—*The Mystery Reader*

**"FANS OF THE THEMED COZY WILL REJOICE."**
—*Publishers Weekly* (starred review)

**"I CAN'T WAIT FOR THE NEXT BOOK!"**
—*Fresh Fiction*

# Polished Off

"Terrific . . . A fast-paced whodunit. This is a winning Georgia peach mystery." —*The Mystery Gazette*

"This first-rate mystery is well written, with smooth dialogue, plenty of action, and numerous suspects. Readers will be guessing all the way to the end as the victims pile up and the spunky and smart Grace stumbles upon a killer and a motive no one saw coming." —*RT Book Reviews*

"Lila Dare . . . once again delights her new legion of fans with a lively, hilarious mystery that will have readers biting their manicures as they try to figure out whodunit. Add in a touch of romance . . . and you've got a cozy mystery that sizzles like the Georgia heat in summer. I can't wait for the next book in this series." —*Fresh Fiction*

"So many twists and turns and side stories are sure to keep the reader engaged in an interesting whodunit. As a bonus, organic skin-care recipes are included. A fun read all-around!" —*The Romance Readers Connection*

*continued . . .*

# *Tressed to Kill*

"Fans of the themed cozy will rejoice as new talent Dare debuts her Southern Beauty Shop series . . . Dare turns this off-the-rack concept into a tightly plotted, suspenseful mystery, and readers will love the pretty, plucky, smart, slightly damaged heroine and the rest of the charming cast."
— *Publishers Weekly* (starred review)

"Humor, heart, and a first-class whodunit . . . Readers will be anxious to make the return trip to St. Elizabeth, Georgia, to check in on the adventures of the girls from Violetta's."
—Casey Daniels, author of *A Hard Day's Fright*

"*Tressed to Kill* sparkles . . . Stylish, swift-paced, and charming. An endearing heroine, delightful characters, and an authentic Southern setting."
—Carolyn Hart, author of *Dead by Midnight*

"Enticing and eccentric Southern characters combined with suspenseful tension and twists."
—Linda O. Johnston, author of *The More the Terrier*

"[A] nicely plotted and well-executed mystery. With its uniquely Southern setting and snappy characters, this mystery is an exceptionally good addition to the cozy genre."
—*Romantic Times*

"Loaded with Southern charm, Lila Dare's first mystery is full of warm, eccentric characters, and hometown warmth."
—*The Mystery Reader*

"The story will grab you, and the ending is fabulous."
—*Once Upon a Romance*

"A lot of twists and turns . . . Ms. Dare pens a winner. Don't miss *Tressed to Kill* if you love small-town mysteries with eye-opening secrets at every turn!" —*TwoLips Reviews*

*Berkley Prime Crime titles by Lila Dare*

TRESSED TO KILL
POLISHED OFF
DIE JOB

# Die Job

## LILA DARE

**BERKLEY PRIME CRIME, NEW YORK**

**THE BERKLEY PUBLISHING GROUP**
**Published by the Penguin Group**
**Penguin Group (USA) Inc.**
**375 Hudson Street, New York, New York 10014, USA**
Penguin Group (Canada), 90 Eglinton Avenue East, Suite 700, Toronto, Ontario M4P 2Y3, Canada
(a division of Pearson Penguin Canada Inc.)
Penguin Books Ltd., 80 Strand, London WC2R 0RL, England
Penguin Group Ireland, 25 St. Stephen's Green, Dublin 2, Ireland (a division of Penguin Books Ltd.)
Penguin Group (Australia), 250 Camberwell Road, Camberwell, Victoria 3124, Australia
(a division of Pearson Australia Group Pty. Ltd.)
Penguin Books India Pvt. Ltd., 11 Community Centre, Panchsheel Park, New Delhi—110 017, India
Penguin Group (NZ), 67 Apollo Drive, Rosedale, Auckland 0632, New Zealand
(a division of Pearson New Zealand Ltd.)
Penguin Books (South Africa) (Pty.) Ltd., 24 Sturdee Avenue, Rosebank, Johannesburg 2196,
South Africa

Penguin Books Ltd., Registered Offices: 80 Strand, London WC2R 0RL, England

This is a work of fiction. Names, characters, places, and incidents either are the product of the author's imagination or are used fictitiously, and any resemblance to actual persons, living or dead, business establishments, events, or locales is entirely coincidental. The publisher does not have any control over and does not assume any responsibility for author or third-party websites or their content.

DIE JOB

A Berkley Prime Crime Book / published by arrangement with the author

PRINTING HISTORY
Berkley Prime Crime mass-market edition / January 2012

Copyright © 2012 by Penguin Group (USA) Inc.
Cover illustration by Brandon Dorman.
Cover design by Annette Fiore Defex.
Interior text design by Kristin del Rosario.

All rights reserved.
No part of this book may be reproduced, scanned, or distributed in any printed or electronic form without permission. Please do not participate in or encourage piracy of copyrighted materials in violation of the author's rights. Purchase only authorized editions.
For information, address: The Berkley Publishing Group,
a division of Penguin Group (USA) Inc.,
375 Hudson Street, New York, New York 10014.

ISBN: 978-0-425-24588-0

BERKLEY® PRIME CRIME
Berkley Prime Crime Books are published by The Berkley Publishing Group,
a division of Penguin Group (USA) Inc.,
375 Hudson Street, New York, New York 10014.
BERKLEY® PRIME CRIME and the PRIME CRIME logo are trademarks of Penguin Group (USA) Inc.

PRINTED IN THE UNITED STATES OF AMERICA

10  9  8  7  6  5  4  3  2  1

If you purchased this book without a cover, you should be aware that this book is stolen property. It was reported as "unsold and destroyed" to the publisher, and neither the author nor the publisher has received any payment for this "stripped book."

*For Paige Wheeler and Michelle Vega,*
*who took a chance on me*

# [ACKNOWLEDGMENTS]

Many, many thanks to all the usual suspects—you know who you are—who sustain my spirits, support my writing life, encourage me in my writing passion, and befriend and love me through it all. I hope I do the same for you.

# Chapter One

ST. ELIZABETH SITS SMACK DAB ON THE GEORGIA coast, so when the weather forecasters start talking about a hurricane headed our way, even if it's still way out at sea, conversation at the salon tends to center on the storm. I knew from prior experience that the Piggly Wiggly shelves would be emptied by people stocking up with enough groceries to last through Armageddon; flashlights and batteries would disappear from the hardware stores; and cars, vans, and campers would clog every road as people headed inland to escape the flooding and power outages. The forecasters were saying Hurricane Horatio would probably turn north before it got to us—as most of the storms did—and come ashore somewhere in the Carolinas, so I didn't plan to panic just yet (although I might buy a box of Twinkies, using the rationale that the preservative-rich sponge cakes would outlast life as we know it, never mind a hurricane-induced power outage). I was in the minority, however, as most of the customers at Violetta's, my mom's salon, joyfully wallowed in worrying about worst-case scenarios.

"I've heard it's going to be as bad as Hurricane Floyd in 1999," one customer said.

"These late-season storms are always the worst," her husband said wisely from the waiting area, which consisted of two chintz-covered chairs, a matching love seat, and a couple of tables.

"I was in Charleston for Hugo," another woman said, "and we lost power for well over a week. This can't possibly be that bad."

"My sister's house was flattened by Andrew," an elderly woman piped up from the Nail Nook, where our manicurist, Stella Michaelson, was painting her toenails a vivid orange.

Ah, hurricane one-upmanship, a popular pastime on the coast whenever the forecasters start talking about named storms.

"I'm evacuating," a client said later that afternoon as I highlighted her hair. "Len and I are going to stay with his folks in Atlanta. I'm not living on canned ravioli like we did before we got the power back after the last storm. Although, the way his mom cooks, it's a toss-up. What are you and Violetta doing, Grace?"

"Oh, we'll ride it out," I said, carefully folding a foil around a section of hair. "This house has lasted almost two hundred years . . . I don't suppose Horatio will be able to blow it down." And my mother, Violetta Terhune, owner of the house and the salon that occupied the front rooms, wouldn't leave for anything less than a tsunami. It was like she believed her presence in the house would help it withstand wind and rain and hail and flooding.

"You're lucky," my client said. "They built to last in those days. We bought in that new area, Delta Bayou, and I swear our condo is made of plywood and tissue paper."

I made commiserating noises as I put her under the heat lamp.

As the last customer left for the day and Mom locked the door behind her, the five of us took a deep breath and relaxed, prepping our stations for the next day. I liked the salon at times like this; it felt more like a home than a business. Dust motes danced in the sunbeams angling through the wooden blinds. The comfy waiting area and the hanging ferns and potted violets clustered on the windowsills made it feel homey, as did the wide, heart-of-pine floorboards. The figurehead from the *Santa Elisabeta*, a Spanish galleon that sank off the Georgia coast in the 1500s, provided benevolent supervision from her spot on the wall behind the counter.

As I swept, our shampoo girl, seventeen-year-old Rachel Whitley, stripped off her smock, revealing her usual black attire. After a brief flirtation with being a beauty contestant this past summer, she had reverted to Goth-type clothes and ragged jet-black bangs flopped into her kohl-rimmed eyes. Her pale face with its slightly lantern-shaped jaw stood out against the black hoodie zipped up to her neck. "Guess what I'm doing tomorrow night?" she asked, her eyes sparkling with mischief. She dropped into my styling chair and spun it in circles.

"Going on a date?" Stella asked, aligning her polish bottles in the cabinet and closing it. Her white Persian, Beauty, swiped at her shoelace, and Stella shooed her away. "With that nice Braden?"

"We're just friends now," Rachel said.

I couldn't tell if she was sad or not that they weren't dating anymore.

"Studying for your AP History exam," Mom suggested teasingly. Her periwinkle blue eyes twinkled behind rimless glasses. Comfortably rounded, she had short gray and white hair she gelled into soft spikes that framed her face becomingly, giving her the look of a kind Beatrix Potter hedgehog.

"You're close," Rachel said. "I'm going on a ghosthunting field trip with my science class!"

Oh, yeah, that sounded educational. What was on the schedule for next week—a monster-hunting trip to Loch Ness? A snowshoe adventure to find the Abominable Snowman?

"You're going on a field trip to do *what*?" Althea Jenkins, our part-time aesthetician, asked. Her brows crinkled her chocolate-colored skin clear up to the hairline of her short, gray-flecked afro.

"Ghost hunting. Debunking, really," Rachel said, a huge grin splitting her face. "But we need another chaperone," she said, pleading with Mom with her Nile green eyes. "My mother was going to go, but her boss got, like, sick and is sending Mom to a convention in Lexington this weekend in his place, so we need to find someone else to chaperone or we won't be able to go."

"In my day," Althea said, putting avocado, olive oil, and a handful of herbs in a stainless steel bowl for a new moisturizer she wanted to try, "we read *King Lear* and did algebraic equations and dissected frogs in school. We didn't go gallivanting about the countryside, chasing after spirits. Fah!" She shook her head, more bemused than angry. A tall woman about my mom's age, she wore a red tunic over black jeans. She pushed the tunic's sleeves up before mashing her ingredients with a pestle.

"Where are you going to do your, um, debunking?" Mom asked, plopping combs into the jar of blue germicide at her station.

"Rothmere," Rachel said. Forearms on her thighs, she leaned toward Mom. "There's this absolutely awesome ghost out there, Cyril Rothmere, who haunts the house looking for his murderer! Dozens of people have seen him over the years and, like, the Discovery Channel did a special on him a few years back. How cool is that?"

"Pretty cool," Mom said solemnly. "I can't think of anything I'd rather do on a Saturday night than go ghost hunting with your class, Rachel," she said, "but Walter's got tickets to *Wicked* in Jacksonville and we're headed down there right after my last client."

Rachel swiveled in the styling chair and opened her mouth.

"Don't look at me," Althea cut her off, holding up an avocado-gooped hand. "Kwasi and I have plans."

"Grace?" Rachel turned to me. "Please?" She drew the word out into three syllables and clasped her hands together prayerfully.

Why was I the only one in the room without plans for a Saturday night? Mom and Althea, both widowed and sixty, had boyfriends and were headed out for wild nights on the town. Okay, maybe "wild" was an overstatement, but at least they were going out. My sort-of boyfriend, political reporter Marty Shears, had moved from Atlanta to DC two months ago for a new job with the *Washington Post*, leaving my weekends pretty darn empty. So, at thirty, and divorced for a year, I had rented a Julia Roberts DVD for the evening's entertainment and was considering purchasing a pint of Chunky Monkey to add to the festivities. If I really

wanted to peg the excitement meter, I would study the
MLS listings my new Realtor had given me and decide
which houses I wanted to view, even though, if the last few
months of house hunting were any indicator, none of them
would work for me. My friend Vonda said that was because
I wasn't sure about settling in St. Elizabeth, but that's just
silly. Other than my two years at UGA and my time in Atlanta with Hank, I'd lived in St. Elizabeth all my life. Marty
*had* mentioned it would be easy for me to get stylist work
in DC, but that hardly constituted a proposal, and our four
months of weekend dating—Atlanta was a half-day drive—
didn't justify a cross-country move. Maybe I'd really like
DC, though, when I visited Marty next weekend . . . I
shook off my thoughts.

"Oh, all right," I told Rachel. "I suppose I can cancel my
plans and go ghost hunting." I tried to make it sound like I
was passing up the opportunity to attend an inaugural ball.
Althea's snort of laughter told me I hadn't succeeded.

Rachel squealed and threw her arms around me. "Thank
you, thank you, Grace! It'll be a blast."


NOT KNOWING EXACTLY WHAT TO EXPECT FROM A
ghost-hunting field trip, and not having plans for tonight,
either—I needed to get a life, as Vonda was always
saying—I drove out to Rothmere half an hour later to
get the lay of the land. Remembering field trip high jinks
during my senior year, not all *that* long ago, I wanted
to be one step ahead of the teenagers I was going to be
responsible for.

St. Elizabeth sits in the crook of a backward L bordered
by the St. Andrew Sound to the east and by the Satilla River
to the north. Being surrounded by all that water is partly

why St. Elizabethans get all worried about hurricanes; it's the flooding more than the winds that we fear. Rothmere lies west of town, up the long arm of the L, and its acreage slopes down to the Satilla. The pure, white lines of the Greek revival building stood out against the cornflower blue of the sky—you'd never know there was a hurricane brewing—and the columns glistened as the sun's slanting rays gilded them. Venerable magnolia and pecan trees provided pools of shade suitable for Southern belles to hold court in with their beaux gathered around, a la Scarlett O'Hara.

Conscious that it was near closing time, I parked beside the aging Audi in the lot and trotted up the wide stone steps to the portico. Double doors of carved oak swung inward at a touch. A fiftyish woman with a long nose and protuberant eyes glided forward, her mid-1800s skirt swishing. The long-sleeved maroon dress with its tight bodice emphasized her stocky waist, but the sway of the skirt made her look graceful. A lacy white cap half covered frizzy brown hair pulled back into a bun. "Welcome to Rothmere," she proclaimed.

"Hi, Lucy," I said.

"Oh, it's you." A sour expression erased the gracious Southern hostess look she'd been wearing. Edging me out of the way, she stepped onto the portico, pulled the massive door closed, inserted a modern key into the lock, and shot the deadbolt home. She turned to face me, crossing her arms over her chest.

I must have missed the lesson on hospitality that included locking guests out. "Nice to see you, too."

"I'm closing up. What do you want?"

"Information."

"Come back tomorrow."

"Cyril Rothmere. Do you know anything about him?"

"Of course." She looked incensed. "I'm the country's premier expert on all things Rothmere."

Like there were dozens of historians competing for that title. "So, what can you tell me?"

"I'm busy."

"Lucy! I'm chaperoning the high schoolers coming for the field trip tomorrow and I want to know at least as much as they do." Lucy had been snippy with me ever since May when I'd discovered she was "borrowing" jewelry and other mementoes that had belonged to the Rothmere clan for her own use. She'd returned the items when I encouraged her to, but she hadn't been in for a haircut since.

"They shouldn't be coming. I told the board of directors it was a bad idea to let teenage hooligans run wild in the mansion—chasing ghosts, of all things—but one of the board members is also the PTO president and she talked them into it. Nothing good can come of it." She made it sound like the board of directors had authorized the students to hold a rave in the ballroom. "They have no respect for the fact that Rothmere is a family's *home*."

"But the family members are all dead."

"I beg your pardon?" Her protuberant eyes widened.

Ye gods. She was in full "Amelia" mode. I wasn't sure if she sometimes thought she *was* Amelia Rothmere, chatelaine of the plantation during the Civil War years, or just a descendant, even though, as far as I knew, not a drop of Rothmere blood ran in her veins. Either way, I didn't want to pursue it. "I understand the Discovery Channel did a special on antebellum ghosts a while back."

"I was the technical consultant." She preened.

It crossed my mind that Lucy probably didn't get a lot of

appreciation for what she did. "I'm sure you gave them excellent information. Any chance I could borrow a tape of the show?"

She heaved a put-upon sigh. "You might as well come with me. I was about to close up the museum. I'm writing a paper, you know, on the impact the local button factory had on the post-war economy. I'm on a panel at the Business History Conference, and I've got to get it done by the end of the weekend. So I don't have time to give you a tour now."

Finally! Someone whose social life was more stunted than mine. A Julia Roberts DVD was several rungs up the ladder from buttons. Maybe I should try one of those online dating services. I grinned to myself at what Mom's reaction would be if I told her I was even considering hooking up with someone from cyberspace.

Twenty yards brought us to the old carriage house, now a museum. It smelled a bit musty inside and I wondered if bits of hay from the days of horse-drawn carriages or motor oil from when the building served as a garage were trapped under the flooring. The long, narrow room held displays highlighting aspects of plantation life, mementoes in glass-topped cases, and a glossy carriage in one corner with a sign identifying it as a barouche. Long-dead Rothmeres gazed placidly or sneered down their noses from portraits on the walls. A round portrait of Amelia Rothmere, her hair a richer brown than Lucy's and her chin a bit more prominent, but otherwise enough like Lucy to be her sister, smiled closemouthed from behind a wooden counter. Maybe she had bad teeth. The room smelled faintly of mint and I finally decided it came from the china cup on the counter with a teabag hanging out of it.

"I've told the docents time and again to clean up after themselves," Lucy said with exasperation, picking up the cup and heading for a small storeroom at the rear of the museum. I trailed her.

We passed a display case filled with 3D art of some kind, featuring framed scenes and jewelry woven out of twisted fibers.

"What are those?"

"Funerary hair art," Lucy said matter-of-factly. "It was fairly common to use hair from a deceased loved one to make these remembrances: rings, brooches, even bonnets."

"Really?" I peered at the labeled pieces, not sure if the idea grossed me out or intrigued me. One ornate still life of flowers made with gray strands threaded through a rich brown was labeled "Cyril Rothmere." Another, blonder piece that looked like a brooch read, "Reginald Rothmere." I didn't have time to study them all as Lucy unlocked the storeroom door.

A sink and microwave occupied one corner. Shelves crowded with books and boxes lined the walls, and a small worktable occupied the room's center, with only a foot-wide alley between it and the shelves.

"Was Cyril really murdered?" I asked as Lucy clattered the cup and saucer into the sink.

"His death is one of the plantation's great mysteries," she said, pulling a VCR tape off a bookshelf and handing it to me. "A house slave found him dead at the foot of the stairs one morning. The official verdict was accidental death, partly, I suspect, because he was known to like his brandy and it makes sense that he imbibed too freely and fell. Or maybe . . ."

"How do you know all this?" I asked when she didn't

continue. "About the house slave finding him and the brandy?"

"I'm a PhD historian," she said, puffing her chest out. "There are primary sources—letters, journals, household accounts, newspaper reports, personal artifacts, portraits—that allow the trained historian to put the pieces of the past together like a puzzle."

I'd bet the whole day's tips that she'd used that line before.

"In fact," Lucy went on, "I just got a box of documents from Cyril's time. Well, they were willed to the Rothmere Trust by a descendant who died in California. Can you believe she kept them in her attic all these years without proper environmental controls for temperature and humidity? Criminal!" She shook her head, freeing a wisp of hair to tickle her cheek. "I only wish I had time to catalog them now, but I've got to get my paper done."

"Do you think I could look at them?" I asked, surprising myself and, from the look on her face, Lucy.

"You?" Lucy asked doubtfully. The way she studied me made me think she was going to demand fingerprints and a background check. "I don't see why not," she said finally. "I went through them quickly and there's nothing of monetary value, like a letter from President Davis or one of the Confederate Army's heroes. Maybe you'll get interested enough in the family to want to become a docent." Her eyes brightened at the thought.

"Maybe," I agreed. Not. At the University of Georgia, I'd taken more business and music classes than history or sociology.

Bending, Lucy dragged a cardboard box a little larger than a case of wine from under the table. She hefted it with a grunt and handed it to me. "Don't eat or drink anything while reading these," she cautioned, "and wear gloves so the oils on your hands don't damage anything, and—"

"I'll take good care of them," I promised, heading for the door before she could change her mind.

The carton cut into the flesh of my upper arms as I lugged it to the car, and I wondered what there was in this small box of history to make it so heavy.

# Chapter Two

✂

[Saturday]

*October 12, 1831*

*My dear Felicity,*

*I write briefly but you will forgive me when I tell you I
have sad news to impart: my papa died last night. I have
written you over the past months, telling you of his dys-
pepsia, but that had seemed better in recent days, and it
was not that which took him from us. One of our maids,
young Matilda, found him at the foot of the stairs at
dawn this morning, lifeless. She set up such a screech I
thought the house must be afire. I know not what to
think. Surely it must be an accident, and yet I have such
a feeling of foreboding. I cannot confide in my mother*

*or my brothers. I hesitate to relate my fears even to my
beloved Quentin. I beg that you will come for the funeral and give me the benefit of your counsel.*

*In haste and with love,
Clarissa*

"WHAT DO YOU THINK OF THAT?" I ASKED MOM AND
Althea as we prepped the salon for opening early Saturday
morning. I looked at them over the letter, the first one I'd
pulled from the box Lucy had loaned me the previous
night. I couldn't get the VCR tape to play—my machine
was on the fritz—so I'd started on the box of documents. I
slipped it back into the manila envelope I'd used to protect
it. Although the paper was thicker than I thought it would
be, it had yellowed and the brownish ink had faded.

"It's fascinating, isn't it?" Mom said. "Getting a glimpse
into history like that. I feel sorry for poor Clarissa and she's
been dead for more than a hundred years most likely. How
terrible to lose her father so suddenly."

I nodded, a lump rising in my throat. I'd felt an immediate bond of fatherlessness with Clarissa. My own father
had died of pancreatic cancer when I was under five, and I
had few memories of him. At least Clarissa had her papa
until adulthood. "I meant to read more letters last night," I
said, "but I fell asleep."

"I'll bet that Matilda she mentions was my great-great-
something-granny," Althea put in, coming over for a look
at the letter.

"Your great-grandmother was a slave at Rothmere?" I
asked. "How come I didn't know that?"

Althea shrugged. "I didn't know it myself until Kwasi and
I did some genealogical research a couple months back."

Wooden bangles clacked on her wrist as she pulled the letter gently from the envelope, read it, and handed it back.

Kwasi Yarrow was a professor of multicultural studies at Georgia Coastal College and Althea's boyfriend. She'd experimented with finding her African heritage at his urging, and although she ended up explaining to him that her roots were in south Georgia and she returned to First Baptist after attending his African Methodist Episcopal church for a month, she retained some of her traditional African fashions and accessories, saying they "suited her."

"You're not surprised that I come from slave stock, are you?" she said, jutting her chin out.

"Of course I'm surprised," Mom said, running a dust cloth over the wooden blinds. "Any slave that gave her master the kind of lip you give everyone from clients to friends would probably have been sold to some unsuspecting owner out of state."

"Hah!" Althea laughed. She tapped on the lid of the Mr. Coffee to encourage it to brew quicker. "You're probably right about that. We Jenkinses are known for speaking our minds. Kwasi and I couldn't find out a lot about Matilda, but it seems she got her freedom and lived to be a hundred and two."

"Good for her," I said, putting the letter in my purse and accepting a mug of coffee from Althea.

"If you come across any more references to Matilda, I'd be interested in seeing them, Grace," Althea said.

"I'll let you know," I promised.

THE DAY PASSED QUICKLY IN A BLUR OF CUTTING AND coloring and highlighting. Once again, conversation revolved around Horatio, which was still on course to

hit the Georgia coast by Wednesday night. People who
weren't fussing about the hurricane were talking about
their Halloween costumes for trick-or-treating Sunday
night. Mom and Walter left for Jacksonville, Althea cleared
out an hour early to meet Kwasi, and after I closed up
the salon, I walked the six blocks from my apartment to
the high school to catch the bus as dusk was falling. A
bat flapped past just overhead and I wished her luck with
catching a mosquito dinner. The sky was still relatively
clear, but it felt like the pressure had dropped a bit and
a headache niggled at the back of my skull. It grew more
forceful as I took in the students milling about the yellow
bus in the parking lot, several of the boys tossing a football
around and other students chatting in clumps of three or
four. Rachel broke away from one of the groups when she
caught sight of me.

She grabbed my forearm. "Grace! We've just had the
most, like, splendiferous idea. The student council"—she
nodded toward the group she'd been talking to—"has been
trying to come up with a fund-raiser idea for the Winter
Ball. Ari suggested we do one of those head-shaving things;
you know, where people contribute money to get certain
teachers or popular kids to shave their heads. And then I
said we could, like, contribute the hair to Locks of Love,
and everyone was, like, 'Yeah!'" She looked at me expec-
tantly.

"Sounds like a good cause," I said, looking around for
the science teacher who was supposed to be in charge of
tonight's outing.

"Great! Then you'll do it?"

I looked at her eager face. "Do what?"

"Come to the school and shave the heads of the kids
who 'win' and cut girls' hair for Locks of Love. Ari looked

it up on her iPhone and you have to have at least ten inches of hair, so I s'pose it'll mostly be girls doing the Locks of Love thing."

It *was* a good cause—Locks of Love makes wigs for children who lose their hair to cancer treatments or other causes—and I didn't mind helping out. "Sure," I said. "I could leave the salon a little early and come to the school. And I can mail the hair to Locks of Love; I've cut hair for them before."

"Great! We'll set it up so we can do it every day this week—maybe over lunch or during last period. I don't know how we'll do the voting, yet . . ." She bounced back to her student council buddies and they began to argue about how to talk kids into participating.

"You must be Rachel's friend," a voice said from behind me.

I turned to see a soap opera–handsome man holding out his hand. Soot-colored lashes and brows made a striking contrast to ice blue eyes that glinted in a way that would have gotten him cast as the guy with just enough bad boy in him to be interesting. He had the kind of full, shapely lips that combined sensitivity with sexy, and smallish ears set close to his head. Strands of silver in his collar-grazing dark hair and crow's feet put him in his late thirties, I guessed. "Grace Terhune," I said, liking his firm grip as we shook hands.

"Glen Spaatz. Science teacher and amateur ghost-buster." He had a dazzling smile that produced a sexy dimple on his right cheek. "Ready?"

"As I'll ever be."

He gestured me toward the bus with a courtly gesture and I climbed the steps with their ridged rubber matting, feeling like I was stepping into a time machine. Letting my hand slap against each seat as I passed, I settled in by a window three-quarters of the way back, just like in high school. The teens filed on, laughing and joking, slinging their backpacks onto the bench seats. Rachel waved to me from her seat near the front, then scooted over as Braden McCullers, her former main squeeze, slid onto the seat. They immediately fell into conversation, her dark head close to his blond one.

"Is this seat taken?" Before I could answer, a short woman with dark hair pulled into a low ponytail so it emphasized her widow's peak sat down, jeans stretching over stocky thighs. "I'm Tasha Solomon." She offered her hand across her body and we shook awkwardly. She smiled, revealing straight teeth with the yellowy gray of tetracycline staining near the roots. "That's my daughter, Ari." She pointed with her chin to a plump, auburn-haired girl seated three rows ahead and studiously avoiding her mother's eyes. "It's really Ruth-Ellen, but she's been going by RE—Ari, get it?—since she started high school. Heaven forbid that I sit with her!" She rolled her eyes as if amused, but I caught a hint of hurt in the way she studied her daughter's back.

"No teenager would be caught dead with a parent at a school function," I said, remembering my own feelings the time my mother had volunteered to chaperone a Sadie Hawkins dance my sophomore year. I'd told her she might as well stab me through the heart since my social life was over. At least she'd had the decency not to actually *dance* like one of the chaperone moms had.

"Oh, I know," Tasha said, waving a would-be casual hand. "Which one is yours?"

"Pardon?"

"Which kid?"

Ye gods. Did she actually think I looked old enough to have a high schooler? "None of them," I said through gritted teeth. "Rachel Whitley is a friend."

"Oh, nice girl," she said. Her gaze followed a pair of youths in letter jackets as they made loud, fist-bumping progress toward the back row. "Those boys look like trouble with a capital T," she said in a low voice. "That Lonnie Farber asked Ari out once, but her father and I put a quick end to that. He's headed to no good end. His brother's actually in *prison*."

The kid she indicated was a six-foot-four African American teen, lithe and muscular, with a cocky air and short dreadlocks draping across his forehead. The bus lurched forward, but he swayed with the motion, settling his backpack between his feet as he sat. The bus trundled out of the lot and picked up speed.

Lonnie Farber didn't look like an immediate threat, and I turned back around as Tasha said, "My husband was against this field trip from the moment Ari mentioned it, but I'm trying to be open-minded. I am a scientist, after all." She paused a brief moment so I could ask about her career but continued when I stayed silent. "The ghost-hunting shtick might be a bit unorthodox, I told Aaron, but I'm sure there's no harm in it."

"How could there be?" I agreed.


THE STUDENTS STAMPEDED OUT OF THE BUS WHEN we reached the plantation. I followed more slowly with Tasha Solomon and Wally Peet, the high school football coach who'd also been a PE teacher when I was in high school. I couldn't figure out if he was there because he was doing Spaatz a favor or because he wanted to keep an eye on some of his players. Several of the boys wore football letter jackets, including the three from the bus's back row, plus Braden McCullers and a couple of others.

The Satilla River flowed past the plantation down beyond the cemetery, and although I couldn't see it, I could smell the wetness in the air. Spanish moss dripped from many of the trees, swaying with the breeze. I had to admit it was an atmospheric setting; if I were a ghost, I'd have hung out here. Five jack-o'-lanterns glowed from the wide Rothmere veranda; with a start, I realized Sunday was Halloween. Why had Spaatz planned the ghost-hunting trip for the night before Halloween? Surely he knew the teens would find it impossible to resist a Halloween prank or two.

"Isn't this fun?" Rachel skipped up beside me, accompanied by Braden McCullers.

A good-looking blond kid, he smiled at me and said, "Hi, Miss Terhune. Thanks for coming." They seemed easy in each other's company as Rachel linked her arm through his and drew him up to the front of the group.

"About as much fun as a root canal," Coach Peet muttered from my left, having overheard Rachel's question. A fiftyish man no taller than five-ten, he looked more like a long-distance runner than a football player. He had a tonsure of gray-tinged brown hair growing around a shiny bald spot and a beak of a nose; combined, the hair and nose made him look a bit like a condor.

"You got drafted, too?" I laughed, holding out my hand. "Grace Terhune. I let Rachel Whitley talk me into this."

"Hunh," he said, ignoring my hand. Hunching his shoulders, he quickened his pace until he was three or four strides in front of me and I was staring at his back.

I let my hand drop, stunned by his boorishness. Not exactly Mr. Friendly.

"Don't mind him," a voice said from behind me.

I looked over my shoulder and Glen Spaatz fell into step beside me, his long stride making me pick up my pace.

"He's like this every year during the season. Two of his star players got ruled ineligible last year after a DUI and a vandalism charge—separate incidents, both Halloween weekend—and he's trying to keep it from happening again. He's a really friendly guy after the playoffs."

Yeah, sure. I didn't trust people who were Dr. Jekyll one moment and Mr. Hyde the next.

Flashing another killer smile, he sped up to reach the veranda ahead of the students. He held up a hand to halt their progress just as one of the wide double doors swung open, spilling light into the gathering dusk.

Lucy Mortimer stood in the doorway. Tonight's dress was blue and topped with an apron. A velvet band with a cameo circled her freckled neck. "I guess you'd better come in," she said. Clearly, the teenagers didn't merit her "lady of the manor" routine.

We all fit easily into Rothmere's foyer. My whole apartment would have fit. With original wood floors, deep baseboards and crown molding, a crystal and porcelain chandelier now wired for electricity, a sprinkling of oil-painted family portraits, and a grand staircase wide enough to let at least two Southern belles in hoop skirts descend side by side, the foyer made a strong first impression. "Wow," and, "Dig that chandelier," came from the students seeing the place for the first time.

"I understand from Mr. Spaatz that you're hoping to encounter Cyril tonight," Lucy said, motioning to us to gather under the chandelier, "so let me tell you his story." She spoke in a low, husky voice, and everyone leaned forward to hear her. "Cyril Rothmere came to Georgia from Yorkshire, England, in 1796 when he was twenty-five. Old letters suggest that he was banished by his family for ruinous gambling debts and he came to America to seek his fortune. He had a knack for farming, and once he acquired some land—winning it in a card game, ironically—he built a house and turned his plantation into the most successful one in southeastern Georgia. In 1801, he met a woman named Annabelle Latham and she broke her engagement to a neighboring landowner to marry Cyril."

"The money-grubbing witch," someone muttered under his voice.

Lucy backed up toward one of the portraits on the wall. "This is Cyril," she said.

Everyone crowded around the portrait of a middle-aged man with a ruddy face, thick brown hair with wooly looking sideburns, and an air of consequence. He stood beside a horse with a hound fawning in the foreground. Rothmere graced the background.

"He's nearly as ugly as you, Lonnie," someone quipped.

Lonnie Farber gave the speaker the finger.

Lucy ignored the byplay; it was probably no more than she expected. "Cyril had this mansion built when the previous house burnt to the ground. Some say the blaze was arson, set by the neighbor who had also courted Annabelle. However it started, the fire consumed the entire house and everything in it, and Cyril started from scratch when he rebuilt. Follow me."

Lucy, obviously in her element talking about "her" family, unhooked the velvet rope which kept the second story off-limits. Although the rooms on the ground floor had been refinished, funding had run out and the upstairs bedrooms remained pretty much as they'd been when Phineas Rothmere willed the place to the city in the 1950s and were off-limits to the public. Explaining this, Lucy led us up two flights of stairs with a half landing where they turned. I was a step below Braden and another kid in a letter jacket and crew cut. Braden leaned toward the other guy and said in a low voice, "Don't do it, man."

Oh, great. What kind of prank was brewing? I hoped it didn't involve alcohol, nudity, or combustibles of any kind.

"Mark—" Braden started.

The crew-cut kid shook his head and called, "Wait up, Lindsay." Taking the stairs two at a time, he caught up with a tall brunette. He put his arm around her waist and she snuggled up against him. Braden's shoulders slumped as he watched the pair.

Lucy paused in a gallery that overlooked the ballroom. A collection of portraits hung on the walls, barely visible in the dusky gloom. "Stay away from the railing," Lucy cautioned. "It's why we can't allow visitors up here. We're in the process of moving the family portraits to the museum."

When she flicked a light switch, I could see lighter patches on the walls where paintings had hung.

"But Cyril's family is still here," Lucy said.

Cyril and an anemic-looking blonde I took to be Annabelle were seated in the middle of a large family that included four sons and three daughters. I edged closer to the painting she pointed at and tried to figure out which of the three young ladies posed in hoop skirts and ringlets was Clarissa. I decided she was the youngest, a sweet-faced girl of maybe sixteen, with chestnut curls, a pale complexion, and a shy smile. I could see her writing the letter I'd read last night.

"Rothmere was the largest plantation home for miles around when it was finished in 1831," Lucy continued, "and Cyril and Annabelle hosted a huge engagement party for their daughter Clarissa shortly after it was completed."

"When do we get to the ghost?"

It was the tall girl Mark had his arm around, Lindsay. Spaatz frowned her down.

Lucy led us back the way we'd come, her skirt swaying as she descended the stairs, one slow step at a time. "There was a huge storm that night, and many of the guests who weren't staying over left early. That may explain why nobody heard it."

"Heard what?" a breathless voice asked.

"Cyril's fall," Lucy said. She stepped off the final stair and looked up at us. "In the morning, a maid found him, dead." She paused to let us absorb the image. Then, with a *shush* of heavy skirts, she turned and gestured to the floor at the base of the stairs. "His neck was broken."

Students jostled for position on the stairs and someone bumped me, hard. I teetered on the edge of the step, unable to grab the banister because of people on either side of me. As I toppled forward, Glen Spaatz hauled me back with an iron hand around my upper arm and turned to glare at the teens behind us. He gave my arm a reassuring squeeze before letting go.

"Was Cyril murdered?" This came from Tasha Solomon, her brow creased with concern.

We all made it down the stairs alive and circled Lucy. "No one knows," she admitted. "What we do know is that Annabelle remarried as soon as her year of mourning was up. She married the neighbor she'd been engaged to when she met Cyril. And Cyril's eldest son, Geoffrey, inherited the plantation just in time for his last son to be born here. Rumor has it the inheritance was timely because his business in Savannah was failing and they were about to lose their house.

"Cyril's buried in the cemetery out back, but many of the sightings of his ghost have been in the house, including on the landing, the spot from which he fell . . . or was pushed."

Ari Solomon and I spoke up simultaneously. "What happened to Clarissa?" I asked.

"Have you ever seen him, Dr. Mortimer?" the redhead asked. "Cyril's ghost, I mean?"

Lucy hesitated. Her fingers strayed to the cameo at her throat. "I'm not the fanciful type." Clearing her throat, she said, "I'll be in my office. Remember, I'm locking up at ten o'clock sharp." She turned on her heel and bustled off down the left-leading hallway.

"Thank you, Dr. Mortimer," Spaatz called after her. He took her place in front of the semicircle of engrossed high schoolers, some of whom carried weird electronic gadgets about the size and shape of a GPS.

"Okay," Spaatz continued. "Find your partner and I'll let you know where you're stationed for the evening." He waved a clipboard with a sheaf of papers on it. "Take baseline EMF and temperature readings as soon as you get to your observation point. Cell phones will screw up the readings, so everyone dump your phones in here." He held up a plastic tub.

"The lights will be off to make it easier for Cyril to manifest, if he wants to," Spaatz said. "Use your red light flashlights if necessary. Any questions?"

"Where do you want the chaperones?" I asked. "And what's EMF?"

Spaatz smiled. "Good questions. EMF is electromagnetic field. Our Mel 8704s"—he held up the GPS-like gadget—"read fluctuations in the EMF. Without getting too technical, certain readings that can't be correlated to household electronics like microwave ovens or TVs suggest the presence of a spirit. Or, at least that's what ghost believers maintain. Got it?"

Sure, I was ready to do a dissertation on the subject. I shrugged and he grinned.

"As to where the chaperones should hang out, you're floaters—no pun intended. Just wander between the positions where our researchers"—he gestured to the kids—"are stationed. I've got flashlights and a diagram for each of you."

Coach Peet stomped forward, taking the sheet that Spaatz handed him. The kids lined up to get their stations from Spaatz. I noticed Rachel was paired with Braden, and Mark and the tall brunette stuck together. I wondered uneasily if boy-girl pairings would lead to . . . indiscretions (as Mom would put it) in a darkened house.

"We're on the landing," Lonnie Farber's buddy crowed. "We're gonna be in on the action." The two youths bumped fists.

"'I ain't afraid of no ghosts,'" Lonnie sang in a tuneful baritone.

Spaatz frowned. "Lonnie, Tyler, this isn't a game. It's a legitimate science experiment. Take it seriously, or take a hike."

When Spaatz turned away, Lonnie cut a sly glance at his buddy. I knew they were planning something, probably some prank that would make me sorry I had agreed to chaperone. Lonnie caught me staring at him, and instead of looking away like I thought he would, he winked.

It was going to be a long night.

# Chapter Three

TRAIPSING AROUND THE OLD MANSION IN THE NEAR total dark was slightly unnerving, even though, like Lucy, I didn't believe in ghosts. Frankly, the thought of what some of the high schoolers might get up to scared me a lot more than the prospect of an encounter with Cyril. In the hour I'd been "floating," I'd caught one couple necking, found one pair snoozing, discovered one pair missing from their assigned spot, smelled beer on one boy's breath, and hadn't run into any of the other chaperones. Just outside the ballroom, I stopped to get my bearings. A film of moonlight made a path across the polished wood floor to the French doors that opened onto a raised stone terrazzo. A breath of a breeze stirred the hair at my temples and I frowned. One of the doors must be open. As I crossed the floor, faint giggles sounded from my left and someone hissed, "Sssh."

I was halfway across the floor to investigate the giggles

when a hideous wailing moan stopped me. Ye gods! The giggles turned to shrieks.

"What was that?" a girl's voice asked.

I didn't answer because I was across the room, trotting toward the front hall where I thought the sound had come from. Another moan rose to a screech and died away, sending shivers down my spine. I skidded into the front hall to see fog spilling off the landing and wafting down the staircase. I gasped. Dimly aware of a couple of other people gathered in the darkness of the hall, I kept my gaze riveted to the landing.

Another eerie scream rent the air and I clapped my hands to my ears. Even before it died away, a white form rose from the mist and staggered along the landing. Hm, weren't ghosts supposed to glide or flit? This one moved more like Frankenstein's monster. My suspicions aroused— not that I'd ever thought there was really a ghost—I started for the stairs.

"Is someone recording this?" a voice whispered.

I had just reached the landing when Spaatz's voice asked, "What the hell is going on here?"

Three or four voices answered him, saying "The ghost!" "Did you hear that scream?" and "Cyril's up there."

My eyes adjusting to the dimness, I took in Tyler crouched by a machine spilling fog into the hallway, a boom box that emitted another loud shriek as I moved toward it, and a tall figure in white ducking into the nearest bedroom.

I ran after the "ghost" as it made for the window, the floor boards shuddering with its heavy steps. Not very wraithlike. It slung a leg over the sill and I lunged. My fingers brushed what felt like cotton. Definitely not ectoplasm or slime or whatever spirits were supposed to be made of. I stuck my head out the window. At the back of the house, the room faced the garden and cemetery. The roof sloped gradually beneath the window and a heavy drainpipe three feet to the left would provide a reasonably strong and agile teen with all the help he needed in shinnying to the ground. I looked out across the landscape. Heavy clouds blotted out the moon and stars, but I could vaguely make out a dark form sprinting toward the cemetery. He—I was darn sure it was Lonnie—must have shucked the sheet in order to run faster.

I had no chance of catching Lonnie, even if I'd been willing to risk climbing out on the roof, so I pulled my head in and returned to the landing. Spaatz had joined Tyler and one of them had shut off the boom box. Thank goodness. The eerie wailing was giving me a headache. I hoped the pranksters hadn't tortured cats to record such hideous yowling.

"Did you catch Cyril?" Tyler asked when I reappeared. He was shorter than Lonnie but bulky through the shoulders, and had straight black hair and a few acne scars low on his cheeks. His look of affected innocence made me want to smack him.

"Hardly," I said in as damping a tone as I could manage with my breaths coming a bit faster than usual and my heart pounding extra hard in my chest. From running up the stairs, of course. "And I didn't catch Lonnie, either. He was headed for the cemetery last I saw him."

"Where else would you expect a ghost to go?" Tyler asked with a smart-ass grin.

Tyler's smirk vanished when Spaatz grabbed him by the upper arm. He quickly let go as visions of lawsuits, I assumed, raced through his head. He folded his lips together, as if to keep hasty words from spewing out, took a deep breath, and said, "I've taught sixth graders with more sense." His gaze raked Tyler.

"Hey, it was just—"

Spaatz cut him off with a sharp movement of his hand. "Where's Coach Peet? I hope he's not counting on having you buffoons in the starting lineup next Friday."

The front door cracked open, letting in a gust of wind and a scattering of dead leaves. Everyone's heads swiveled and a couple of people flinched as the door gaped wider. Coach Peet stepped in. He glanced around at the crowd, his brows drawing together over his beaky nose.

"Wally." Spaatz spoke from the landing, bringing Peet's head up. "Take this miserable prankster and park him on the bus." He gave Tyler a light shove toward the stairs. "Then go find his partner in crime and lock him up, too. He was last seen heading for the cemetery."

"What happened? Tyler, get—I want to know—" The coach broke off and settled for glaring as Tyler clomped down the stairs. Coach Peet held the door wide and gestured the youth out. He followed, slamming the door so the portraits on the walls shook.

The fog machine was still spewing and I bent to turn it off as the kids dispersed again. The boys' flattened backpacks lay beside the machine.

"Are all your classes this exciting?" I asked Spaatz, trying to lighten the mood.

"Fortunately, no. Mostly it's just dry old stuff out of the textbook. Boring."

"Somehow, I doubt that," I said. I was sure the high school girls, at least, weren't bored in his class.

His smile reached his eyes this time and he studied me with awakening interest.

"Hey, Mr. Spaatz, can we be on the landing now?" Rachel called from the foot of the stairs.

Spaatz shook his head. "No, I think we'll leave the land-

ing open. After all this activity, I can't imagine old Cyril
would want to show up here."

RESIDUAL ADRENALINE FROM MY GHOST CHASE HAD
me hyped up and I decided to check on the students posted
in the outbuildings, including the kitchen, stable, and
carriage house museum. The fresh air felt cool against
my heated skin, and I dawdled along the oyster shell path
hooking the buildings together. An owl *whoo-whoo*ed from
a stand of trees to my left and I looked for her but couldn't
spot her. Three or four minutes spent with the pairs in
the outbuildings convinced me that not even a science
experiment involving ghost hunting could hold students'
attention forever. The kids in the museum were still zealous
about the mission, recording readings from their EMF
monitors every few minutes, but the other students seemed
bored and ready to call it quits.

Reminding the girls in the kitchen that there was only
fifteen minutes to go, I headed back outside. The air seemed
heavier, pressing on my skin in a palpable way. Or maybe
it was just my mood. Lonnie and Tyler's escapade had left
me unsettled and I was wishing I'd stayed home with Julia
Roberts. I had almost reached the front door of the mansion
when a loud explosion made me jump. What in the
world—? A *shreee* split the night and then a burst of green
and gold broke over the cemetery, showering the darkness
with colored light. I laughed with relief. Fireworks. Someone was shooting off fireworks. My money was on the erst-
while ghost, Lonnie.

I jogged toward the cemetery—forgetting that I hated
the place after being knocked into an open grave last
May—as another two rockets went off with ear-jarring

bangs. From the front of the house, the cemetery was quite
a hike, around the side of the mansion and across the slop-
ing garden in back. Students streamed from the house and
the outbuildings, all thoughts of recording spirit data forgotten in the magic of fireworks. Nothing more than dark
silhouettes, they laughed and pointed at the dazzling colors
starring the sky over the graveyard. A device whistled sky-
ward and exploded into ribbons of white that fizzled slowly
as they drifted toward the ground. The lights seemed to
animate the marble angel watching over one of the graves,
making her wings shimmer and her marble robe seem to
undulate in the play of light and shadow.

A couple of minutes later, Glen Spaatz appeared beside
me where I stood outside the wrought-iron fence that
ringed the tiny cemetery. I wasn't sure where he'd come
from.

"I think it's time to call it a night," Spaatz said in my ear.
His arm brushed mine. "I'll let the kids enjoy the show and
then round them up. I must say this hasn't been the most
successful field trip on record."

Over the pops of the fireworks, I heard a faint call and I
shushed Spaatz. It seemed to come from the direction of
the mansion.

"Did you hear that?" I asked Spaatz.

He turned to listen. The sound came again, clearer as the
wind dropped suddenly. "Help! Someone! Call nine-one-
one!"

Spaatz rolled his eyes. "Don't they ever give up? How
many pranks—"

I was running back to the mansion before he stopped
speaking. I knew that voice.

# Chapter Four

MY BREATH CAME IN RAGGED GULPS AS I STRUGGLED
up the slight rise to the mansion where Rachel stood on the
terrazzo, waving frantically. Her hair straggled more wildly
than usual around her face, and tears had smeared her mascara down her cheeks.

She grabbed my arm and pulled me toward the French
doors when I reached the terrazzo. "Oh, thank God! I don't
have my cell phone. I didn't know what to—" She burst
into tears.

"What's wrong?" I spoke as she dragged me across the
ballroom and down the hall toward the huge foyer.

She put one hand to her mouth and pointed with the
other, shaking her head back and forth in denial of what lay
before us.

I gasped at the sight of the body lying at the foot of the
staircase, unmoving, a trickle of blood oozing across the

floor. One arm was flung over his head, the other trapped under his body. A gleam of white poked through a hole in his jeans and, with a sick feeling, I recognized it as his shin bone. His other leg was straight, the foot resting awkwardly on the bottom stair. A boy. Blond hair. Jeans. Braden.

I dug my cell phone out of my pocket and punched in 911. I tossed it to Rachel. "Tell them what's happened." Crossing to Braden, I dropped to my knees and felt for a pulse. Thready, but there.

I didn't dare move him for fear of spinal injuries or other bone breaks, but I needed to treat him for shock. His pallor and jerky breathing, not to mention the still spreading blood, told me he was in trouble. Neither Rachel nor I wore a jacket I could use to warm him. My gaze flashed around the hall. A memory pinged and I dashed into the adjacent parlor. Grabbing hold of the velvet drapes, I ripped them from the rod, bringing it down with a huge clatter. Crumpling a panel of velvet in my arms, I carried it into the hall and spread it over Braden's still form, tucking it as close as I dared.

"What happened?" I asked Rachel.

She had stopped talking and was staring at Braden, her eyes huge with worry. She shook her head. "I don't know. We were in the parlor, doing our readings. I had to go to the bathroom. It took me a while to find it. While I was in there, I heard what sounded like explosions."

"Fireworks," I supplied.

She looked at me blankly, like she'd never heard the word. "I came back to get Braden, thinking we could go see what it was, and I found him like this. I didn't have my cell and no one answered when I screamed for help and . . ." She dissolved into tears again.

I moved to her and hugged her tightly. She was shivering. "You did great," I said. "He's going to be fine." I hoped. I said a quick prayer.

A siren racing up the long drive brought our heads around. Giving Rachel a quick squeeze, I jogged to the double doors and pulled them open. An ambulance, lights flashing, skidded to a stop beside an SUV that hadn't been there earlier, and the EMTs hopped out. I beckoned them in and backed out of their way.

"What in the world—" a disapproving voice said. Lucy Mortimer moved into the foyer from the hallway that led off to the administrative offices and storage areas. Her gaze took in the scene and then she gasped, "My parlor drapes!"

Before she could rip them off Braden—which I feared she might do—the EMTs clattered into the hallway, lugging a gurney and their equipment. They had Braden hooked to an IV and secured in a cervical brace faster than I would have thought possible. They had lifted him on a backboard and were wheeling the gurney out the door as Glen Spaatz and a gaggle of students appeared on the scene, stopping abruptly where the hall met the foyer. Lucy hurried off toward her office, muttering about calling the board of directors.

"Braden McCullers apparently fell down the stairs," I told Spaatz briefly, watching as his face registered disbelief and worry.

"Oh my God! Cyril's ghost pushed Braden!" a girl's voice said from behind Spaatz.

A babble of voices rose up, only to be silenced as the front door thwacked open again and a man appeared on the threshold, eyes wide, gray hair mussed. I'd never seen him before.

"Where's Mark?" he asked urgently. "Is Mark okay?"

We looked around. No Mark. No Lindsay. No Lonnie or

Tyler or Coach Peet, but presumably they were waiting on the bus. I couldn't tell if anyone else was missing.

"Who are you?" Spaatz stepped forward and challenged the stranger. They were about the same height, but the newcomer was bulkier through the neck and shoulders.

"Eric Crenshaw. Mark's dad. I saw the ambulance while I was waiting. Is Mark—"

"Take it easy, Dad." Mark's voice came from the hallway leading to the ballroom. Lindsay's nervous face peeked over his shoulder.

"Goddamnit," Crenshaw said, taking a step toward Mark. "You were supposed to be outside at nine thirty, remember? So we could get on the road to your aunt's? When I saw the ambu—"

"Sorry. I forgot." Mark's voice was sullen; he clearly didn't like being chewed out in front of his friends.

"That's not good enough," Eric Crenshaw snapped, taking a step toward Mark. "You know your mother—"

Rachel's voice in my ear, begging me to take her to the hospital, drowned out the rest of their confrontation.

"Please, Grace, I have to be there. What if he, like, dies?" She whispered the last word.

"He's not going to die," I said firmly. Why did we make statements like that when we had no clue? Denial, I guessed, or hope. I pulled Spaatz away from the group. "When the police show up, tell them Rachel and I have gone to the hospital."

"The police?" He looked startled. "Oh, shit. Of course, the police." He pushed a hand through his hair.

"I'm surprised they're not here already." I said. I dug in my purse for my keys before realizing I didn't have my car. We'd all come in the bus. "Damn!"

At Spaatz's raised brows, I explained my dilemma.

"Take the bus," he said immediately. "Tell the driver. He can come back for the rest of us after he drops you at the hospital. I don't think we'll be going anywhere any time soon."

"Thanks." I gave him a tight smile, grabbed Rachel by the hand, and sprinted toward the bus.

THREE HOURS LATER, COMING UP ON ONE IN THE morning, I sat in the hospital cafeteria, clutching a lukewarm mug of tea in my hands and being grilled by my ex-husband. Braden was still in surgery, his family hovering anxiously in the waiting room, and Rachel's dad had fetched her an hour ago, promising she could return to the hospital in the morning. My ex, Officer Hank Parker of the St. Elizabeth Police Department, had shown up just as I was debating calling my mom for a ride home or lurking in the waiting room until someone looked like they were headed back to St. Elizabeth. Hank and his new partner, Officer Ally Qualls, a short, dark-haired woman, arrived before I could make up my mind. While Officer Qualls talked to Braden's family, Hank steered me to the elevator and down to the cafeteria, where he bought me a fresh cup of tea.

"Thanks," I said with real gratitude, slumping into an uncomfortable plastic chair. The cafeteria smelled like burned toast and was deserted except for a man and a woman in lab coats arguing at a table by the window, and a short-order cook dressed as a mummy yawning over the grill.

"What in blazes were you doing at a high school get-together, Grace?" Hank asked. He leaned back in his chair and stretched his long legs out toward me. He'd thickened a bit through the neck and middle since high school, and his brown hair had thinned a bit, but he still looked sharp in his uniform. He'd applied to the Atlanta Police Department more interested in cop groupies and carrying a gun than protecting the public, but it seemed to me recently that he'd gotten a bit more serious about policing. He'd told Mom he was planning to take the sergeant's exam before long. "You don't have the hots for that teacher, that Spaz guy, do you?" His eyes narrowed with suspicion.

Hank's jealousy, despite our divorce, which happened largely due to his infidelities, got on my nerves. I was sure he'd deliberately mispronounced Glen's name. "It was a field trip," I said. "Surely Mr. Spaatz"—I emphasized the pronunciation—"told you that."

"Yeah. But it still sounds like a stupid-ass idea to me," he said, shaking his head. "Ghost hunting? What's the point of that? I can't see where it matters if there's ghosts or not. What were they going to do if one showed up? Put it in a zoo?"

Maybe it was because I was sleep-deprived and worried, but what Hank said made a certain amount of sense. Scary. "I don't know," I said. "It was for science." I propped my elbows on the table and let my head fall into my hands.

Hank snorted. "So, what were you doing there?"

"Chaperoning."

"Damn fine chaperone you are."

His words scraped my raw emotions. I'd already been beating myself up for agreeing to chaperone in the first place and for failing so miserably at it. It was at least partially my fault that Braden McCullers was in the hospital. "Thanks a lot," I muttered.

"Not that it sounds like you could have prevented the accident," he added graciously. "The fireworks, now . . .

We're going to have to ticket the kid who set those off when we catch up with him. All the other kids say it was"—he checked his notebook—"an Alonso Farber."

I was concerned that Lonnie still hadn't turned up, but it was Hank's first words that caught my attention. "Accident? You're sure it was an accident?"

Hank worked his lips in and out. "Of course. What else would it be? You certainly don't believe that ghost—Cyrus or whatever—"

"Cyril."

"—shoved him off the landing?" He guffawed. "You need more than caffeine, Grace—you need some shut eye. Let me take you home."

Riding home with Hank was not high on my list of things I wanted to do, but neither was sleeping in the hospital waiting room. "Okay, thanks. Just let me see if there's any news on Braden," I said.

When we got back to the ICU, a tall woman in surgical scrubs was talking to Braden's parents. "A coma?" his mother said in a horrified tone, and slumped forward in a faint. The doctor and Mr. McCullers caught her before she hit the floor. A line of plum-sized plastic jack-o'-lanterns strung over the doorway wavered.

"Guess we won't be able to talk to the kid any time soon," Hank said, hooking his thumbs in his utility belt. He approached his partner to tell her he was running me home. She looked over, suspicion in her dark eyes, and I remembered that she'd seemed interested in Hank the last time we met. I couldn't think of a good way to tell her she was welcome to him, so I gave a little wave and tried to look nonthreatening. After the night's adventures, I felt about as glamorous as a manatee and was sure I had circles under my green eyes and a pasty complexion from lack of sleep.

My light brown hair was a tangled mess and my shirt had blood on it from when I'd tended to Braden. Apparently, I looked as bad as I felt because Officer Qualls smiled, said something to Hank, and turned back to the family member she was interviewing.

Hank and I rode home in the patrol car in silence. The loblolly pines lining both sides of I-95 turned the highway into a dark tunnel, and traffic was light at this hour. Hank pulled into my landlady's driveway and got out when I did. "It feels just like old times, Grace," Hank said. "Like when we'd come home from a date and I'd walk you to the door. Remember how your mom used to flash the porch light when we were ki—"

"It's late and I'm beat," I said, not wanting to encourage his romantic reminiscences. I had all those memories locked in a corner of my mind labeled: "Big Mistake. Keep Closed." I started briskly toward my apartment, a former carriage house slightly offset from my landlady's Victorian home.

"Maybe I could come in for a cup of joe," Hank hinted, catching up to me easily.

"No." I stopped at my door, unwilling to open it while he was there.

He looked taken aback but recovered quickly, giving me a broad smile. "Sure. You're tired. Another time."

Before I could tell him there wasn't going to be another time, not in this life or any other where I had free will, he leaned close enough so I could smell the coffee on his breath. "Then how about a good-night kiss, for old time's sake?"

I stared up at him, incredulity and anger fizzing through me. "What part of 'divorced' don't you get?" I asked. "Not married. Not related. Not interested."

He reared back like I'd slapped him and his smile turned to a sulky pout. "You know you don't—"

The radio attached below his left shoulder crackled to life and spouted cop talk. Hank responded and I took advantage of his momentary distraction to open my door and slip inside, closing it firmly and leaning back against it. To think that I'd been anxious to get out and about on a Saturday night, I thought wearily as Hank stomped back toward his patrol car. I should have stuck with my original plan of a DVD, ice cream, and real estate listings.

I stepped into my small living room/dining room combo. The kitchenette sat beyond it and my bedroom was to the right. It was small, but it was more private than a unit at a huge complex and I got a break on the rent for helping Mrs. Jones with her yard and garden. Fixing myself a tuna salad sandwich, I poured a glass of milk and settled at the dinette table, too wired to sleep, despite my weariness. I eyed the packet of MLS listings, but then my gaze drifted to the box from Rothmere. Wiping my hands on a napkin, I opened it. I thought about rummaging through the box to find more letters from Clarissa but decided to enjoy the anticipation of coming across them in turn.

I unfolded the stiff paper, conscious of the creases ironed in by time. Gently spreading it flat on the table, I glanced at the signature. Spikier and darker than Clarissa's rounded script. I began to read.

*October 18, 1831*

*Dear Angus,*

*Your condolences on the death of my husband are much appreciated. My bereavement was sudden, as you know,*

*and you also know how grieved I am by his passing, but
time and God heal all wounds, or so Reverend Johnson
tells me. Geoffrey remains at Rothmere, as the estate
belongs to him now that his father has passed to his re-
ward. My other children have returned to their homes
and all I have left to comfort me is Clarissa, who drifts
through the day like a wraith since her father died,
starting at sudden noises. I fear for her mental health
and must deem it prudent for her to marry Quentin as
soon as may be possible, despite our mourning. I would
welcome a visit from you when your business affairs
permit.*

*Yours,*
*Annabelle*

Huh. Clarissa's mother seemed to think her daughter
was losing it after Cyril's death. Well, wouldn't anyone be
knocked off-kilter by the circumstances? I wondered who
Angus was as I sifted through the box's contents. The next
few items were receipts for household purchases—boxes
of beeswax tapers; sugar; Finest India tea; American secretary cabinet desk of Cherrywood, one hundred dollars; rat
poison; nails; and "a large and muscular black man, Amos,
for seventy and a half." I dropped the paper, realizing it was
the bill of sale for a slave. It gave me an eerie feeling. I'd
enjoyed history mildly in high school and college, but it
had never felt as *real* to me as it did now. Something about
these documents, written by real people who used to live
near St. Elizabeth, made the past seem more immediate
than my stodgy history texts had, despite their glossy photos and scholarly interpretations. History and the present
seemed to merge in a way I'd never noticed before.

# Chapter Five

✂

I MUST HAVE FALLEN ASLEEP AT THE TABLE BECAUSE when the phone rang, I struggled awake, disoriented, feeling stiff from hours spent slumped over the sharp-edged table. I groped for the phone, knocking one of the Rothmere ledgers to the floor. Lucy would kill me.

"How's my favorite hair stylist?" Marty greeted me.

I smiled at the sound of his voice and pushed my hair out of my face. I pictured him relaxed in his leather recliner with his laptop on his lap—he was *always* working on a story—long legs extended, sandy hair flopping onto his forehead.

"I'm good," I said. Well, I would be after a shower and a stretch. "And how's my favorite reporter?"

"Bushed."

I could hear the weariness in his voice. "Big story?"

"Um-hm." Voices from the Sunday-morning talk shows

mumbled in the background. "The usual: politicians, corruption, sex, drugs, and rock 'n' roll."

I laughed, then sobered and told him about the ghost hunt and Braden.

"God, that's awful," he said when I finished. "I hope the kid comes out of it."

"I've been reading up on Rothmere and what happened to Cyril and it's fascinating. Listen to this." I read him part of Annabelle's letter.

"Sounds a little cold, doesn't she?" he said.

I skimmed the letter again. I hadn't been thinking of Annabelle as cold. "How do you mean?"

"Well, the bit about marrying off her daughter rather than trying to help her work through her grief. Who is the Angus guy?"

I admitted I had no idea. "Maybe I could make copies of some of the letters and bring them with me when I come up next weekend."

A moment's silence made my stomach knot up.

"About that . . . I don't know if it's going to work for this coming weekend, Grace." The *squee* of a door opening—his closet?—came over the phone. "This story I'm on is heating up and I'm going to be balls to the wall on it for at least another ten days. You'd be bored sitting in my condo while I chase down sources, so let's postpone, okay?"

"Oh." Disappointment surged through me. Was this a brush-off? I didn't have the guts to ask. "Sure, another weekend will work fine."

"Great." Relief tinged his voice.

Because I hadn't made a fuss? Clicking noises filtered to my ear and I realized he was typing on the keyboard. Anger tightened my jaw. "You sound busy," I said stiffly. "I'll let you go."

"I miss you," Marty said.

But he didn't try to persuade me to talk longer, didn't set a new date for my trip to DC. "Me, too," I whispered.

I hung up and headed for the shower, feeling low. The thought that Marty and I might be growing apart made me sad. I was "in like" with him, if not in love, and I enjoyed spending time with him. The last weekend I'd spent with him in Atlanta, we'd visited the zoo where he had been a volunteer in the ape house for years, apparently. I'd stared at him in astonishment when he told me and he laughed, saying that hanging out with the apes was an intellectual and ethical step up from politicians. He'd taken me "backstage" to visit with a six-month-old orangutan named Tanga, and I couldn't remember the last time I'd had such fun. Marty had an intensity about him, especially when he was probing something, trying to get to the truth, which appealed to me. His eyes fixed on me when I was talking like I was the only person in the world and that was a treat after being with Hank, whose gaze tracked every attractive woman who walked by.

We'd deliberately left things kind of loose when he moved to DC. My divorce was too fresh and his drive to succeed in his new job too powerful for us to push the still-new relationship.

"DC will be teeming with beautiful, interesting women," I'd said on our last morning together before he left, rolling over in bed to prop myself on his chest. His skin was pale, slightly freckled, and sprinkled with wiry, sandy hairs. Sunlight streaming through the vertical blinds of his Buckhead condo striped the floor and the navy sateen coverlet.

"So?" He craned his head up to kiss my chin.

"So, we're not . . . you know."

"Lawyers and lobbyists? No temptation." He pulled me down to nibble on my neck.

"I'm just saying . . ."

"I know. No strings. We're both free to date other people." Threading his hand through my hair, he pulled my face closer and kissed me for a long, long time. "Thing is," he said with a smile lighting his hazel eyes when we broke apart. "I don't want to."

"Me, either," I whispered.

I heard the echo of that conversation now and wondered if he was dating someone else—or a couple of someone elses—or if it was his passion for his job pulling him away from me.

MARTY'S CALL, PLUS ONE I MADE TO THE HOSPITAL, made me late, and I arrived at the First Baptist Church barely in time to pull my choir robe over my clothes and do a few warm-up "mi-mi-mis" with the group. I sang the anthem mechanically, my mind on Marty. Part of me wanted to drive up to DC that afternoon to talk to him face-to-face, and part of me wanted to bury my head in the sand and pretend everything was hunky-dory. Replaying every word of the conversation, I walked over to Doralynn's Café and Bakery to meet up with Mom, Althea, and the salon's manicurist, Stella Michaelson. She goes to St. Joseph's Catholic Church but frequently joins us for breakfast after Mass. Sometimes Rachel comes, too; I didn't spot her this morning and figured she was at the hospital. I'd called to check on Braden before church and been handed off to an aunt who told me he was still in a coma caused by his head injury and that he had a compound fracture of his tibia and three broken ribs. The head injury, though, was the big problem. His aunt cried as she said the doctors didn't know if he'd come out of the coma today, next week, or never.

I reached Doralynn's as a party of at least twelve straggled out the door. A St. Elizabeth's fixture, Doralynn's was hugely popular with tourists and residents alike. Lots of windows and booths and tablecloths in blue and white and yellow made it cheery even on the grayest day. Ruthie Steinmetz, the owner, was chatting with customers at the register. I caught her eye and waved. Although the tourists celebrated Doralynn's as the quintessence of Southern cooking and hospitality, Ruthie described herself as "a Jewish grandmother from Germany by way of New Jersey." She'd opened Doralynn's over twenty years ago and such was the power of suggestion and savvy marketing that many people believed the charming café on the square was a Southern institution.

I slid onto the booth seat next to Althea, across from Mom and Stella. "Sorry I'm late," I said, smiling gratefully at the server who immediately filled my coffee cup. I took a long swallow. Ah, caffeine. "You wouldn't believe what happened at the ghost hunt last night."

I filled them in on the preceding night's events and they interjected, "Oh, no!" and, "I can't believe it!" as I shared my story. I paused my recital to order scrambled eggs, biscuits, and grits, then told them about finding Braden and the trip to the hospital. I left out the bit about Hank putting the moves on me; I didn't want to listen to another refrain of "What did you ever see in him?" He was sweet and he loved me and he got to be a habit . . . what can I say?

Althea shook her head, setting the double wooden hoops in her lobes clacking.

"My, my," she said. "I knew nothing good would come of that ghost hunt. What was that school thinking?"

Stella leaned forward, tucking a strand of red hair behind her ear. Usually accepting of people and situations as she found them, she had a disgusted look on her gentle face. "Education has become nothing more than entertainment," she said. "Teachers have to compete with kids texting and only wanting to play video games or check Facebook. I'm not surprised they go out on a limb with something like a ghost hunt to try and get their students' attention." At forty-one, Stella had a daughter in middle school.

"Is Rachel holding up okay?" Mom asked, cutting into the stack of blueberry pancakes on her plate.

"I haven't talked to her this morning," I said. "She was pretty upset last night. She thinks it's her fault because she went to the bathroom and left Braden alone."

"Well, my goodness," Althea said. "The boy must be eighteen years old. It's not like she needs to babysit him."

"No," Stella put in, "but I can understand how she feels. You can't help but feel responsible when people you care about are troubled or hurt."

"Amen," Mom said with a decisive nod.

"Anyway, Hank says the police are calling it an accident, although no one knows why Braden went up on the landing," I said. I spread homemade strawberry-rhubarb preserves on my biscuit and took a big bite. Heaven.

"Maybe he saw the ghost and went up to check it out," Stella suggested.

Althea stopped eating and looked at her. "Are you saying you believe in ghosts?" she asked.

"I don't *not* believe in them," Stella said after a moment's thought. "There are just too many things that happen in this world that science can't explain. And whether you think of them as ghosts or spirits or 'presences,' you've got to admit there's more going on around us than we can understand."

"I suppose next you'll be saying you believe in zombies and werewolves," Althea said.

Stella's pale skin flushed red. "I didn't say that."

Althea thrust her chin up a hair, defensively, but then lowered it. "Sorry, Stel. I know it's not the same. And it's not as if I haven't thought I felt my William nearby a time or two over the years. I guess I'm just fed up with the way everyone these days seems obsessed with the supernatural. That series all the teen girls are gaga over—the one with the vampire and the high school girl. I took my niece Kendra to the mall last Saturday and all she could talk about was how romantic it was. Fah! And there's that series about the woman who sees the future or the past or some such rot, and that Spirit Whisperer woman, Ava something, who has that talk show where she chats with ghosts—excuse me, 'spirits.' Don't get me started."

"Too late," Mom observed dryly.

We all laughed as Althea stabbed a fork into a sausage patty. "All I'm saying is that keeping up with the people we can see and touch in the here and now ought to be more than enough for anybody."

A woman seated near the window got up to leave and I recognized Lucy Mortimer. She saw me at the same time and veered toward us, tucking the book she'd been reading into her purse. Wearing a shirtwaist dress in a forgettable blue and tan print, and with her slightly frizzy hair loose around her face, she looked very different than she had last night.

"Grace!" she said, stopping beside our table, oblivious to the server trying to slide past her with a loaded tray.

"Good morning, Lucy," Mom said.

"Hello," Lucy said absently, so caught up in whatever she wanted to say that she barely acknowledged Mom and

Althea and Stella. She twisted an opal ring around her pinkie. "Did you hear? They're accusing Cyril of trying to kill that high school boy!" Her voice rose and people at a nearby table looked over.

"Who is, Lucy? The police told me it was an accident."

"A reporter. She called me this morning and said she'd heard Cyril Rothmère's ghost tried to kill someone. She wanted me to give her a quote and let her come out to the mansion to take photos." Lucy fairly quivered with emotion. "As if Cyril would do such a thing!"

"I thought you didn't believe in ghosts," I said.

"I don't—not really—but some people do, and they are going to tarnish Cyril's reputation. I won't stand for it." The tip of Lucy's nose turned pink with indignation.

"Braden McCullers is in a coma," I said pointedly. "He may not recover."

"Who?" Lucy looked confused but then her face cleared. "Oh, the boy who got hurt. Well, it's a terrible thing that he's so badly injured. I certainly hope he gets better soon."

"That's nice of you, Lucy," I said, feeling more kindly toward her. I'd thought her reaction to the incident last night was a bit unfeeling. Maybe she'd just been shocked by it all.

"Of course. When he's able to talk again, he can tell everyone it wasn't Cyril who pushed him!"


AFTER BREAKFAST, I CALLED RACHEL TO SEE HOW she was doing. She was at the hospital, she said, and there was no change in Braden's condition. She sounded woebegone, so I decided to drive up to Brunswick and sit with her for a while. My laundry and real estate listings could wait. State Road 42 led me out of St. Elizabeth to the west where I hooked up with I-95. The trip to Brunswick was painless on a Sunday afternoon and I easily found a parking spot in the hospital lot. High cirrus clouds, the hurricane's advance guard, obscured the sky and seemed lower than when I left St. Elizabeth. I made a mental note to listen to a weather report on my way back. Passing the gift shop on my way through the lobby, I veered in to pick up a small plant for Braden. Maybe some greenery would speed his recovery. The clerk, wearing cat ears on her head and with whiskers drawn across her cheeks, said, "Happy Halloween," when I paid.

The ICU waiting room was depressingly full of people. An Asian family clustered together at one end of the room, adults talking quietly while four children watched cartoons on the television with the volume turned low. Braden's family and friends gathered around a table at the other end of the room, takeout containers emitting the scent of fried chicken cluttering the surface. Rachel sat off to the side by herself, her arms pulling her knees close to her chest, her head bowed. She didn't see me come in.

Braden's mother, a plump woman with her son's wheat blond hair, accepted the plant with thanks. "They don't allow flowers and such in the ICU," she told me, "but I'm sure Braden will enjoy this when he's moved to a regular room. The doctors say they'll move him this afternoon. That must mean he's doing better, that he'll wake up soon, right?" She looked to her husband for confirmation.

He reached over to squeeze her hand. A lanky man with slightly stooped shoulders, he had light brown hair graying at the temples and might have looked distinguished if worry hadn't been dragging down his face, accentuating the grooves in his forehead and the brackets around his thin lips. "That's right, Darla. Thank you for being so thoughtful, Miss Terhune. I'm sorry . . . how did you say you know Braden again?"

"Rachel Whitley introduced me last summer," I said. "And I was a chaperone for the field trip last night."

Darla McCullers's mouth fell open a half inch and tears began streaming down her face. Without a word, she turned away and went to sit with two women I knew from their similar profiles had to be her sisters.

Guilt flayed me, like a thousand paper cuts slicing my skin.

"We know you didn't mean for this to happen," Mr. Mc-Cullers said, pinching the bridge of his nose and squeezing his eyes shut for a moment. "It's not anyone's fault. Accidents happen. We can't protect our kids from everything, can we? From less and less as they get older." He smiled sadly. "Do you have children, Miss Terhune?"

"No," I choked out. Darla's tears and his attempt to absolve me of blame made me feel awful.

"They are life's greatest joy," he said, and drifted over to join his wife.

I stood still for a moment, stricken by their grief and the sense that it was my fault. I could tell myself there was no way I could've kept an eye on all of the students last night, but that didn't make me feel better. Neither did reminding myself that there were three other adults present. We'd all allowed ourselves to be distracted by the fireworks, and Braden might die because of our lack of attentiveness. I took two deep breaths and forced myself to move toward Rachel, where she was huddled on the plastic chair. I sat. She raised her head a fraction when my weight rocked the connected chairs.

"Oh. Hi. You didn't have to come."

"Yes, I did. C'mon. Let's get out of here for a bit. I'll buy you a milk shake at that diner down the block."

Her gaze slanted toward Braden's parents. I forestalled her objection. "You can't camp out here until Braden comes out of the coma. It could be hours or days." Or weeks or never. I was no expert, but I knew enough to realize that moving Braden to a regular room only meant that he wasn't in imminent danger of dying, not that he'd necessarily come out of the coma any time soon.

Unfolding her arms and legs, she stood. The dark circles under her eyes had nothing to do with makeup because her face was scrubbed clean. She looked younger without the heavy eyeliner and mascara. "Okay. But I need to be back here in, like, half an hour."

I was going to try to persuade her to go home and call a friend or get ready for the school week, but I said, "Fine."

A thin cardboard skeleton leered from the diner door and swung loose-jointedly when we walked in. The diner smelled of fried onions and was too warm, so we ordered our shakes to go. This part of Brunswick didn't seem to have a park, so we strolled down the sidewalk heading away from the hospital. Gusty winds tossed discarded plastic bags high in the air and scooted an abandoned comics page from the Sunday newspaper along the sidewalk in front of us. A homeless man, drunk or asleep, leaned against the rough concrete wall of a closed video store. I hoped there was a nearby shelter he could take refuge in if the hurricane hit.

I spooned up a slushy mouthful of chocolate shake and looked over at Rachel. She was working so hard to suck her strawberry shake through a straw that her cheeks were concave with effort. She gave up and started using the straw like a chopstick to scoop shake into her mouth.

"What have the doctors said about Braden?" I asked.

"He's got a lot of brain swelling," she said, concentrat-

ing on swirling her straw through the thick ice cream mix-
ture. "And the broken leg. But it's the brain injury that's
worrying them. I overheard the main doc tell Braden's
folks that with brain injuries, there's just no way of, like,
knowing exactly what's going on inside their heads or how
long they might be in a coma or if there'll be any permanent damage when the person wakes up. Doctors are just
useless!" She yelled the last words, startling a small flock
of pigeons pecking hopefully around a trash can. They
flapped into the air in a flurry of gray, white, and tan feath-
ers, settling to the ground just feet away to fight over a limp
French fry.

I didn't try to argue with her about the utility of doctors.
"I'm sure they're doing all they can. And Braden's young—
resilient."

"Like I haven't heard that thirty times this morning," she
said sullenly. Kicking at a pebble, she watched as it skipped
over the curb and clattered down a storm drain.

Her anger and moodiness seemed out of proportion. I'd
expected her to be worried about Braden, but her reaction
seemed a bit off. I eyed her profile, noting the way she
gripped her lips together and tugged at a lock of hair behind her ear.

"What's wrong, Rach?" I asked.

"My best friend is, like, sucked into a black hole in his
brain, and you ask me what's wrong?" She hurled the remains of her shake at a metal trash can, but missed, splat-
tering strawberry goo across the sidewalk and into the
street. Drawing in a quick breath, she started to run, arms
pumping hard, black hair flopping against her shoulders.

Depositing my cup in the trash, I jogged after her, not
trying to catch up with her, but wanting to keep her in sight.
She didn't run long. After only two blocks, she wrapped an

arm around a light pole and spun around it, sinking to the ground. As I stopped a few feet away, I asked myself, What would Mom do?

I, of course, had been a delightful teen, helpful, courteous, and happy all the time. I never obsessed over acne or feeling fat. I never sobbed my heart out when Hank flirted with another girl or my best friend, Vonda, deserted me for a whole week to hang with Stephanie Matejka. I never overreacted to a bad grade or imagined slight. Hah! I remembered Mom's technique for kicking a little sense into me and Alice Rose when we let our moods or hormones get the better of us.

"Enough, Rachel," I said in as unsympathetic a voice as I could muster. "Stand up, blow your nose, and tell me what the heck is eating at you."

She looked up, surprised at my tone. Sniffing, she dug in her jeans pocket for a tissue and scrubbed at her tear-stained face. I held out a hand, and when she took it, I hauled her up.

"Let's sit." I pointed to a bus stop and we settled on the bench with its back advertising a local Realtor. The red metal bench had a woven look to it, with holes for water to drain through. "Talk to me."

She fixed her eyes on mine and bit her lip. Finally, she said, "I'm not sure Braden's fall was, like, an accident."

"What?"

She pounded her fists on her thighs. "See, I knew no one would believe me!"

"Wait a minute." I held up a calming hand. "I didn't say I didn't believe you. Why don't you think it was an accident? Did you see something?"

She didn't answer; instead, she shoved a hand into her pocket and came out with a crumpled piece of paper. As she smoothed it out, I could see it was an article torn from a newspaper.

"Did you see this?" she asked. "It was in today's *Brunswick News*."

I shook my head and she passed it to me. "Depressed Teen Injured during Ghost Hunt," the headline read. I glanced at Rachel, but she had her head bowed, her hair a dark curtain obscuring her expression. Scanning the brief article, I read that "Braden McCullers, eighteen, suffered head and other injuries in a fall at the Rothmere mansion near St. Elizabeth Saturday night. He was taking part in a school-sponsored field trip to scientifically dispute the presence of a nineteenth-century ghost in the antebellum home, according to Merle Kornhiser, principal at St. Elizabeth High School. Police sources are calling the fall an accident but say the teen had a history of depression. He remains in intensive care."

I folded the page carefully along its creases, playing for time. Newspaper articles and TV reports about teen depression flashed into my head. I thought I knew what was troubling Rachel. "Are you afraid Braden tried to commit suicide?" I finally asked.

"No! But that's what people will say. And it's not true. He told me about his depression when we were dating. Not many people know. He was taking antidepressants and was involved with a study to, like, test a new drug."

A bus slowed but I waved it on. Belching diesel smoke, it picked up speed. The fumes drifted around us and I coughed. "If you don't think it was a suicide attempt, then what—"

"He was worried about something this past week." She plucked at the metal strands of the bench seat with a fingernail. "But not in a sad kind of way. He wasn't worried about himself. He said he knew something and was wondering if he should intervene."

"Knew what? Intervene how?"

"I don't know!" She flung her head up and her eyes, worried and defiant, met mine.

I hoped Rachel was making a mountain out of a mole hill, but she clearly needed someone to take her fears seriously, so I did the best I could. "What, exactly, did he say?"

"He gave me a ride home on Thursday. We stopped at the marina and walked all the way out the boardwalk in the marsh, out to where those benches are where the bird watchers like to sit?"

I nodded. I knew the spot she meant. It was a peaceful place surrounded by cattails and swamp grasses, home to dozens of bird species. A wooden bench, with the names of many visitors etched into its boards, looked out over an expanse of marsh to where the St. Andrew Sound glinted in the distance. I liked to sit there myself at this time of year, when the tourists were mostly gone, and inhale the slightly sulfurous scent of the marsh and listen to the cries of the water birds.

"Anyway, he recited a bit of that Donne poem, you know, the one about 'No man is an island'? He was always doing that when we were together—saying bits of poems. He even wrote a few. And then he talked about, like, our responsibilities to each other and said he had a hard decision to make. He said that sometimes knowledge is a curse and that he felt he needed to intervene."

"'Intervene'? That's the word he used?"

Rachel nodded. "Yeah, like, he said it two or three times."

"But he didn't say what he was referring to?"

"No. I asked him. He said he had a responsibility to be discreet until he'd made up his mind about what to do."

"And you have no clue what he was talking about? He didn't bring it up again on Friday or Saturday?"

"I didn't see him Friday," Rachel said, "and he was all jumpy last night. When I asked if he'd made a decision, just concerned-like, you know, not trying to be nosy, he told me to drop it."

I heard the hurt in her voice and reached over to squeeze her hand. "And now that's he been hurt, you think this plays in somehow?" Like maybe he was dealing with something he couldn't handle and he tried to kill himself? I didn't say it aloud, but the thought crossed my mind.

"I don't know," Rachel said, frustrated. "I just don't want people saying he tried to kill himself, and I don't see how it could've been an accident. He wouldn't have gone up the stairs just for nothing. And he wouldn't have fallen for no reason!"

"You think there was someone else there?" I asked slowly.

"It's the only thing that, like, makes sense," Rachel said. "Isn't it? Some*one* or some*thing* got him to climb the stairs. And who knows what happened then?"

# Chapter Six

✂

BY THE TIME I STARTED BACK TO ST. ELIZABETH, HAV-
ing failed to get Rachel to come with me, I was confused
and disturbed. Traffic on the interstate flowed freely, giving
me plenty of opportunity to chew on what Rachel had said.
Despite Braden's history of depression, I was inclined to
agree with her that he hadn't seemed suicidal at the ghost
hunt. Preoccupied, maybe, but not suicidal. Besides, who
would choose such a bizarre place to end their lives? And,
throwing oneself down a couple of flights of stairs was
hardly a guaranteed ticket to the cemetery, as Braden's fall
proved. Surely, anyone intent on ending his life would pick
a more effective method? Without even wanting to, I
quickly thought of three or four better methods.

And an accident seemed almost as unlikely as suicide.
Braden was a football player, an athlete, for heaven's sake.
How likely was it that he would trip going up the stairs or

stumble coming down and not be able to catch himself on the rail or regain his balance? And why had he gone upstairs in the first place? I tried to think it through from his perspective. Rachel goes to the bathroom, leaving Braden in the parlor. He's tired of doing EMF readings. He wanders into the hall and looks around, maybe studies some of the paintings. Then . . . what? He hears the booms from the fireworks and decides to go upstairs to get a better view. I shook my head. That didn't make sense. He'd have gone out the front door to see what was going on.

I realized the speedometer had crept over eighty and eased my foot off the accelerator. Despite not wanting to be, I was more than half convinced that Rachel's answer was right: someone else had been there. Someone being on the landing wasn't necessarily a problem, but where had they disappeared to when Braden fell? Why hadn't they gotten help? An itchy feeling crept up my back and I wriggled my shoulders against the seat back to erase it.

Without my consciously planning to, I ended up in front of Mom's house rather than at my apartment. The light purple Victorian with the dark purple and white gingerbread had been my home until I went to the University of Georgia. When I left college after two years to go to beauty school, I'd moved back in and lived there until I followed Hank to Atlanta and began working at Vidal Sassoon. The magnolia trees with their spreading branches and glossy leaves, the hammock swinging gently, and the spacious veranda with its mismatched chairs and elephant plant stand cum table were so familiar I frequently didn't notice them. Right now, maybe because I'd spent time in the fear-clogged and antiseptic hospital environment, I felt a rush of affection for the place. Fire ant hills and fallen pecans dotted the yard and I avoided the former and scooped up a handful of the latter as I took the walkway around the side of the house and let myself into the kitchen.

"Mom?"

"Up here, honey." Her voice came faintly down the back staircase that went from the kitchen to the upstairs hall.

Leaving the pecans on the counter, I grabbed a banana and peeled it as I climbed. I found Mom in the guest bedroom, ripping wide strips of packing tape from a roll and crisscrossing them over the window panes. She wore black knit slacks, a white tee shirt with black stars on it, and white sneakers and was standing on a step stool. She looked over her shoulder as I came in and smiled.

"You really think Hurricane Horatio is going to hit, huh?" I asked around a mouthful of banana.

"Well, that's what the forecasters are saying. And it might be a category three before it hits the coast, so I think it's best to be prepared, don't you?"

"Probably." I plopped the banana skin in the trash can. Tearing some tape off the roll, I handed it to Mom. The tape didn't keep the windows from breaking if a tree limb or flying lawn chair hit them, but it helped keep the glass from scattering all over the room.

She stuck it on the highest window and tried to smooth out a wrinkle as I told her about my conversation with Rachel.

"That poor boy," she said when I finished. "And his poor parents. I'm so blessed that neither you nor Alice Rose ever had any problems like that, although I did wonder if Alice Rose might not have been a teensy bit depressed after Owen was born."

"Really?" I hadn't noticed anything different about my younger sister after she had Owen.

Mom nodded. "Don't you remember how weepy she

was, and how she kept worrying that the house was going to burn down or that Wade would get in a wreck on the way home from work?"

I remembered; I'd put it down to her usual drama-queen tendencies. Alice Rose was an awfulizer: if one of my nephews had a rash, she was convinced it was smallpox; if her CPA business had a slow week, she knew they would lose their home.

"Anyway," Mom said, folding up the stepladder, "I think you should look into it, Grace."

"What? You do? Look into Braden's accident?"

She nodded. "Yes. If nothing else, it might help Rachel feel better about the incident, poor thing. Or, maybe you'll find out that someone *was* on the landing and did see what happened. Knowing for sure that it wasn't a suicide attempt would probably give the McCullerses real peace of mind. You could call John and see if the police know anything else." She sent a sly smile my way.

John Dillon was the special agent in charge of Region Fourteen of the Georgia Bureau of Investigation, head-quartered in Kingsland. Mom had a soft spot for him since he'd helped rescue me from a murderous Realtor in August. I fought to control the betraying heat that rose to my cheeks.

"The GBI isn't involved with this case, Mom," I said. "It's strictly a local police thing." Before she could say anything else, I added, "I suppose I could go back to Rothmere and look around. And maybe talk to Glen Spaatz and a couple of the kids who were there. I'll be out at the school this week, anyway, shaving heads for the school fund-raiser. What could that hurt?"

\* \* \*

**IT WAS FOUR O'CLOCK WHEN I PULLED UP IN FRONT** of Rothmere.

A handful of cars sat in the small lot near the carriage house museum and I figured some off-season tourists were visiting the mansion. Crossing the oyster shell driveway, I pushed open one of the heavy oak doors and stepped into the hallway. Voices came from somewhere to my right, maybe the ballroom. The cadence sounded like a docent lecturing about the house. I stood for a moment, taking in the feel of the place. What must it have been like to own all this, to stride across acres and acres planted with tobacco and sugar? To entertain a hundred friends and neighbors in the ballroom? I could almost hear the notes of a Virginia reel if I strained my ears. To sit down to a family dinner in the glow of candlelight, waited on and pampered by servants? I made myself consider the less romantic aspects of plantation life: visiting the outhouse in all weather, dying in childbirth, women having no more rights than a dairy cow, the horrors of slavery. All in all, I'd take working for a living in the twenty-first century over the life of a nineteenth-century plantation owner.

Shaking off my fanciful mood, I strolled around the hall, not sure what I was looking for. I guess I was hoping that a moment of intuition would tell me why Braden climbed the stairs to the landing. I studied the oil paintings, as Braden might have, and tilted my head back to enjoy the sparkle of sunlight on the chandelier's crystals. I avoided looking at the floor until I neared the staircase; then, I didn't see any sign of the bloodstain. I let my breath out, not aware I'd been holding it. The old oak planks were so darkened, scarred, and stained with who knew what across the centuries that Braden's blood had already blended with the mansion's history. I tentatively put one foot on the lowest stair.

"What are you doing here?"

I jumped. The voice came from above me and I looked up to see Glen Spaatz peering over the railing, dark hair flopping across his forehead. "What are *you* doing here?" I countered.

"Same as you probably." A slight smile banished the sternness from his face. "Come on up."

I didn't need his invitation. The rope that normally barred access to the stairs hung limply against the newel post, so I marched up the stairs until I was level with Spaatz on the landing. "Find anything?" I asked.

He shrugged. "Not really. I cast around up here, but I didn't find anything out of place. Not that I know what I was looking for. Something to explain what happened, I guess. My ass is on the line here. My principal is *not* happy with, and I quote, 'an incident so full of negative energy' happening on a school outing."

I felt a pang of sympathy for him. If I felt somehow responsible for Braden's situation, how much worse must it be for him?

"I was just about to check that bedroom where Lonnie went out the window." He jerked a thumb over his shoulder.

"Has Lonnie turned up yet?"

"I don't know." He pushed open the door to the room and it squeaked. "If he has, no one's told me. I did hear that they're moving Braden out of the ICU, though. That's got to be good news." With a sweeping gesture, he invited me to precede him over the threshold.

"Yeah." And it would be even better news if he woke up. I swiveled slowly two hundred seventy degrees to take in the room. It hadn't made any impression on me when I was trying to catch Lonnie.

A ten by ten square, the room had the same wood floors

as the rest of the house. A rag rug added a splotch of color by a single bed with a threadbare quilt on it, and wallpaper featuring overblown roses covered the walls. A stuffed doll with button eyes and yarn hair slumped against an embroidered pillow. A walnut armoire took up most of one wall, and the window filled most of another. It didn't look like this room had been restored to its pre–Civil War origins. Rothmere descendants had lived in the house until old Phineas Rothmere willed it to the city upon his death in the 1950s, and some of the rooms were a confusing mix of Victorian, Art Deco, and other design sensibilities. Lucy Mortimer burned to restore it all to its original splendor, but that took money. Spaatz moved to the window and threw up the sash easily. The movement sparked a memory.

"The window was already open when Lonnie came in here," I said. "He jumped right through it." I thought for a moment. "Is Lonnie a good student?"

Spaatz looked over his shoulder at me. "He's very bright, but he's . . . shall we say 'unmotivated'? I don't think his home situation is good."

"Bright enough to come check this place out before last night? How long has the field trip been planned?"

"You think he cased the joint?" Spaatz turned and half sat on the windowsill, stroking his chin. "Could be. It's been on the calendar for over a month. Had to give enough time for the kids to get their permission slips filled out and ante up five bucks each so we could pay for the bus." Sarcasm tinged the words.

"You know, he went out that window like a shot. Never even looked to see if the roof sloped or if there was something to hang on to or anything. I think he and his cohort—"

"Tyler Orey. Not as bright as Lonnie—more of a follower, I'd say."

"I think they had this all planned out, the fog machine, the sheet, the escape route—everything."

Spaatz straightened. "Could well be, but where does that get us relative to Braden's fall? Nowhere. Tyler and Lonnie were out of the picture long before Braden's accident."

I deflated a little. "True enough." I scanned the room and crossed to the armoire. It towered over me, easily eight feet tall. I tugged on one of the metal pulls and the door swung toward me, emitting a faint scent of camphor. A few wire hangers rattled on the metal pole that stretched across half the opening. Drawers marched down the left side of the cabinet and I opened them idly. Liner paper with a faint gold stripe and a few rodent pellets were all I found until I got to the last drawer. It didn't open as easily as the others and I gave it a sharp jerk, nearly falling on my fanny when it slid toward me to reveal white fabric crammed into the drawer.

Spaatz and I exchanged a glance and I scooped my arms under the material and pulled it out in a crumpled ball. I found an end and flapped it, unfolding a white sheet. I arched my brows and poked a finger through one of two perfectly round holes, golf ball sized, in the middle of the cloth.

"The Ghost of Christmas Past, I presume?" Spaatz said dryly.

"Boo."

We stared at the sheet draped over my arms for a moment.

"It must be Lonnie's costume," Spaatz said, rubbing a corner of the cloth between his thumb and two fingers.

I was shaking my head before he finished. "Uh-uh. Lonnie was still wearing his ghostie disguise when he went through the window. He got rid of it out there somewhere."

I tilted my head toward the gardens and the cemetery beyond.

"So who left that in there?"

I bit my lower lip. "I don't know, but it seems to me that more than one of your students wanted to make sure you would find 'spirits' on your ghost debunking field trip."

A troubled look settled on Spaatz's face "This might explain why Braden came upstairs."

I nodded. "If someone was playing ghost on the landing, with or without special effects like Lonnie's, Braden might have come up to investigate. Trouble is, even though this explains why he came upstairs, it doesn't explain how or why he fell."

Spaatz widened his ice-blue eyes. A faint, half-moon scar curved from the outside corner of his right eye. "It must have been an accident, like the police said. He ran up to catch the ghost, caught his shoe on a tread, and fell."

"So why didn't the ghost get help, instead of stuffing his costume in this armoire and disappearing?" I asked quietly.

"Scared?"

"Maybe." The situation made me uneasy. I hadn't liked it when there was no obvious reason for Braden to have come upstairs. I liked it less now that we knew someone else had been up here, someone who hadn't bothered to get help for a critically injured teen.

Spaatz and I descended the stairs and walked to the now-deserted parking lot.

"What should we do with that?" he asked, nodding at the sheet I still carried.

I chewed the inside of my cheek, undecided. "I guess we should take it to the police," I said finally, "and tell them what we figured out about someone playing ghost on the landing." I dumped the sheet into the trunk.

"It probably won't change their minds about it being an accident," Spaatz warned, pushing the trunk lid down so it closed with a clang.

"I know." I sighed. "But we can't just leave it here. I'll take it by the station first thing in the morning. Then it will be the police's problem."

# Chapter Seven

DUSK HAD FALLEN BY THE TIME I PULLED UP TO THE curb in front of my apartment, the remodeled carriage house offset from my landlady's Victorian home. Clumps of trick-or-treaters carrying flashlights and pumpkin-shaped plastic containers for collecting candy ran excitedly down the sidewalks. Parents trailed behind, assuring the safety of the tiniest princesses and ninja warriors. A huge jack-o'-lantern with a goofy grin on its face glowed from the bottom step of Mrs. Jones's veranda.

"Yoo-hoo! Grace!" Mrs. Jones called. She waved a broom to attract my attention and I saw she was dressed as a witch, complete with pointy hat on her head. "Come help me hand out candy."

I obediently climbed the steps to the veranda and helped myself to a Snickers bar from the basket at her feet. "Had many customers yet?" I asked.

She nodded happily. "Oh, my, yes. Quite a few. I do so enjoy Halloween!"

In her mid-eighties, Genevieve Jones was still a go-getter, taking Meals on Wheels to shut-ins, practicing tai chi in the park, and generally meddling in the lives of her numerous nieces and nephews and their children. Tall and skinny and with a frill of white hair standing up from her head, she reminded me of a crowned crane.

"Such a shame about the McCullers boy," she said.

I wasn't surprised that she'd heard; Mrs. Jones's network of family and friends kept her posted on all the good gossip.

"He wasn't really possessed by a spirit, was he?" she asked, leaning forward.

I sighed. Mrs. Jones might get all the good gossip, but the rumor mill had usually distorted it beyond recognition by the time she repeated it. "Of course not. He tripped and fell on the stairs at Rothmere," I said.

"Twick or tweat," a tiny bumblebee with blond curls said, holding out a pillow case. Two other youngsters stood behind her, a skeleton and a diva with a feather boa, over-sized sunglasses, and chunky jewelry.

"Aren't you all so sweet?" Mrs. Jones said as I plunked a couple of pieces of candy into the bee's bag.

"Are you really a witch?" the skeleton asked apprehensively, his words muffled by his mask.

"Just like you're really a skeleton," Mrs. Jones replied with a twinkle.

The boy thought about it for a moment and then gave a satisfied nod before scampering after the bee and the diva.

"They moved him out of ICU this afternoon." I picked up our conversation.

"I had a friend whose son was in a coma for twenty-four years," Mrs. Jones said sadly. "Such a tragedy."

"And then he came out of it?"

She shook her head as a posse of teens—way too old to be trick-or-treating—came up the walk. "Then he died."

"Hand over a treat or I'll make you walk the plank," a female pirate said. She had a red bandanna tied around her head and a lot of leg showed under her skimpy skirt with its ragged hem.

A costume was no excuse for her rude tone. I skipped over the chocolate bars and gave her a packet of candy corn. She backed down the stairs and a Frankenstein's monster, complete with green face and penciled-on stitches, replaced her. He looked a bit familiar . . . Recognition dawned in his eyes at the same time I realized who he was. I half stood, spilling some candy onto the veranda. "Lonnie!"

He turned, like he might run off, but then I could see him decide to brazen it out. "The name's Frank. Frank N. Stein," he said as his buddies scooped up the spilled candy and put it in their bags.

Mrs. Jones said, "Aren't you a bit old for trick-or-treating, young man?"

"I'm a kid at heart," he said, getting a laugh out of her. "I still believe in Santa and the Tooth Fairy . . . and ghosts." He shot a sidelong glance at me on the last word.

"Where'd you disappear to last night? The police are looking for you." Should I call the police, try to detain him? I gave the thought up almost immediately. No way could I keep the six-foot-four, two-hundred-pound Lonnie here if he didn't want to stay.

"Let 'em look." Lonnie gave me a slow, lazy smile, green makeup caking in his smile creases.

"Ooooh, the po-po," the pirate girl said with a mock shudder.

"C'mon, Lon," said a short Obama. Tyler Orey. "Let's split, dude. The party starts in an hour."

"Happy Halloween," Lonnie told me and Mrs. Jones. He poked a green finger at me. "You. Don't go messing with stuff that ain't any of your business. You hear what I'm saying?" He sauntered back down the stairs and followed his friends across the street.

I stared after him in disbelief. Had he just threatened me?

"There goes a bunch of kids who're going to get into mischief before the night is over," Mrs. Jones said, shaking her head so the witch hat tilted rakishly over one eyebrow. "Just you mark my words. They'll be TPing houses or knocking over mailboxes or worse."

I dialed the police number on my cell phone and asked for Officer Parker. Not that I wanted to talk to Hank, but he and his partner were working the case.

"There's no point in calling the police on them yet, dear," Mrs. Jones said. "I don't think the police will take action until those kids *do* something. And maybe not even then," she ended.

"Hi, darlin'," Hank said loudly into my right ear. "Did you want to pick up where we left off last night?"

The smirk in his voice slimed my ear. I sighed and moved the phone an inch from my head. I quickly told him about Franken-Lonnie.

"Now, Grace," he said, a *tsk-tsk* note in his voice, "you shouldn't be trying to do our job for us."

I'd heard that before, from Special Agent Dillon, and it stung. "I'm not—"

"We interviewed Alonso Farber this morning at his home in that trailer park south of the old cemetery. He 'fessed up to setting off the fireworks without a permit and we ticketed him. Case closed."

"Oh. Well, that's good," I said, feeling a bit foolish. I remembered the sheet. Before Hank could hang up or, worse, ask me out, I told him about Spaatz and me finding the sheet. "I can bring it by in the morning," I said.

"You know I always enjoy seeing you," he said, "but we don't need that sheet. That boy's fall was an accident, pure and simple."

I hung up with a growl.

"You sound quite ferocious, dear. What is it?" Mrs. Jones asked.

"Nothing," I gritted between my teeth.

More trick-or-treaters arrived, and I had calmed down by the time they left with their bags a bit fuller of teeth-rotting booty. I handed out candy for another fifteen minutes, chatting with Mrs. Jones between waves of Hannah Montanas, stormtroopers, witches, ghosts, and Disney princesses. She was happily quizzing an aluminum-foil robot when I said good night and strolled toward my apartment. I hadn't reached the door when a horn honked. I turned to see my friend Vonda Jamison's old station wagon with its Magnolia House logo on the side panel. A vampire waved from behind the steering wheel.

"Vonda?" I approached the car and peered in through the passenger window. "What did you do to your hair?"

My best friend had had me dye her hair red a few weeks back after a spat with her ex-husband, Ricky, who was also her on-again, off-again boyfriend. Now, Vonda's short hair was jet-black and spiked around her gamine face. Her heavily made-up eyes twinkled.

"It's not permanent. I'm making a grocery run . . . we've run out of candy for the trick-or-treaters. Wanna come with?" She lisped the words around a pair of plastic fangs.

Why not? I hadn't talked to Vonda all weekend. "We've got to stop meeting like this," I said, sliding onto the station wagon's bench seat and buckling up.

"I know. It's just been crazy at the B and B this week. Which is a good thing, I guess. But I was missing my best bud." She patted my hand. She and Ricky owned a twelve-bedroom B&B, Magnolia House, and lived on opposite sides of it so they could run the business and share custody of their son, RJ.

"You and Ricky . . . ?"

"We're good." She turned her head to grin at me.

"Good." I was relieved. Vonda and Ricky belonged together, but they both had tempers and their arguments were the stuff of legend in St. Elizabeth. As Vonda slid the car into a slot at the Winn-Dixie, I told her about my weekend. "I should've kept a closer eye on the kids."

She didn't argue like I hoped she would. Giving me an incredulous look, she liberated a shopping cart from the train of them near the store's entrance. "You chaperoned a ghost hunt? And Rachel's boyfriend fell down the stairs?"

I walked fast to keep up with her as she charged toward the candy aisle, not distracted by the lopsided pyramid of pumpkins at fifty percent off. Several shoppers, their carts piled high with bottled water and canned goods, strolled the aisles. One man gave Vonda, sexy in her clinging black vampire dress with the plunging neckline, the once-over. She bared her fangs at him and he jumped back into a cereal display, knocking boxes to the floor.

"Or was pushed. Either way, it shouldn't have happened," I said, flinging a bag of Snickers into the cart.

Vonda pulled them out and restored them to the shelf.

"No chocolate. Only icky stuff. Otherwise, I'll eat all the leftovers for breakfast and blow up like a blimp."

Vonda was a petite slip of a thing, no wider than an angelfish, who'd never been two ounces overweight, and right now her focus on the candy was beginning to irritate me. I flung a couple of bags of caramels into the cart. Vonda added some gum and candies the size of ping-pong balls that advertised themselves as "so hot they'll burn through the roof of your mouth into your brain." Irresistible.

"So, do you think it was?" I prodded.

"Was what?" Vonda wheeled the cart toward a cashier.

"My fault."

"No, especially not if he was pushed. Do you think he was?"

"I don't know. Maybe. Rachel said he was depressed."

"Suicide attempt?" *Thunk, thunk.* Bags of candy landed on the conveyor belt. The bored-looking cashier scanned them without comment.

I shrugged. "I don't know how anyone with an IQ over forty could think that a fall down a couple flights of stairs would be guaranteed fatal."

"A gesture? A call for help?"

I hadn't thought of that. "Possible." I looped my fingers through the bag's handles and walked with Vonda back to the parking lot. A man and a woman stood arguing by the open tailgate of a Chevy Tahoe. The man looked vaguely familiar . . . It took me a moment to realize he was the man who'd shown up at Rothmere looking for Mark Crenshaw. His dad? The couple wasn't shouting, but their faces were mere inches apartment and I could tell from the rigid way they held themselves that they were quarreling.

". . . last time," the woman, dark-haired and petite, said in a louder voice.

As I watched, Crenshaw flung up a hand and stalked toward the grocery store. The woman hesitated only a second before jumping into the driver's seat, gunning the engine, and pulling out recklessly, clipping a shopping cart with the rear bumper as she peeled out of the lot. Tottering over the asphalt, the cart crunched into a motorcycle. Crenshaw spun when he heard the SUV take off, chased it for a couple of futile steps, then kicked at a discarded soda can, using his whole leg like a World Cup midfielder aiming for a goal half a field away. It sprayed caramel-colored liquid onto his slacks before rolling off the curb and under a sedan parked in a handicapped slot. I watched to see if Crenshaw would retrieve the can, but he headed back toward the store, pulling a cell phone from his pocket as he walked. Glancing at Vonda, I saw she'd missed the whole byplay, busy putting the groceries into the backseat of the station wagon.

It didn't seem worth mentioning, so we chatted about hurricane preparations as she drove back to my apartment. We arrived safely, not even clipping any of the trick-or-treaters dashing heedlessly across the road in search of enough candy to keep them on a sugar high until February.

"Sorry this had to be drive-by catch-up," Vonda said as I opened the door. "Let's do lunch later in the week. Keep me posted about Braden."

"You bet." I slammed the door shut and patted it twice. "Thanks for dropping by."

She grinned her silly vampire grin and pulled away.

I went in and watched a bit of the Julia Roberts DVD but couldn't get into it. Noise from the Halloweeners had tapered off, and when I peeked through the blinds, I didn't see any costumed figures making the rounds. A dim glow to my left told me Mrs. Jones's jack-o'-lantern was still on duty. I went to bed feeling unsettled and a bit weepy, and I knew the morning's conversation with Marty was driving my mood. It wasn't like Marty and I had been dating for eons; we'd known each other only since May, and our relationship had always been a long-distance one, with him in Atlanta and me here. And I'd known from the start that his work was paramount to him. Still, I'd gotten used to thinking of him as my boyfriend, and he was the first man I'd slept with since Hank and I divorced and . . . Oh, hell! I punched my pillow.

I must've drifted into an uneasy sleep because a loud bang wrenched me upright some time later. I looked around, disoriented, and heard another bang—coming from the direction of Mrs. Jones's house— followed by a cut-off shout and the squeal of tires. My bedside clock read 12:30 as I unwrapped myself from the sheet. The wooden floor was cold against my bare feet as I raced toward my door. Pulling it open, I peered toward Mrs. Jones's house. A line of vertical light slit the darkness on her veranda—her door was open. Uneasy, I headed across the yard separating my apartment from her house. Acorns and twigs cut into my feet and I hoped I didn't stumble into a fire ant hill in the dark.

"Mrs. Jones?" I called as I got closer.

Nothing.

I put my foot onto the bottom step and felt something sticky. Oh, my God! Blood? I scrambled up the steps to push the door wider but stopped when I saw a crumpled form lying across the threshold.

Mrs. Jones.

# Chapter Eight

THE OLD WOMAN LAY HALF IN, HALF OUT OF THE door, a thin form in a floral flannel robe. I knelt beside her and groped for her wrist. A pulse hammered under my fingers. Thank God. I kicked backward at the door with one foot to open it wider and get more light. I didn't see any blood. The sticky stuff on my foot seemed to be pumpkin, and now that I looked around, I saw chunks of pumpkin scattered across the veranda and steps. I didn't have time to figure out what had happened; I was afraid Mrs. Jones had had a heart attack. I rose and was about to enter the house to call 911 when a hand closed around my ankle. I jumped.

"Grace?"

Mrs. Jones sounded confused and querulous. I knelt again so she could see my face.

"Yes, it's me. I'm going to call nine-one-one. I'll be right back." I brushed a tendril of wiry hair off her face.

"Oh, don't bother them," she said, pushing up on one elbow. "I'm okay."

"Are you sure?" I asked doubtfully. "Does your chest hurt? Your left arm?"

"I haven't had a heart attack, if that's what you're worried about," she said, reaching up a hand. "Pull me up, there's a dear."

I helped her to a sitting position, still unsure about what to do.

She gathered the robe around her. "It was just the suddenness of the explosion," she said. "I admit it gave me quite a jolt. I must have fainted. I can't think how I came to do that; I never do so."

"Explosion?" I was anxious to know what had happened, but first things first. "Never mind. Let me at least help you into the house and make you a cup of tea. If you won't go to the hospital, I think I should stay with you tonight, make sure you don't have a concussion or something."

"That's sweet of you, Grace," she said as I put an arm around her waist and helped her up.

For someone who wasn't much more than a bundle of bones, she weighed a lot. I guided her to the pink damask sofa and steadied her while she sank onto it. Spotting a crocheted afghan on the nearby love seat, I spread it around her frail form.

"You don't need to stay," she said. "I can call my niece Varina and she'll be happy to come over. She's an RN, you know. And her son is just about your age. Have I told you about him? He's an architect."

Even injured she was still trying to fix me up. I smiled as I studied her face. She was paler than normal, but her blue eyes were bright and her pupils seemed to be the same size. "I'll call her," I said, reaching for the phone.

After the phone call, I traipsed through what seemed like half a mile of halls and rooms to reach the kitchen, where I poured water into a dented copper teakettle and set it on the gas range to boil. Ransacking the cupboards, I didn't find any tea but came across envelopes of instant hot cider. I emptied one into a mug and inhaled the tangy apple steam when I added boiling water. Carrying the steaming mug back to the parlor, I found Mrs. Jones lying on the couch, a cushion under her head, fast asleep.

Varina, a short, no-nonsense-looking woman in her early sixties, arrived before I had to make a decision about whether or not to wake Mrs. Jones to make sure she was all right. "That cider will hit the spot," she said, taking the mug from me. She gazed fondly down at Mrs. Jones. "Aunt Genny's going to have to slow down one of these days, but I don't want to be the one to have to tell her!"

I told her as much as I knew about what had happened and she nodded her gray head. "Halloween pranksters, no doubt. I raised three boys of my own and it's a wonder they got to adulthood with all their parts still attached and no police record." She took a noisy sip of cider. "Boys just don't understand the damage some of their 'funny' pranks can do. You go on back to bed, Grace. I'll take care of things here."

I wasn't so sure the exploding pumpkin had been a random prank, but I didn't say anything to Varina about Lonnie's semi-threat. It crossed my mind, though, that he might have thought I lived in Mrs. Jones's house since he'd seen me handing out candy there. I trudged across the lawn, my mind fuzzy with lack of sleep and worry. I'd talk to Mrs. Jones in the morning and find out what had really happened.

## [Monday]

THE SUN WAS CREEPING INTO MY BEDROOM WHEN something next jolted me awake. I lay still for a moment, trying to figure out what had awakened me. *Bam, bam, bam.* Someone was knocking—loudly—on my door. Maybe Varina needed something. I prayed that Mrs. Jones hadn't taken a turn for the worse. Trotting to the door, I opened it.

A man, six feet of lean muscle, plus a slightly crooked nose, short brown hair graying at the temples, and posture that would make a Marine jealous, stood on my tiny stoop, wearing a serious expression and a handsome navy suit. Special Agent John Dillon of the Georgia Bureau of Investigation. A little thrill lilted through me before I remembered I had morning breath, bed head, and was wearing my old red University of Georgia tee shirt, which showed way too much leg. Unshaved.

Dillon's gaze traveled the length of me, starting with my Cherry Flambé toenails and working his way up. An almost smile dented his left cheek and lightened his grim look. "Good. You're up," he said.

"How could I not be with all the racket you were making?"

The serious expression returned. "Invite me in."

"I'm not dressed." I tugged at the hem of my tee shirt.

"I've seen you in less."

Yeah, but only by accident, not because we'd ever even been on a date. He'd invited me to meet his horse once, but that hadn't panned out and I'm not sure it would have counted as a date anyway.

"Grace!" Dillon recalled my wandering thoughts. "Invite me in. Offer me some coffee, or anything with caffeine, for that matter. This is official business and I'd rather not go into it on your doorstep."

I pulled the door wider in silent invitation and preceded him to my compact kitchen. In my search for a house, I'd learned that "compact" was Realtor-speak for "smaller than a gumdrop." I'd also learned it was all I'd be able to afford, unless I was willing to settle for appliances that predated the moon landing and "mouse" holes in the walls big enough to admit a puma. I was afraid to ask what brought Dillon here; that's why my mind kept leaping to inconsequential things. Nuking two mugs of water, I plopped Irish breakfast tea bags into them. It felt like I'd been making hot beverages all night. Okay, technically it was morning, but it still felt like night.

Dillon blew on his tea and took a long sip. Finally, I could stand it no longer.

"What?" I prompted, leaving my tea untouched on the counter. "Is Mrs. Jones okay? Is it about the exploding pumpkin? Because if it—"

"I understand you have evidence in a murder case. I need it."

"Wha—Oh, no! Mrs. Jones died? She said she felt okay. Her niece was with her! She—" Tears started to my eyes.

"Whoa!" Dillon grabbed my shoulders and gave me a little shake. "Mrs. Jones is fine, as far as I know. It's Braden McCullers."

"He died?" My brain was swirling, trying to absorb the news. I paced around my kitchen, working out my agitation. "When? What happened?"

"Last night. Someone smothered him in his hospital bed."

His grim tone shocked me into stillness. Grabbing up my mug, I held it to my chest, trying to absorb its warmth into my sudden coldness. "So you think his fall was a murder attempt, too," I said, my brain beginning to function again. "You want the sheet. Hank told you about me and Spaatz finding the sheet."

"Right."

I tore a paper towel from the roll and dabbed at my eyes. I didn't know Braden that well—hardly at all—but his death saddened me, largely because it would devastate Rachel. I wondered if she'd heard. "Do you have any leads on who did it?" I asked. "Surely, someone saw something in the hospital."

"It was a werewolf," he said.

I threw the crumpled paper towel at him, but it drifted ineffectually to the floor between us. "It's not something to joke about!"

"Do I look like I'm joking? The nurse on duty walked into Braden's room to take his vitals and saw a werewolf holding a pillow over his face. She grabbed at it, but it shook her off and bolted for the stairs. Whoever it was, was long gone by the time she tried to revive Braden and raised the alarm."

"A Halloween costume," I said, catching on.

"Right." He drained his mug and set it on the counter. "The sheet?"

"It's in the trunk of my car," I said. "Let me get my keys."

While I was in the bedroom fetching my keys, I pulled on a pair of sweatpants and ran a brush through my hair. A glance in the mirror told me it wasn't enough, but it would have to do. Dillon was poking through the box on my table when I reappeared. I raised my brows at him.

"Occupational hazard," he excused his snooping. "Are you switching careers? Changing from beautician to historian?"

I explained why I had the box.

"Interesting. My mom gave me some letters my great-grandfather wrote to my great-grandmother during World

War I and they were fascinating . . . They made history more personal, somehow."

Having found myself getting attached to Clarissa after only one letter, I completely agreed with him.

"I'll need a statement about Saturday night," he said as I led him out to my car.

"Okay." Unlocking the trunk, I pulled out the sheet. "I'm afraid we probably messed up any evidence," I apologized. "Spaatz and I both handled it, and we pulled it out of the drawer and—"

"Get over it," Dillon said, flapping open a large plastic bag to contain the sheet. "This case isn't going to go unsolved because of anything you did or didn't do. You've been watching too much *CSI*. Hair and fiber and DNA evidence aren't of any use until we have a suspect."

"Thanks." I smiled slightly. "Do you know who all's been told about Braden's death? I mean, some of the students—"

"We let the high school principal know. He's making all the usual arrangements for grief counselors and what-have-you. No memorial, though; the parents have said they don't want one for a while. In fact, the McCullers family has left town for a week or so to come to terms with their loss." Dillon tossed the sheet onto the passenger seat of his brown Crown Victoria. "My investigators will need to talk to everyone who attended the ghost hunt to see what they might have observed, and to kids who were close to the vic."

We made arrangements for me to give my statement later that afternoon and said good-bye. As he drove off, I walked toward my apartment to dress; I wanted to get hold of Rachel before she heard about Braden's death on the news or, God forbid, via the public address system at school. I could hear it now: the Pledge of Allegiance would be followed by announcements about the lunch menu, an upcoming swim meet, and the death of a classmate. Not the way to learn that someone close to you has died.

"Grace!"

A voice brought my head around as I opened my door. Varina stood on Mrs. Jones's veranda, waving. Darn, I'd forgotten to tell Agent Dillon about the exploding pumpkin.

"I made banana nut muffins," she said, holding one up, "and Aunt Genny would like to talk to you if you have a mo."

"Sure," I said. "Just let me throw some clothes on."

I approached Mrs. Jones's house fifteen minutes later, showered and dressed in dark-wash jeans and a lightweight yellow sweater. I looked around, noting the large chunks of pumpkin strewn across the veranda and into the yard, as well as what looked like plastic bits from a soda bottle or something similar. What on earth had Lonnie and crew—if it had been them—used to make such a mess? Something thunked onto my shoulder. I brushed off a yellow orange clod. It was raining pumpkin. Looking up, I saw globs of the former jack-o'-lantern adhered to the veranda ceiling.

"I called the police this morning," Varina said matter-of-factly when she opened the door. "TPing a few trees is one thing; this"—she gestured to the veranda and yard—"is something else. I didn't quite get the extent of it last night in the dark. Aunt Genny's lucky she wasn't injured by the explosion—it had to be a pretty big one. Anyway, the police said it might be a few hours, but that they'd send someone over."

She led me back to a breakfast nook off the kitchen where Mrs. Jones sat, dressed in neat navy slacks with a pink blouse. Her color was much better than last night and her eyes twinkled like usual as she greeted me. The scent of warm banana bread filled the room.

"I hate to eat and run," I said, accepting a large muffin from Varina, "but I have to do something before work." I told them about Braden's death and my desire to break the news to Rachel.

"Oh, my, trouble certainly comes in threes, doesn't it?" Mrs. Jones said. "That poor McCullers boy, and my incident last night, and now that hurricane is bearing down on us, they say." She shook her head.

"What, exactly, happened last night?" I asked, sliding into a chair. Real butter tempted me from a china butter dish, but I passed it up. I'd been doing well with diet and occasional gym visits since helping out at the Miss Magnolia Blossom pageant in August and I didn't want to undo all my hard work. The muffin was evil enough.

"Well, I don't know what time it was because I was asleep," she said, "but the doorbell rang. I couldn't think who it might be at that hour, but I got up to answer it."

Varina shook her head at her aunt's foolhardiness.

"Don't look at me like that, Varina. I'd like to know where you'll find a safer town than St. Elizabeth." Mrs. Jones took a swallow of orange juice. "When I opened the door, there was no one there. Just as I was closing the door, my poor jack-o'-lantern went ka-blooey!" She flung her hands wide apart. Her frill of hair quivered. "Next thing I knew, you were standing over me. Did I say thank you?"

She held out her bony hand and I took it. "You're very welcome," I said, squeezing her cool fingers gently. "Did you see anything else? A person? A vehicle?"

A frown crinkled her brow. "Now that you mention it, I think there was a truck or an SUV—something big— parked at the curb."

That fit with the squeal of tires I'd heard. "Well, you tell the police everything when they get here, Mrs. Jones. I'm so glad you weren't seriously injured. I'll hose the pumpkin guts off the veranda for you when I get home." I rose, brushed muffin crumbs off my jeans, and said good-bye. I was going to have to hustle to catch Rachel before she left for school.

# Chapter Nine

✂

HALF AN HOUR LATER, HAVING BROKEN THE NEWS TO Rachel and her mother and feeling like I'd been up all night, I dragged myself into the salon and told Mom, Althea, and Stella. As if sensing my distress, Beauty, Stella's white Persian who usually doesn't consort with lowly humans, leaped onto my lap and purred while I absently stroked her head.

"I hope you told Rachel not to come in today," Mom said.

"I told her not to come in all week if she didn't feel like it, but she said she'll be back tomorrow."

"I'll bet Rachel's really freaked out that one of her friends is a murderer," Stella said with a shiver.

The three of us stared at her.

"Well, it has to be, doesn't it? There weren't any tourists at Rothmere on a Saturday night, so it must have been one of the kids who pushed Braden. Or a chaperone." She looked questioningly at me.

"You're right," I said slowly. I hadn't gotten around to puzzling through who might have done it. "But the kids were all paired up. And as for the chaperones . . . I can't imagine a reason why Glen Spaatz or Coach Peet or the other woman—she was some girl's mother—would want to kill Braden. Oh, and Lucy was there, too, but she was in her office."

"That woman's a few pecans shy of a pie," Althea said.

"Thinking she's the reincarnation of Amelia Rothmere doesn't make her a murderer," I said. Beauty jumped off my lap and went to intimidate squirrels with her evil cat glare through the front window. I brushed long, white hairs off my jeans. "Although, if she happened to see one of the kids damaging the house or its contents in some way, there's no telling what she might do. I thought she was going to slap me for using the parlor drapes to keep Braden warm."

"That was good thinking." Mom nodded approvingly. "And Lucy's harmless. Just a little . . . eccentric."

Althea looked unconvinced. It was opening time so I unlocked the front door and greeted Euphemia Toller, an octogenarian who came weekly to have Mom set and curl her thinning hair. She was a small woman with a dowager's hump that threatened to topple her over.

"I'm leaving early to help the school with their fund-raising head shaves," I reminded Mom as she fastened a violet cape around Mrs. Toller's hunched shoulders.

"I'm leaving, too," Mrs. Toller said in the overly loud voice of the near-deaf. "My son's driving over from Albany to take me back with him this afternoon. He says he doesn't want to have to worry about Horatio blowing me away."

"You're lucky to have such a loving son," Mom said.

I pulled up the wooden blinds and stared at the sky. It was leaden today, a surly gray, and the wind had picked up. I knew there'd be whitecaps on the sound. My first client came in and I tried to focus on cutting and coloring for the rest of the morning, but my mind niggled at the mystery of Braden's death whenever I wasn't talking to someone.

I left shortly after noon to keep my appointment with Agent Dillon at the Georgia Bureau of Investigation Regional Headquarters building in Kingsland, a town a few miles south of St. Elizabeth and just west of I-95. The familiar single-story building with narrow windows not much bigger than arrow slits in a medieval castle sat in a square of grass that almost matched the tan brick. Shrubs clipped by someone with a ruler and a level stood between the windows like prisoners lined up against an execution wall. The inside was not so grim: standard waiting room fare, a reception desk, and doors leading to interior offices. Propped against the desk and holding a mug of coffee, Agent Dillon was talking to Officer Kent, an earnest young cop with jug ears who hero-worshiped his boss.

"Marshal, how's it going?" I said by way of greeting, watching the tips of Officer Kent's ears turn red at what he took to be a slur on his hero. Dillon sighed at my *Gunsmoke* joke, clapped Kent on the shoulder, and led me to a conference room. It consisted of a long table, rolling chairs, a window looking to the lot behind the building, and photos of former special agents in charge hung on the walls. Bureaucratic blah. He'd interviewed me in his office in the past, and I raised my brows as he indicated blueprints spread on the table. I stepped closer to examine them, brushing past Dillon and catching the male scent of him, spiked with a lime aftershave and soap. I flushed and made a show of shifting the documents on the table to get a better view.

"Rothmere," Dillon said. "I need you to show me where everyone was Saturday night. I understand the students were supposed to be paired up, but our interviews at the high school yielded surprisingly few hard and fast alibis. Only a couple of the teams stuck together the whole time and could alibi each other." Frustration sounded in his voice. "It seems everyone had to use the bathroom at some point or wander off to chat with a friend stationed in another room, or go outside to watch the damned fireworks. I'm hoping you can help."

"I'll try. I don't even know all the kids' names, though, so I don't know how much help I'll be."

I showed him where I'd encountered various kids and the route I'd taken chasing Lonnie. I gave him times as best as I remembered them and closed my eyes to try to remember who I'd seen outside watching the fireworks.

"That's it?" he asked when I finished.

"What do you mean?"

"Pretty loose supervision. You only saw each pair of kids—what? Ten minutes in an hour? One of them could've driven to Disney World and shot Mickey for all you know."

"It's not like I was the only chaperone," I said hotly, mad at him for remarks that pricked my already sensitive conscience.

"Where were the other chaperones?"

"Coach Peet took Tyler to the bus," I said, "and I assume he stayed there."

"No, he didn't," Dillon said, tossing the pencil down. "He took Tyler to the bus but left him with the bus driver who then fell asleep. Tyler snuck away, so we can't account for Peet, Tyler, or for that matter, the bus driver."

"What about Tasha Solomon? Her daughter was part of the class."

"*Dr.* Solomon. Mother of Ari Solomon. Spent most of the evening in the carriage house museum with a couple of teens who got excited about an owl hooting and thought it was the ghost. She and they split up when the fireworks drew everyone outside, though."

I nibbled on my forefinger, thinking. "Do you think someone deliberately set off the fireworks to create an opportunity to . . ."

"To kill McCullers? Possible. Although Lonnie Farber copped to the fireworks and vehemently denies going back in the mansion."

"And if it was him, up on the landing when Braden got hurt, there'd be no need for another ghost costume, would there?" I said, thinking about the sheet Spaatz and I had found in the armoire.

"You're right."

The faint hint of surprise in Dillon's voice told me he hadn't made that connection and I felt a flash of triumph at having helped. "What about Sunday night?"

"What about it?"

His face got that closed look that told me I wasn't going to learn anything, but I persevered anyway. "What were the"—I stumbled over the word "suspects"—"what was everyone doing? Who had the opportunity to get to the hospital?"

He gave me the "we don't share investigation details with civilians" look. It was an eloquent look; he practiced it a lot. "Where were you last night?"

"When?"

Dillon just looked at me, brows slightly elevated. I sighed. "Six thirty—handed out candy with Mrs. Jones.

Seven thirty or so—ran to the store with Vonda. Eight o'clock—home alone, watching a DVD, then sleeping. Midnight—investigating an explosion at Mrs. Jones's house."

"What?" He spluttered coffee on the blueprints and dabbed at the spots with a sheet of paper.

Pleased at having startled him, I explained.

"I'll see what the SEPD came up with," he said, making a note and asking me to spell Varina's name.

"What about you?" I asked, feeling daring.

"What about me what?"

"Where were you last night?"

"I'm not a suspect." He said it with a purposely smug expression.

"And I am?" I asked indignantly, even though I was sure—pretty sure—he didn't really think I'd killed Braden McCullers.

A certain light in his eyes told me he was amused. "I was helping my troop learn first aid techniques."

"You're a Scout leader? Don't you have to have a son?"

"Who says I don't?"

I goggled at him and the grin he'd been suppressing spread across his face. "I've got another appointment," he said, rolling up the blueprint.

Fine. If he wouldn't volunteer information about his kids—if he had any—I wouldn't give him the satisfaction of asking. I looked at my watch. "I've got to get over to the school. If I think of anything else, I'll call you." I kept my voice cool, but it didn't seem to faze him.

"Do that," he said. Picking up his mug, he said, "I haven't seen Shears around recently. Is he staying busy up in Atlanta?" His tone was so casual I knew his interest was more than that.

"He got a new job—in DC," I said, equally casually. "I was supposed to visit next weekend, but that fell through." I rubbed at a smudge on the glossy table.

"Really?"

"Um-hm."

The conversation trickled to an awkward halt. I looked up from under my lashes to see him staring at me intently. His gaze lingered on my mouth. "I'm going to be late," I said, bolting for the door.

In my car, I pounded the steering wheel. Why had I run out like a nervous high schooler? I drove too fast on the way back to St. Elizabeth and parked outside Mom's; I knew from experience that parking within two blocks of the high school was impossible on a school day. Mom's house is situated on Bedford Square, the historical shopping district in town, and the high school was only six blocks away. It was actually a relief to walk to the high school and let the pre-hurricane bluster blow away my confusion and frustration. The wind kicked up leaves no one had bothered to rake this fall and flung them at me. Stepping into the gutter and scuffing leaves up with my feet, I watched the wind swirl them away. It was fun and I arrived at the school feeling better than I had all day.

St. Elizabeth High School, a characterless rectangle of red brick from the '60s, housed about a thousand students. The school's mascot, a sabertooth tiger, leered at me from the wall beside the office. A strange orangey color, the sabertooth's paint was flaking off in spots, revealing a mint green layer beneath that made him look like a Dr. Seuss character. The hall surged with jean-clad teens, laughter, and the clanging of locker doors as the students switched classes. Many of them stopped at a large display on a folding table that said: "Winter Ball Fund-raiser!! Vote for Your Favorite Teacher or

Friend to Shave His/Her Head!!! Each Vote $1." Coffee cans with slits in their plastic covers were placed beneath photos of five people I took to be SEHS students and teachers. The kids in the hall were egging each other on to put money in the cans. As the crowd thinned out, I looked into one coffee can; it was crammed with bills. A bored-looking kid with severe acne sat behind the table, probably to ensure money got put into the coffee cans and not taken out. Sad. He eyed me suspiciously but didn't say anything.

Putting a dollar into each of the cans, I approached the office. Standing at the half door, I told the heavyset woman at a computer terminal why I was there.

"Oh, yes, Miss Terhune," she said in a high-pitched voice that didn't match her generous build. "The principal wants to see you."

Ye gods! I'd only been back in the building two and a half minutes and already I was being sent to the principal's office. It was weird how those words made my tummy do a little flip. Not that I'd spent much time in the principal's office when I went here, but still. The woman motioned me through a full-sized door to my right and then led me past two unoccupied desks, a water cooler, and a dying philodendron to a door with "PRINCIPAL" and "Merle Kornhiser" stenciled in gold. Rapping once on the open door, the woman said, "Merle, here's Miss Terhune."

I walked in not knowing quite what to expect. The massive oak desk and straight-backed leather chairs I remembered were gone, replaced by an acrylic or glass desk that looked like a drafting table and a rounded, armless love seat in pale orange with matching chairs. A stack of three large pillows upholstered in a bright geometric print suggested some lucky visitors got to sit on the floor. During my years at SEHS, Mr. Iselin, a tall, spare man with a

Hitler-type mustache, had been principal. He knew all the students by name and always addressed us as "Miss Terhune" or "Mr. Parker," but with an inflection that made the titles more snide than respectful. When I entered, Mr. Kornhiser came around his desk and held out his hand. He was the anti-Iselin: short, with thinning blond hair pulled back into a stubby ponytail, and wearing a turquoise and pink Hawaiian shirt. He could've been any age between forty and sixty, judging by the crinkles around his eyes and the gray threading through his hair.

"Grace—I can call you Grace, can't I?—I want to welcome you to St. Elizabeth High and thank you for helping with our fund-raiser." He pumped my hand.

"I'm happy to do it, Mr.—"

He held up a hand. "Ah-ah. Merle. Call me Merle."

"Okay. If you'll just tell me where—"

"Actually, Grace, I was hoping we could chat for a few minutes. About the incident Saturday night." He motioned to one of the orange chairs and I sank into it gingerly. He dropped gracefully to one of the pillows and crossed his legs.

I had to look down at him to converse and it felt very weird.

"It makes you uncomfortable, doesn't it?" He grinned, revealing a gap between his front teeth. "I like to play with our cultural notions of power. In most meetings, the grand poobah sits at the head of the table, or behind a desk, while the lesser minions sit along the wall. I consider myself a servant of this school and our students so I sit here." He patted the pillow.

I made no response. What could I say? Very democratic of you? I like your pillow? What kind of drugs do you take with your corn flakes and OJ?

After a long moment of silence, he continued, "It was very servant-minded of you to volunteer your time Saturday night to chaperone our field trip. Really. I, personally, appreciate it. And I'm more sorry than I can say that the evening ended on such a negative note. You didn't happen to observe anything, did you, that would clear up what happened?"

He sat back, seemingly relaxed, bracing himself with his hands behind him, but his eyes watched my face carefully. I decided he was probably in his fifties and worried about school liability just like any other administrator in his position would be. The "I'll sit at your feet approach" wasn't going to cut much ice with a jury if the McCullerses sued him.

"Not really," I said. "What have the students told you? Did any of them have a grudge against Braden?"

"A grudge?" He blinked his eyes rapidly several times. "You're not implying that one of our students could have *intentionally* harmed Braden? It must have been an accident. Or maybe someone else was in the house. Tourists."

I gave the man an A plus for grasping at straws. "I don't think it gets much more intentional than smothering someone with a pillow," I said. Merle was living in la-la land if he thought the police could hang the murder on a random tourist from Topeka, visiting Rothmere hours after it closed, who decided on the spur of the moment to toss Braden down the stairs and then finished the job with a pillow in the hospital.

"Braden McCullers was a good kid," he said. "A real servant-leader. Captain of the football team, a GPA that got him accepted to MIT, homecoming king, state-level debater. I can't imagine any of the students had a beef with him."

"Have you asked?"

"No. The police have been interviewing the field trip students all day," he admitted, "creating a lot of negative energy in the school."

I thought it was probably Braden's death that was bumming the students out, not the police investigation. "Did the McCullers family say anything to you about when the funeral would be?" I asked, standing, "I'd like to go."

Merle reached a hand up to me and I took it reluctantly, helping him to his feet. His knees crackled. "I explained to them how Braden's friends, all of us at SEHS, need closure, but they said they preferred to say their good-byes privately. They wouldn't even authorize a memorial service."

He sounded personally affronted. It was a little strange, but maybe the McCullers family couldn't face Braden's friends and classmates right now; the sight of all the seniors going on to graduation, college, marriage might remind them too painfully of milestones their son would never reach.

"Let me walk you down to the auditorium," Merle said. "I expect I'll be losing this"—he tugged at his ponytail and grinned—"before the week is out."

He delivered me to Rachel at the door of the auditorium and hustled off to "brief the school board on the situation." Rachel looked wan, her face paler than usual against her black hair and clothes. A camera dangled from a strap around her wrist. "Thanks for coming, Grace," she said, managing a tiny smile.

I gave her a quick hug, glad she'd mustered up the courage to come to school. Being around her classmates was the best thing for her right now, I was sure. Much better than crying alone at home. "Happy to do it," I said. "Are there a lot of takers?"

For answer, she pushed open the auditorium door. Eight girls waited on the stage with a chair positioned in the center. "They're all here for Locks of Love. We'll do the head shaving at the pep rally on Friday. I'm supposed to take photos for the yearbook." She indicated the camera.

I surveyed the girls, a lonely clump on the bare stage surrounded by the echoing emptiness of the auditorium. I advanced toward them and thanked them for donating their hair to Locks of Love. "Tell you what," I said. "These are hardly ideal hair-cutting conditions."

They bobbed their heads in agreement. "How about if y'all come down to Violetta's after school and we'll do it there? That way, we can give you a shampoo and make sure you get a style you're happy with. You can tell all your friends that they can get a free cut at Violetta's if they're donating their hair to charity, okay?"

The girls looked relieved. "I only have study hall last period," said Lindsay, the tall brunette from the field trip. "Can I come now?"

"Sure," I said. "If that's okay with the school. And I'll see the rest of you later this afternoon?"

They nodded and headed for the hall. "I should've thought of that," Rachel said. "It's, like, a way better idea than cutting hair here." She swung the camera moodily.

"Either way would've worked. You've done the hard part by motivating them to part with their hair," I said. "Want me to take pictures today?"

"Sure." She handed me the camera and trudged down the hall, a slim figure in black, looking very alone.

"She's taking it hard. Braden's death, I mean," said Lindsay's voice beside me.

I looked up at the athletic girl who topped my five-six by several inches. Her brown eyes were fixed on Rachel.

"They were very close," I said. "But I'm sure it's hard on a lot of Braden's friends."

"Oh, yeah," she said, grief in her voice and face.

She fell into step beside me and we left the school. "No homework?" I asked when she didn't stop by her locker to pick up any books.

"I have to be back later for volleyball practice," she said. "I'll pick up my backpack then."

"Do you like volleyball?" I asked as we cut across the parking lot. She certainly had the height for it.

"Love it. I've got a full ride to the University of Maryland. I signed my letter of intent a couple weeks ago." She mimed a signature in the air.

"Congratulations."

"My boyfriend's going to Annapolis, so it'll work out great."

"Mark?" I said, remembering the name from Saturday night.

"Yeah, he's got an appointment to the Naval Academy. It's been his dream forever. And his dad's. His dad's a navy captain down at Kings Bay. His stepdad, really, although his real dad was in the navy, too."

Kings Bay was the submarine base about twenty miles south of St. Elizabeth. "I think I saw him at Rothmere," I said. And at the grocery store, fighting with his wife.

Lindsay nodded again, a curtain of brown hair swinging across her face. "Yeah. Mark was Braden's best friend." She kicked at a fallen pecan, sending it skittering into the road. "He's really broken up about it, but he's not talking about it. You know how guys are."

She sounded both worried and a bit peeved. I tried to remember what it was like to be eighteen and in love. Had I resented it when Hank didn't share something with me? I couldn't remember. "Give him time," I said. "It's probably just about the hardest thing he's ever had to deal with."

"I don't know about that," Lindsay said. She clamped her lips together and lengthened her stride.

I hustled to keep up with her and we climbed the steps to the salon's veranda together. Mom was using a curling iron on a customer's hair and Stella had a client in the Nail Nook. Althea sat on the love seat in our waiting area, flipping through the pages of a magazine. She looked at us from under her brows as I shut the door. "You dragging clients in off the streets now, baby-girl?" she asked.

Lindsay looked startled. I motioned her toward my chair, saying, "No. The Locks of Love girls are coming here." I explained the change of plan.

"That's a good idea, Grace," Mom said. "Shasta here is my last client of the day, so Althea and I can help when the other girls get here."

I flipped a cape around Lindsay's shoulders and brushed her hair back from her forehead. She had enviably clear skin and strong bones. She was pretty now, but I figured she'd be striking once she hit her late twenties or thirties. I secured her hair with an elastic at the nape of her neck and quickly braided it. "You're sure?" I said, lifting my shears.

She gave a sharp nod. "Yeah. This was really important to Braden—his little sister died of leukemia—and I really feel I should do it for him. I owe him this."

I stood there stunned. "I had no idea. His poor parents. That's awful!" I shut up; there weren't any words that could begin to address the McCullerses' family tragedies.

"Yeah." Lindsay bowed her head and I thought for a moment she might be praying, but when she slanted me a look, I realized she was waiting for me to chop off her hair.

I cut off the braid and put it aside to be mailed to Locks

of Love with the others when we'd collected them. Then, I led her to the shampoo basin and washed her hair, enjoying the fragrance of our new lavender-scented shampoo as it bubbled in the sink.

By the time I'd finished giving Lindsay a jaw-length bob, the other girls were trickling in, looking around curiously. "This is way cozier than Chez Pierre out on the highway," one of them observed, running a hand through the fern fronds dripping from a hanging basket. "I need to tell my mom about this place."

Mom beamed and swept her off to the shampoo sink. Althea and I each hooked up with a teenager, and the three of us were busy for an hour and a half. By the end of the afternoon, we had ten braids of varying length and thicknesses to send along to Locks of Love. I'd even remembered to take photos so Rachel could use them in the yearbook.

"I'm bushed," Althea said when the last girl left. She sat on the love seat, kicked her shoes off, and began to massage the ball of one foot.

"Let me do that for you, Althea," Stella said. She brought over the foot basin she used for pedicures and gently submerged Althea's feet.

Althea leaned back and closed her eyes. "Thank you, Stel. That feels right good. I don't know what's more tiring—being on my feet all day or listening to all that chatter. Bunch of magpies!" But she said it with a tolerant smile.

"It reminds me of when you and Alice Rose were in high school," Mom said, plopping her combs into the container of blue germicide. "And all your friends used to come around. Maybe we should do some kind of promotion to attract a younger clientele. Maybe Rachel would have some ideas. I hope she's doing okay."

"Nobody's okay ten minutes after someone they cared about dies," Althea said testily, opening one eye. "You of all people should know that, Vi."

"I do." She thought for a moment, standing with a comb forgotten in her hand. "I guess I was guilty of thinking that things like this don't hit young people as hard because youth is so resilient. But they do. Sometimes harder."

The salon door creaked open and we all turned, surprised, to see a young man on the threshold. He was tall, with a football player's broad shoulders and thick neck. He wore the same letter jacket he'd had on at Rothmere. Mark Crenshaw. He shifted from foot to foot, looking uncomfortable in the feminine salon, with four pairs of female eyes—five, if you count Beauty—staring at him.

"Um, is Lindsay here?" he asked. "Lindsay Tandy?"

"She left almost two hours ago," I said. "She said something about volleyball practice."

"That's just it," he said, bringing his thumb to his mouth to gnaw on the cuticle. "I was supposed to meet her after practice, but coach said she never showed. She'd never skip practice. Something's happened to her."

# Chapter Ten

IMAGES OF A GHOSTLY FIGURE PUSHING BRADEN down the stairs and a werewolf smothering him in his hospital bed jumped into my mind. Could some deranged killer be after all the kids who were on the field trip? What if—

Mom cut into my lurid thoughts with her usual calm good sense. "You say she's only been 'missing' for a couple of hours? I doubt anything's happened to her. Maybe she had more homework than usual and skipped practice to do it, or maybe . . . was she close to Braden McCullers?"

"He was more my friend than hers," the teen said, looking less tense than he had.

"Well, but she knew him. Maybe she just needs a little space to come to terms with his passing."

Althea nodded in agreement. "Uh-huh. I'll bet your gal's holed up somewhere having a good cry."

"You could be right," he said, doubt and hope in his voice. "She was a real mess when we first got the news."

"Have you checked at her house?" Stella asked, rocking back on her heels. Using a towel, she dried Althea's feet.

"I called, but no one answered. Both her folks work. Maybe they're home now." He rubbed at a dark bruise that discolored his left cheek, then winced.

I could see why Alice Rose didn't want to let my nephews play football. "You get hurt playing football," she declared every time her husband, a second-stringer during his time at Auburn, tried to persuade her to sign six-year-old Logan up for a league.

"You're right," Mark said. "I'll run over there. I'm sorry for interrupting."

"Don't worry about it," Mom said to his back as he pushed through the door and pounded down the veranda steps.

"That young man is strung way too tight," Althea observed. "If my William had fretted himself like that every time I was late or not where I was supposed to be, he'd have worried himself into an early grave and Beau Lansky wouldn't have had the chance to murder him."

"Now, Althea—" Mom started.

Althea had convinced herself that Georgia's governor, Beau Lansky, with or without the help of the DuBois family, had killed her husband and his friend Carl. Their bodies had turned up in the old DuBois bank this past May, sealed into a wall, lending some credence to her obsession. Still, there was no evidence to tie Lansky to the crime, and Mom had tired of listening to her friend's conspiracy theories.

"I'm just saying that boy needs to relax," Althea grumbled.

Even though I agreed with her, I could see how it would

be difficult to chill out when your best friend had been murdered in his hospital bed.

I said good night to Mom and Althea, who were planning to see the new Robert Downey Jr. movie, and to Stella, who was headed home to hem her daughter's marching band uniform. "How's it going with Darryl?" I asked Stella as we descended the veranda steps together. Beauty slunk behind us, stalking a mockingbird under the magnolia.

"One day at a time," she said, but she sounded more happy than sad. "We're still going to counseling; I guess we both had a lot of stuff to get out on the table." She held her hair back against a gust of wind. "Funny how you can be married to someone for twenty years and talk all the time without saying the things that really need to be said. Or maybe we just weren't listening. Either way, it helps that he's got a job again."

Darryl was a mechanic who'd been out of work for several months and he'd used his down time to have an affair. "I'm sure it does," I said. I waved as she scooped up a frustrated Beauty and got into her car. I was about to head for my apartment when another car pulled to the curb. A white Corvette with California plates. The passenger-side window buzzed down. "Grace?"

The voice was familiar but I didn't place it immediately. Curiosity warred with caution. I peered through the open window. Glen Spaatz leaned toward me, smiling. "Hey, I'm glad I caught you. The kids told me you were cutting their hair for free and I wanted to stop by and thank you." He must have seen my puzzled look because he added, "I'm the senior class sponsor and I okayed the head-shaving fund-raiser."

"Oh, well, you're welcome," I said. "Locks of Love is a great organization."

"Do you have dinner plans?"

His question caught me off guard.

"Uh . . . no."

He pushed the passenger-side door open. "Why don't you join me? I've got a stack of exams to grade, but I was going to get a quick bite at The Crab Pot."

Why not? He was attractive, single (I assumed), and I had nothing more exciting waiting at my apartment than a tuna sandwich or canned ravioli. "Okay," I said, sliding into the low-slung seat. Leather. They must be paying teachers more than I realized. He put the car in gear and pulled smoothly away from the curb before accelerating well past the speed limit.

"What's the point of having all those horses under the hood if you don't let 'em run?" he said, apparently picking up on my discomfort by my white-knuckled grip on the dashboard.

His mention of horses brought John Dillon to mind for a moment, but I pushed the thought aside. Glen pulled into a spot in the lot across from The Crab Pot a few minutes later and we walked into the restaurant, a cozy place with high-backed booths and décor that ran to strategically strung nets populated by plastic crabs and fish. I considered The Crab Pot a tourist haunt and rarely went there during the summer, but it was okay at this time of year. It sat on Ocean Drive and had a lovely view of the sound from the second-story deck. White caps made the sea look like a dark meringue tonight, and we opted to sit inside, out of the growing wind. A sprinkling of customers provided a background hum of conversation.

"Have you thought about evacuating?" Glen said. "I guess the storm's supposed to hit late Wednesday."

"If it doesn't veer north like they usually do," I said,

opening my menu. No surprise: nearly every entrée featured crab in some form. "What about you?"

"I've never seen a hurricane—we don't have them in California. I'm going to stick around to see what it's like." He flashed a white smile, clearly jazzed by the thought.

"No power or running water is not the stuff of high adventure," I said prosaically, giving my order to the waitress: she-crab soup and a Caesar salad. "So you're from California?"

"LA. Land of palm trees and movie stars, daahling. Kiss-kiss."

"I take it Hollywood wasn't your cup of tea?" I asked, smiling at his air kisses.

"Oh, I gave it a whirl," he said, "but it seems I don't have that star quality." His grin this time combined both self-deprecation and a hint of bitterness.

"Were you in a movie?" I asked, surprised.

"Several. Infinitely forgettable." He waved the topic away. "I got tired of doing auditions and brown-nosing casting directors and decided it was time to grow up and do something useful with my life. My degree was in biology and I heard there was a shortage of science teachers, so I picked up my teaching credential and taught for a couple of years in LA before moving out here. No wife or kids to worry about—like how I worked that in?—so I could suit myself and give Georgia a whirl. What about you? Are you living the life of your dreams?"

His question took me aback and I sipped my water, grateful that the server's appearance with our salads gave me a chance to think. "I like my life," I temporized, trying to think if I even had a dream. Once, it had been to marry Hank, have children, and live a life not unlike Mom and Dad's, except for that whole Dad-dying-young thing. Now . . .

He apparently read my confusion because he said, "I'm sorry. That's too deep a question for a first date. We should start with the basics. Ever been married? Children? Favorite color? Hobbies?" He forked up a bite of his salad.

I laughed, relieved to abandon soul-searching. "Divorced. No. Green. Singing."

We chatted easily through the rest of the meal and I enjoyed his company, but the evening's easy camaraderie dissipated when we pulled up behind a police car parked outside my apartment.

"What's a copper doing on your doorstep?" Glen asked in a tight voice.

"My ex," I said, having recognized Hank even in the near dark as he turned away from my door and tromped toward us. I got out of the car.

"I thought you'd be home, Grace," Hank said, scanning the Corvette suspiciously. "I needed to follow up with you on the incident Halloween night. The explosion. Who's that?"

"A teacher from the high school," I said. I did not need a run-in with Hank to cap off my evening and I prayed Glen would have the good sense to just go. "Bye," I encouraged him with a wave.

Glen climbed out of the car and came around to the sidewalk. He and Hank were of a similar height, but Glen was far less bulky, looking almost willowy beside Hank's body-armored and uniformed figure. I introduced the two men and they shook hands, Hank glowering and Glen smiling easily. "Looks like the officer needs to talk to you," Glen said. "We'll do that nightcap another time." And he astonished me by ignoring my outstretched hand and kissing me on the cheek, just at the corner of my mouth. Before I could recover, he was back in the car and zooming off in a way that must have had Hank itching for his radar gun.

He jotted down the car's license number and turned to me. "What the hell—"

"Don't start with me," I warned him, trying to puzzle out Glen's strange behavior. It was almost as if he were deliberately taunting Hank since neither of us had mentioned a nightcap. Why would he do that?

"Oh, good, you found Grace." Mrs. Jones's voice came from her veranda. "Now you can tell us what you found out. I'm dying to know."

Turning my back on Hank, I trotted over to Mrs. Jones, who looked fully recovered from her ordeal in a plum-colored velour lounging suit, her hair frilled around her face. Hank trailed up the steps after me, saying, "I wouldn't trust that man, if I were you, Grace. My cop instincts tell me he's trouble."

Your cop instincts or your jealous ex-husband instincts? I wanted to ask but didn't since Mrs. Jones was standing there. "I can take care of myself," I said instead.

"What man?" Mrs. Jones asked, her eyes wide. "Do you have a new young man, Grace? Was that him that just drove off? I liked that snazzy car. A pretty young thing like you should be playing the field, living it up. It's about time you got over your divorce and moved on. Life doesn't stand still."

I could feel the frustration building in Hank as she spoke and I edged away from him.

"She was married to me," Hank said, his jaw jutting forward pugnaciously.

"Well, of course she was," Mrs. Jones said, eyeing Hank like he was a bit dim. "But you blew that all to bits with your philandering, didn't you? Ka-boom! Just like my pumpkin."

I bit back a giggle as Hank gobbled incoherently.

Mrs. Jones blinked at him innocently. "What did you find out about the explosion?"

Hank pulled out his notebook, either to hide behind or refresh his memory. "The lab tested some of the residue. It was aluminum and hydrogen chloride."

"My goodness! Where would one get that, I wonder?" Mrs. Jones asked.

"There's a toilet bowl cleaner that has it," Hank said, clearly pleased to be able to demonstrate his knowledge. "Kids mix some of the cleaner in a container—like a plastic pop bottle—add aluminum foil, and run like crazy. If it explodes in your hand, it can blow off a few fingers. Well, you've seen what it did to your jack-o'-lantern." He glanced up at the ceiling where a few pumpkin strings still clung.

"Mercy." Mrs. Jones put a hand to her chest. "But why *my* jack-o'-lantern?"

"It was most likely random—kids playing pranks on Halloween," Hank said with a wrapping-it-up air, returning his notebook to his pocket.

"Did you talk to Alonso Farber?" I asked.

"We know how to do our jobs, Grace," Hank said huffily.

I took that to mean no and resolved to make sure Agent Dillon had the info on the pumpkin bomb. I couldn't shake the suspicion that it had been meant as a warning to me, with Mrs. Jones an accidental victim.


I ENTERED MY EMPTY APARTMENT WITH RELIEF, ready for a shower and an hour reading one of my favorite Georgette Heyer novels. I'd read all her Regency romances a half dozen times or more, but they were still the books I went to when I was stressed. My answering machine blinked at me and I listened to a message from Marty, feeling vaguely guilty about having been out with Glen, but it's not like we were ever exclusive and the dinner with Glen hadn't really been a *date*. The message only said, "I'm off to Phoenix and then Houston for my story. It's heating up. Check my byline this week. I'll catch up with you later."

It made me sad. Not a word about missing me or about rescheduling my trip to Washington. I reached for the phone but pulled back my hand. I wasn't up to cheery enquiries about what he was working on when all the time I was worried that more than geographical distance separated us. Trailing to the bathroom, I remembered what Stella had said about all that goes unsaid in a relationship. Certainly with Hank I'd kept my innermost feelings to myself. Oh, we'd had it out about his affairs, but I'd never once told him how his screwing around made me feel little and worthless. Yes, it had hurt my feelings and finally dried up my love for him, but it was more than that.

I stepped into the shower and let the pounding spray wash away my unusual melancholy. I put it down to the aftereffects of Braden's death—was it only this morning Dillon stopped by to tell me about it? Towel-drying my hair, I pulled on my UGA tee shirt and traipsed barefoot into my tiny kitchen. Glass of milk in hand, I headed for the orange and cream recliner, which didn't match anything in the room but had cost me only fifteen dollars at a garage sale. I read *Faro's Daughter* for a few minutes, but found that Ravenscar's attitude toward Deb was depressing me instead of amusing me. My gaze fell on the box of documents from Rothmere.

I rooted through the box, looking for something with
Clarissa's handwriting. I found a slim packet of letters tied
with a blue ribbon and slid one out. Bolder and slantier
handwriting than Clarissa's.

*30 October 1831*

*My darling Clarissa,*

*Your most recent letter convinces me you are over-
wrought, my dear. I'm afraid the tragedy of your father's untimely death has upset the balance of your
mind. Your suspicions do you no more credit than they
do your family. Let us be married at once, my love, so I
can carry you off to my plantation and you can immerse
yourself in household tasks that will distract your mind.
You are too much alone at Rothmere, with no serious
responsibilities to occupy you. Let us not wait out the
year of your mourning, but be married quietly at once.
We can discuss it further when I arrive on Saturday
next.*

*Everlastingly yours,
Quentin*

I folded the letter thoughtfully. Quentin sounded like a
nice guy who truly cared about Clarissa. I hoped they'd
married and lived happily ever after. But what had he meant
about her suspicions? Clearly she'd written to him about
her father's death. Had she implicated a family member?
Who? One of her brothers? Her mother? Extracting the
next letter from the pile, I carefully spread it open.

*22 November 1831*

*Dear Clarissa,*

*I am sorry to hear that you are unwell. What has the physician said about your condition? Perhaps you can visit me in Savannah when you have recovered and we can add to your trousseau. It delights me greatly that you and Quentin are going to marry after the New Year. It will give me great pleasure to stand up for you at your wedding, as you stood up for me. Let me know when you are feeling more the thing and we will arrange your visit.*

*Your dear friend,*
*Felicity*

I found myself worried about Clarissa's illness and had to shake my head to remind myself that she'd been in her grave—from one cause or another—for well over a hundred years. Maybe she'd made herself ill by worrying about her father's death. Suddenly overcome with tiredness, I tucked the letters into the box and crawled under my quilt. My last thought as I drifted off to sleep was not of Clarissa, but of Lindsay Tandy. I hoped Mark had found her at home.

# Chapter Eleven

[Tuesday]

TUESDAY MORNING, PUFFY CLOUDS WERE CREEPING across the sky from the east, forerunners of Horatio, and a slight headache behind my eyes told me the barometer was falling. For the first time, I began to worry that Horatio really was going to hit St. Elizabeth. I needed to run by the Piggly Wiggly and scoop up some supplies before the shelves were barer than Mother Hubbard's cupboard. Midway through the morning, a woman I didn't know came in looking for a haircut. Dark brown hair, too flat a shade to be natural, hung around a thin, tanned face that matched her thin, tan body clad in a long-sleeved blouse and Bermuda shorts that showed wiry, muscular legs. In her forties, I guessed, she had the nervous energy of a sparrow, her sunspeckled hands fluttering as she talked, her gaze darting about the salon, taking everything in. I was able to accommodate her without an appointment because we'd had many cancellations as people fled inland. Evacuations weren't mandatory, but many people left anyway, dodging the inconvenience of no electricity as much as true danger.

As I led the woman back to the shampoo sink, she introduced herself as Joy Crenshaw. "My son mentioned what you were doing for the high school girls and since I needed a cut myself . . ."

"Mark's your son? Did he ever catch up with Lindsay yesterday?"

She rolled her eyes but smiled. "That boy. He's such a worry wart. Lindsay was fine. She hadn't felt well, so she'd skipped practice and gone home to take a nap. I don't know where he gets that worry gene. Certainly not from me, and not from his father, either. Mark Sr. was intrepid until the day his F-14 went into a flat spin and crashed into the Pacific."

"I'm so sorry," I said, taken aback by the easy way she introduced her husband's death into the conversation. "I had no idea."

"It was a long time ago," Joy said. "Mark was only eight. Eric's been a good father to him." She relapsed into silence as I massaged her scalp but began to chatter again when I wrapped her head in a towel and showed her to my station.

"What a shame about Braden, huh?" she said, using the towel to dab at some water in her ears. "Mark's absolutely distraught about it. And even Eric and I—well, we've known the kid for years. It gets to you, you know?"

"It makes me sad, too." I worked my fingers through her damp hair. "What are you looking for today?"

She cocked her head, looking at her reflection in the mirror. "Something shorter maybe, and really wash-and-go. I play tennis and it's just such a pain having to blow-dry my hair in the morning when I get up and then after a match."

I showed her a couple of photos from a style magazine and she pointed to a short, layered bob. "Like that."

As I sectioned her hair and twisted it up with clips, she prattled on, drowning out the quiet conversation Mom was having with a client and the rattling of the door blinds as Stella's nail client left and another one came in. "Even though Mark plays football and not tennis, he gets his sports drive from me. That boy is disciplined! That's how he got into the Naval Academy—with discipline. Eric, well, he works out, but he doesn't set goals the way I do. And I've taught that to Mark. 'Set a goal and work your butt off,' I tell him. 'Never give up! That's the way to success. It's how your father became a naval aviator.' Mark's always wanted to be a pilot like his dad."

"Congrats on his getting into Annapolis," I said. "It's hard to get into one of the military academies, isn't it?"

"You wouldn't believe! All the usual academic tests, plus physical fitness tests, interviews, psych profiles, and background checks. Pretty much anything can get you disqualified: asthma, a DUI . . . you get the picture. But that's where Mark Sr. went to school, so nothing else would do for Mark." She smiled proudly.

"And Mark's stepfather is in the navy, too, right?"

"You betcha. I guess I have a thing for men in uniforms." She laughed. "Eric's a submariner, though, not a pilot. We're PCSing to the Pentagon next summer. The traffic will be awful—everyone says so—but we'll be that much closer to Mark. And if Eric's going to make admiral, he's got to do his time in the Pentagon."

"PCSing?"

"Permanent change of station. Navy talk for moving," she said.

"It feels like half the town is moving north," I said.

She gave me a puzzled look.

"Lindsay told me she's going to play volleyball at Maryland," I explained.

"She's one of the top ten or fifteen high school players in the country," Joy said with what sounded like reluctant admiration. "She's mastered the never-give-up philosophy. Unfortunately, her latest goal seems to be Mark."

"Don't you like her?"

She dodged the question. "I think they're too young to be so serious. And I think getting too attached at eighteen will get in the way of both of them achieving their goals."

Couldn't argue with that. Look how hooking up with Hank had sidelined my college plans. No, that wasn't fair. Hank wouldn't have minded if I'd finished college before we got married; I was the one who decided two years in that I preferred the chemistry of hair dye to a biology lab, and the art of hairstyling over the history of Renaissance artists. I had no one to blame but myself for not having my degree. Certainly, my mother had encouraged me— strongly—to finish college before going to beauty school or marrying Hank.

I trimmed Joy's bangs to mid-forehead, opening up her face more, and blew her hair dry. After a few more snips to texturize the crown, I said, "How's that looking? Want to see the back?"

Shaking her head and watching the hair fall back into place, she said, "I love it!" She took the hand mirror from me as I turned the chair around. She held the mirror up to see the back of her head, and her sleeve slipped down a few inches to reveal a bruise on her right forearm that almost encircled it.

Joy caught the direction of my gaze and shook the sleeve back down. "Ugly, isn't it? My doubles partner clocked me with his racket when we both went for the ball. We still won the match. Like I said, never give up!"

"SHE NEVER GIVES UP TALKING, I'LL SAY THAT FOR her," Mom observed as Joy headed for her car.

The salon was temporarily empty of customers and Stella had stepped into the bathroom. I grabbed a diet A&W from the fridge behind the counter and popped it open. "She was on the chatty side," I agreed. I watched Beauty whisk her tail back and forth as she debated whether or not to pounce on the pile of hair Mom was accumulating with the broom. "Don't you do it," I warned her.

She gave me an affronted "I don't know what you're talking about" look and leaped onto the windowsill.

"Have you thought about evacuating, Mom? They're saying Horatio could be a category—" I started, but footsteps pounding up the stairs and across the veranda interrupted me.

Rachel burst through the door. At first, I thought she had a black eye, but then I realized her mascara had run because she was crying. Flinging herself onto the love seat, she buried her face in a throw pillow.

"Rachel! Honey!" Mom hurried to her side. "Whatever is wrong?"

Sobs were the only answer. Mom looked at me. "Grace, why don't you make some tea. Put in some of that lemon honey I got at the farmer's market last week."

Mom thinks honey, especially in tea, is a cure for almost any emotional distress. She'd have done well to set up her own hive in the backyard when I was going through my divorce. I hurried back to the kitchen and put on the teapot, listening to Mom's comforting murmurs. When I returned to the salon, bright yellow mug in hand, Rachel was sitting up, a pile of used tissues on the cushion beside her. Mom sat next to her, patting her hand.

When I handed Rachel the cheery mug, Mom said, "Tell us what's wrong, honey."

Blowing her nose, Rachel said, "Mkdz tink," into the tissue.

"What?"

She looked up with tear-sheened eyes. "The kids at school think I pushed Braden."

"No way!" I gasped.

"Way," she said sadly.

Mom put her fists on her hips. "That is the meanest, ugliest, most hateful thing I've ever heard. And the most ridiculous!"

"Who said it?" I asked.

"Everyone," Rachel said. She gulped some tea and coughed. "My friend Willow told me," she added after Mom pounded her on the back. "Everyone's saying that I was mad at Braden for, like, breaking up with me and so I pushed him. I was the one who was with him, so I'm the one that did it. Except I wasn't with him—I was in the bathroom. And I would never have hurt him—I cared about him. He was my friend!" She looked wildly from Mom to me.

"Of course you didn't do it," Mom soothed.

"And that's not the worst of it," Rachel said. "The police think I did it, too!"

"The police? How did they find out?" I pulled up a hassock and sat in front of Rachel. The magnolia's branches danced in the rising wind, casting faint shadows across the floor.

"One or more of the kids from the field trip told them about me and Braden breaking up and about how I was, like, his partner for the ghost hunt. They pulled me out of class today and, like, *interrogated* me for an hour!" She started to breathe in quick, shallow gasps, and I was afraid she'd hyperventilate.

"Deep breaths," I said, demonstrating.

Beauty sauntered over, looked into Rachel's distressed face, and jumped onto the girl's lap. Rachel's breathing calmed as she stroked the satisfied cat.

"Who talked to you?" I asked.

"Not Agent Dillon," Rachel said. "Some other agent from the GBI. A woman."

"Did she read you your rights?"

"No."

I heaved a sigh of relief. "They don't really consider you a suspect," I told her, not sure they didn't, but wanting to make her feel better. "If they did, they'd have had to Mirandize you." I had learned a few useful things while married to Hank. "They were probably just trying to figure out where everyone was that night and who had alibis."

"Well, I don't," Rachel pointed out. "I was in the bathroom. I *could* have pushed Braden, but I didn't!"

"What were you doing when . . . the night that . . ." I was reluctant to put it in words.

"The night the werewolf smothered Braden?" Rachel asked.

I nodded.

"The GBI agent asked that, too. I told her I was in my room studying. She said I could've sneaked out of the house, ridden my motor scooter to the hospital, killed Braden, and gotten back without my folks even knowing I was gone. And, like, I could have, because they were out to dinner. But I didn't!" Tears welled again and Mom silently offered the tissue box.

Anger snaked its way from the pit of my stomach to my

chest and made it hard to breathe. I was going to have it out with Agent Dillon before the day got much older. His agents didn't need to terrify an innocent teenager to learn what happened to Braden.

"What about the other kids? Do you know where any of them were Sunday night?"

"The party." Rachel sniffed.

"What party?"

"Ari Solomon had a Halloween party. Everyone went. I was supposed to—I had a Lady Gaga costume—but with Braden in the hospital . . ."

A Halloween party. Costumes. People coming and going. Great. I'd bet none of the kids had a decent alibi. No wonder Dillon was frustrated.

"I don't want to go back to school," Rachel said.

"Let's call your mom," Mom answered.

"I already tried. She's in a meeting and not to be disturbed, her secretary said."

"Well, maybe I can convince them to 'disturb' her," Mom said grimly. "C'mon." She gave Rachel a hand up and the two of them headed for the kitchen—to refill Rachel's honey tea, I was sure, and make the call. I felt sorry for any secretary who tried to tell Mom she couldn't talk to Mrs. Whitley.

A phone call of my own to the GBI netted the information that Agent Dillon was at the high school. Yelling, "I'll be back soon," toward the kitchen, I stormed out of the salon without waiting for a response. My anger carried me the six blocks to the high school in less than ten minutes. Spurts of wind dashing dust and pine needles at me matched my mood, and I merely gathered my hair into a ponytail and wrapped an elastic around it to thwart the wind's attempt to tangle it. Hah!

I straight-armed the high school's glass door and found myself in an empty hall. Class must be in session. Marching to the office's Dutch door, I asked the fat woman making copies where I could find Agent Dillon.

"In the gym," she said, never taking her eyes off the copier. "Damn machine," she muttered as I left.

I stalked down the hall toward the gym, slamming an open locker door shut with a satisfying clang as I passed. The gym floor was empty, its bleachers collapsed against the wall as I entered. A stray basketball lay under the backboard at the far end. Crossing the slick floor, I turned into the hallway leading to the locker rooms. The sounds of running water and faint laughter, and the scents of sweat, mildew, and soap snapped me back to my high school days. I'd always enjoyed gym class and had played on the volleyball team. I missed volleyball and the camaraderie of a team, I suddenly realized. Maybe after I'd given Special Agent John Dillon a piece of my mind, I'd call around and see if there were any adult volleyball leagues in the area. Passing the locker rooms, I peered into the glassed-in offices that came next. When I reached Coach Peet's, the door swung open and the coach emerged with Agent Dillon.

Coach Peet frowned when he saw me, and Agent Dillon raised his brows slightly. "Grace? What are you doing here?"

"I'd like a word with you, if you have a moment," I said as pleasantly as I could manage.

Coach Peet disappeared into his office and closed the door hard, leaving Dillon and me facing each other in the narrow hall.

Wearing a navy suit with a pale yellow shirt and striped tie, he looked tired and severe in the cheerless fluorescent light.

"What in the world do you and your people mean by browbeating a seventeen-year-old girl about Braden's death? How could you think a teenager would—"

"If you're talking about Rachel Whitley," he interrupted me, "she had motive, means, and opportunity, which means I'd be remiss in not interviewing her. *Interviewing*," he emphasized. "Not browbeating."

"She didn't do it." I glared at him.

"Fine. But before you rip into me about interviewing poor, innocent teens, who do you think did it? Statistically, it's likely to be a teenager because there were more of them at Rothmere when Braden was pushed than there were adults. The only adults were you, the science teacher, Coach Peet"—he nodded toward the closed door—"and Dr. Solomon." He leaned close to me as he talked, keeping his voice low with an effort. "You think I like investigating the murder of a teen? Well, think again." He pulled back suddenly, walked three paces away, then whirled and came back.

"I'm sorry, John," I whispered. "I wasn't thinking. Rachel was crying and upset and I reacted emotionally. Of course you have to interview everyone who was there. And I can see how it looks like maybe Rachel is a likely candidate. But I've know her for almost four years, since she started part-time at the salon when she was fourteen, and she couldn't kill someone. She couldn't walk into a hospital and smother someone in cold blood! And certainly not Braden. Their breakup was amicable and they were still friends."

"That's not what the other kids say." Dillon crossed his arms over his chest and eyed me grimly, his eyes the cold navy they got when he was angry.

"Well, they're lying," I said hotly. "I saw the two of

them together that night and they were comfortable with each other—pals."

"Would you go to dinner with me Friday night?" he asked.

"What?" I wasn't sure I'd heard him right. Had he just asked me on a date? Right in the middle of my railing at him?

"I asked if you'd go on a date with me," he confirmed.

A warm feeling that had nothing to do with anger coursed through me, making my fingertips tingle. "What about the hurricane?" I asked stupidly.

"What about it? It'll be blown out by then, or on its way to the Carolinas." He smiled, his teeth a flash of white in his tan face, his eyes lightening to a marine blue. "Well?"

"Okay."

"Just 'okay'?" He arched his brows quizzically.

"I'd like to go to dinner with you, John Dillon," I amended. "Thank you for inviting me."

"Much better." He leaned forward, catching me by my upper arms, and before I could move, he pressed a hard, brief kiss on my lips. "I really like the way you're so passionate about your friends."

And before I could react—kiss him back? push him away?—he had turned and was striding down the hall. The bell rang and the hall flooded with students, hiding him from my sight.

# Chapter Twelve

I STOOD IN THE HALL, AN OBSTACLE THE STUDENTS flowed around, for a good thirty seconds. In that time, my mind flitted from the zing I'd felt from Dillon's two-second kiss, to the way his eyes changed color with his moods, to wondering what I should wear on Friday. I should've asked where we were going. Ye gods, you'd think I'd never been on a date the way I was letting it disrupt my thoughts. As students filtered into the locker room behind me to dress for gym, I knocked on Coach Peet's door. If Agent Dillon thought asking me out would distract me from clearing Rachel's name by figuring out who really killed Braden McCullers, he had another think coming.

"Come," Coach Peet called in a gruff voice.

I pushed open the door. His metal desk was relatively bare of papers, but football trophies of varying heights stood along two sides of the desk's top, like soldiers on guard. Three folding metal chairs sat in front of the desk, and a pile of what looked like lost-and-found stuff—shoes, jerseys, an umbrella, some books—cluttered one corner. "Do you have a moment?" I asked.

He looked down at me over the condor nose. "Who are you?"

"I'm—"

"Oh, you were at the ghost hunt. What do you want?"

His tone and manner were less than welcoming, but I plowed ahead. "It's about what happened—"

He scraped back his chair and stood, revealing a yellow and white St. Elizabeth Sabertooths jersey and basketball shorts over hairy legs. A whistle hung midway down his chest. "I don't have time," he said, scooping up a basketball from under his desk. "Got a class to teach."

"I'll walk with you," I said, backing up so he could get past me into the hall.

"Unh," he grunted.

I took that as permission and walked beside him as he strode toward the gym. "I just want to know more about Braden McCullers. Was he a good student? A good football player? Did he get along well with the other guys on the team?"

Peet shot me a sideways glance. "You went to school here, didn't you? Eight or ten years back? Played volleyball, right?"

It was more like twelve years ago, but I just said, "Right."

"What the hell's in this for you?"

I gave him a puzzled look. "In it? Nothing. But there are some ugly rumors going around about Rachel Whitley and I want to dispel them."

He worked his lips in and out. "Whitley. Don't know the name. She's not an athlete."

So that made her a second-class citizen? Or worse, a suitable murder suspect? I tamped down my rising irritation. "Being an athlete isn't everything."

He gave a crack of laughter, the sound Columbus must have heard when he announced the world wasn't flat. "Okay. McCullers. Outstanding wide receiver. Recruited by Notre Dame and LSU but hadn't committed yet. He was considering MIT."

His tone said what he thought of that choice. "Good student. At least, I never had to go to bat for him, try to get teachers to bump his grades up so he'd stay eligible. Wish I could say that for a few more of my players." Rubbing a hand across his jaw, he pinched his lower lip between his thumb and forefinger. "A bit too much of a straight arrow, though. You know what I mean—turning in teammates who might have had a coupla beers before driving home after a game, testifying against a buddy who was up on vandalism charges—"

"And that's a bad thing?" Keeping drunk drivers off the street was a darn good thing, in my opinion. Ditto for vandals.

He frowned at me. "Hell, yeah. Undermines the teamwork. Makes players doubt your commitment. Hard to win unless all the guys on the field trust each other."

Ye gods. I let that one pass without comment because Coach Peet was pushing through the gym door and a straggly line of high schoolers in gym clothes quieted as he came in. From the smell, I was betting some of these kids hadn't run their tee shirts through the wash in at least a couple of weeks.

The coach turned to face me, putting his back to the students, and spoke in an undertone. "You want my opinion, it was suicide. He threw himself down the stairs at Rothmere. That bit about a werewolf smothering him at the hospital"—he shook his head sharply—"that reeks of cover-up. Maybe he managed to smother himself and the hospital's afraid of being sued. Or maybe one of his folks did it if the docs told 'em he was going to be a vegetable. I think he did himself in. Ever since he got into that study—the one testing the new antidepressant—he's been real unpredictable with his moods."

The coach's words left me with my mouth agape. Was it even possible to smother yourself? I didn't know.

"Where were you Sunday night?"

His eyebrows crinkled his brow. "None of your—Oh, what the hell. Home. Reviewing film from last week's game. Happy?"

He was half turned away from me when I got in my final question. "Who gets Braden's spot on the roster?" I asked.

"Farber." And the coach blew his whistle, either to signal the end of our conversation or the start of gym class.


I LEFT TO THE SOUND OF BASKETBALLS DRIBBLING ON the slick floor. Walking back toward Mom's, I thought about what I'd learned. Braden was a good student and, apparently, an honorable kid. Too honorable for the coach's taste, and probably for his teammates' taste. He was participating in a study for an antidepressant drug. How could I find out more about that? I thought I'd read somewhere that antidepressant meds could, paradoxically, increase the chance of suicide, especially in teens. Was it possible that Coach Peet's speculations were right? No way. A hospital wouldn't make up a story like that to avoid a lawsuit . . . would they? I wished I could talk to Braden's parents again, but they'd gone out of town.

Mark Crenshaw was supposedly Braden's best buddy. Maybe he'd know something. Maybe he'd even know what was bothering Braden the week before he died, what Braden was talking about when he told Rachel he might need to "intervene" in something. And Lonnie Farber would probably be worth talking to as well. How badly did he want to be a starter? He'd certainly done everything he could to confuse things at Rothmere. Had there been more intent behind his pranks than just stirring the pot?

Arriving back at the salon, I took a moment to look at the line of clouds bearing down from the east. The puffy harbingers from earlier had clearly invited their friends and relatives to join the party. The sky was a hazier blue and the sounds of a weather forecast greeted me as I entered Violetta's. Mom had brought down the twelve-inch television from her bedroom and balanced it atop a stack of fashion magazines on the counter. A weatherman with a grim face was pointing to a swirling mass in the Atlantic north of the Bahamas. Rachel, Mom, and Althea gathered around the TV.

"Where's Stella?" I asked.

"Darryl came by and picked her up," Mom said. "I guess he's decided that they're going inland for a couple of days. He said something about having a reservation at a Red Roof Inn outside Macon."

"Oh. Well, it doesn't look like her customers will miss her," I said, looking around at the customer-free salon. "Maybe we should think about evacuating," I added as the weatherman started talking about Horatio becoming a category three storm and about winds and storm surges.

"Don't be ridiculous, Grace," Mom said shortly. "This house has withstood a century and a half of storms. It's not about to collapse on us now."

"What about you, Althea?" She lived much closer to the beach than we did in a cottage she and William had bought for a pittance when they wed and which was worth a quarter million or more now.

"Vi's offered to put me up for a couple of days, and I'm going to bring my stuff over early tomorrow, if it still looks like Horatio is headed toward us. Personally, I think it's just playing chicken with us and it'll make landfall way north of here."

I didn't ask Althea when she'd had time to pick up her meteorology degree, knowing I'd only get blasted for sassing her.

"I want to go down to the beach," Rachel announced. "I'll bet the waves are, like, awesome."

"I'll drive you down," I said, earning disapproving looks from Mom and Althea. "We won't go in the water," I reassured them.

"Cool!" Rachel said. She looked much better than earlier, with the smeared mascara scrubbed off her face and a grin replacing her woebegone look. What had Mom said a couple of days ago about youth being resilient? Here was proof.

THE WAVES DIDN'T ACHIEVE THE HEIGHTS OF THOSE on Hawaii's north shore or anything, but they rolled onto the beach with tremendous crashes, sending up a spray that misted Rachel and me as we walked along the beach a couple of miles south of St. Elizabeth. I loved the briny smell that filled the air, the smell of salt and water and

seaweed and something mysterious dredged up from miles
beneath the surface. Surprisingly, we weren't the only ones
out there; a couple walked a golden retriever who was busy
keeping the gulls off the sand, and a lunatic in a wetsuit
rode a surfboard in almost to the beach before paddling
back out to catch another wave.

"I wish I could do that," Rachel said, watching the
surfer.

"You have a death wish? We'll be hearing about that guy
on the news tonight," I said.

"You sound like my mom."

This was apparently not a compliment. Stifling the
thought that I might be getting stodgy, I said, "Your mom
just wants to keep you alive long enough to spend all her
savings on college tuition."

Rachel grinned at that and took off running down the
sand toward the water. I fought the urge to call her back.
She was barefoot and let the surf just lick her toes before
running back toward me as another series of waves boomed
on the beach.

I pulled my white cardigan around me against a chill
that came from the wind rather than the air temperature.
My feet were bare, too, and I worked them into the sand,
searching for yesterday's sunny warmth stored somewhere
beneath the top layer. "I need you to tell me about the kids
who were on the ghost hunt, especially those who might
have wanted to harm Braden," I said.

"Nobody would want to hurt Braden," she protested au-
tomatically, then made a moue of disgust. "Like, I sound
really stupid, since obviously someone did hurt Braden."

I pulled my feet out of the sand and we walked, Rachel
scanning the ground for shells. "Start with Mark," I suggested, when she didn't say anything.

"Mark is—was—his best friend," she said, tucking a strand of black hair behind her ear. "They do everything together—football, classes, even dating. Braden and I double-dated with Mark and Lindsay a few times; in fact, I think Braden may have dated Lindsay a couple years back, before she and Mark got together."

That was interesting—could there be some unresolved jealousies or a teen love triangle at work? "Do you like Mark?"

Rachel shrugged. "Sure. He's okay. A bit . . . intense, but that might be because his folks, like, put so much pressure on him."

"What do you mean?"

"To hear Lindsay tell it, they're always after him about his grades and being involved in the 'right' clubs and doing volunteer stuff and taking on leadership roles so he can get into the Naval Academy and carry on the family tradition. His dad is really keen on him being in the navy."

"You mean his stepdad?"

"I guess." She hesitated, kicking up some sand, which the wind promptly blew back at us. "Sorry. You know . . ."

"What?"

"Lindsay told me once that she thinks maybe his dad . . . Mark's dad hits him," she said in a rush.

"Did Mark tell her that?"

"Oh, no." She shook her head violently. "He told her that she was crazy, that he got his bruises playing football."

"Plausible." But not necessarily the truth. I thought of the bruise on Joy Crenshaw's wrist. "Did Lindsay tell anyone, like her folks or a teacher?"

"I don't think so. I'm sure not. I mean, it's not like she was sure or anything."

Shoot. What was I supposed to do with this information,

if anything? Lindsay was a teenager; it was understandable that she would feel uncomfortable making an issue out of possible abuse, especially if her boyfriend denied it. I, however, was an adult who might be expected to do something, although I only had secondhand hearsay plus my observation of Mark's bruised face. Surely, I argued with myself, his teachers would have noticed if there were a problem. Pushing the dilemma aside to deal with later, I tried to return to my original line of thought. "What about the others—Lonnie, Tyler, Lindsay, the other kids who were at Rothmere? How did they get along with Braden?"

"Lonnie had, like, issues with him," Rachel said, bending to pick up an interesting shell. Turning it over in her hand once or twice, she rejected it and let it fall. "Braden testified or talked to the police or something about Lonnie's brother being the one who vandalized those cars at the high school last year. His brother got sent to juvie and Lonnie was really pissed about it. They got into a fight in gym, but Coach Peet broke it up. Lonnie broke Braden's nose, though."

"Lovely. Did he get suspended?"

Rachel shook her head. "Nope. Coach said Braden, like, had it coming and didn't tell the principal. Coach said now they were even and could go back to being teammates. Go Sabertooths!" she finished with an ironic fist pump.

We turned around to head back toward where I'd parked my Ford Fiesta. The wind at our backs grabbed at my ponytail and flicked it into my face. It pulled Rachel's black hair over her eyes until she looked like Cousin Itt. She pushed her bangs back with one hand, then made a visor of it, scanning the ocean. The surfer was up again, a mostly black splotch atop a green and yellow board that stood out against the heavy gray green of the waves. He carved a path along the inside of the wave, trailing his hand in the water, and Rachel clapped, laughing delightedly. "I'm going to learn to surf," she announced, turning to me.

"Lindsay?" I prompted.

"She's amazing," Rachel said. "She set a school record for kills last year when she was a junior. She and Mark are, like, the perfect couple."

"Are you and Lindsay close?"

She waggled her hand. "You know. Not, like, BFFs, but not enemies or anything. They run with a different crowd." She didn't sound jealous or bitter about not being part of the popular crowd. I'd never minded, either. I'd been happy with my semi-nerdy friends in chorus and my best friend, Vonda.

"What do you know about Braden taking part in a drug study?" I asked.

"Look!" Rachel pointed toward the water. The surfer was up again, zipping toward the beach, when suddenly the front end of his surfboard flipped up and seemed to hit him. He toppled into the water, disappearing from sight. After a moment, the brightly colored board popped to the surface, but there was no sign of the surfer. Both of us scanned the waves and shore anxiously for thirty seconds. I willed the man to appear. Nothing. I looked up and down the beach, but the couple with the dog were gone.

"Call for help," I told Rachel, stripping off my cardigan. I was a mediocre swimmer, not in any way qualified to undertake a rescue in conditions like this, but there was no one else. I sprinted the twenty yards to the waterline, pulling my tee shirt over my head as I went. My feet slapped against the hard, wet sand as I neared the water. A wave broke, sending a surge of water over my feet and halfway up my shins. It was colder than usual, pulled up from the depths by Horatio's winds. I stood there, torn, not wanting to dive in, but unwilling to just watch as the sea took the surfer. Between swells, I thought I spotted something black. He wasn't too far out. The beach sloped gradually into the water and normally I'd have been able to walk out to where he floated. Without further thought, I waded into the angry surf.

# Chapter Thirteen

THE COLD SMACKED ME. MY SKIN SEEMED TO SHRINK around my frame as I struck out toward where I thought I'd seen the surfer. I couldn't last more than ten or so minutes. Ducking under a wave about to crest, I popped up for another look. There! In the trough between two waves, I spotted the surfer's head bobbing just at the surface. One of his arms flailed before another wave cut off my view. I spit out a mouthful of salty water and went under again, finding it easier to swim beneath the waves, even though roiling sand and shell bits made a muddy scrim I couldn't see through. The next time I surfaced, the surfer was barely a body length away, his face twisted in panic, his mouth open as if he were screaming something.

"I'm coming," I screamed back pointlessly.

The current pulled him away even as I breaststroked toward him, trying to keep him in sight. Stretching out my hand, I brushed what felt like the slick skin of his wet suit—his ankle, maybe—before the current yanked him away. A wave began to swell behind him, pulling him up above me. It looked like one arm was useless, dangling helplessly as he tried to stay upright by paddling with his left arm. Then the wave swept me up and I gulped in a deep breath before it smashed me down toward the sea floor, rolling me over and over against the sand. I needed air. I tried to orient myself, tried to get my legs beneath me. Just as I got my legs upright underneath me and pushed as hard as I could, something heavy thudded into me. The surfer.

Frantic to grab him, I hooked a hand around what felt like his knee. Knocked off-balance by his weight, I pushed up with the one foot still touching the sand. I didn't get much leverage and clawed desperately at the water. Air. I needed air. My head broke the surface and I gulped a mouthful of seawater, choked, and gasped for air. Then, I let my hands climb the surfer's body, desperate to lift his face from the water. Tangling my fingers in his hair, I pulled his head up. His eyes were shut. Blinking salt out of my eyes, I tried to see if he was breathing, but I couldn't tell.

Another wave broke over us, but to my relief it seemed to be pushing us toward the shore, not pulling us away. The tide must be coming in. My toes scraped sand and I tried to stand, but the surfer's weight and the sucking of the water as the wave receded kept me down.

"Hold on," strong voices called from the shore. "We're coming."

Water blurred my vision, but I thought I saw three men pounding toward us, carrying the yellow and green surfboard and a flotation ring. One of them flung it toward me and it bounced off my forehead. I hardly registered the pain. Still holding the surfer by his hair, I grabbed for the ring just as the men splashed up to me in what turned out to be only waist-high water. Two of them grabbed the unconscious surfer while the third helped me stand. My every muscle trembled, and he put his arm around my waist to keep me from falling. I looked up into his face, at blue eyes framed by bushy white brows and seamed skin that spoke of decades in the sun, and thought I'd never seen anything so wonderful.

BACK IN MOM'S KITCHEN AN HOUR LATER AFTER A shower, shampoo, and change of clothes, I spooned up chicken noodle soup and defused Mom's worries.

"You said you wouldn't go in the water," she said, ladling more soup out of the pot into my bowl.

"I'm full," I protested. I cupped my hands around the bowl, letting the heat seep into me. The room exuded warmth with its brick wall, yellow paint, copper pans hanging from a rack overhead, and a faint scent of vanilla. "And it's not like I planned to go swimming. What did you want me to do—leave the poor guy to drown?"

"Of course not. Whatever possessed him to trying surfing with a hurricane off the coast? Didn't he know how dangerous it was?"

I rather thought that was the point. The surfer had turned out to be a man in his mid-twenties who worked for some government organization in Atlanta. He'd regained consciousness and thanked me and the fishermen for rescuing him as the EMTs prepared to load him into the ambulance to have his broken arm set at the hospital. Over his shoulder, I noticed a reporter speaking with a police officer who had responded with the medics.

"You saved my life," the surfer said, surprising me with a kiss on the cheek. "My parents thank you."

"The surf was pushing you toward the beach, anyway," I said, embarrassed by his gratitude. My hair dripped onto the blanket the EMTs had wrapped around him, and I shivered.

"Still. If there's ever anything I can do for you, let me know." Brown-flecked hazel eyes looked into mine with grateful sincerity. "And next time you're in Atlanta, I'm taking you to dinner." He pressed a business card into my hand, fishing it from the pocket of khaki shorts the fishermen had retrieved, along with his shoes and wallet, from a heap down the beach. His gaze strayed to the heaving water behind me. "What a rush!"

He was certifiably insane. I told him so and he grinned. As the ambulance started down the road, I glanced at his card: "Stuart Varnet," it read, "Agency for Toxic Substances and Disease Registry." Sounded like a cheery job.

Rachel had driven me to my apartment in my car, where I'd cleaned up and put Band-Aids on a couple of places scraped raw in the surf. The worst spot was high on my cheekbone, and any facial movement—smiling, frowning, laughing—tugged at it and made me wince. Now, while Rachel and Althea dealt with a client up front, I brought Mom up to speed on what Rachel had told me and what I'd learned from Dillon and Coach Peet. I didn't mention my upcoming date with Dillon; that was a development I wanted to keep private for the moment.

"I can't believe Braden was participating in a pharmaceutical study," she said. "Aren't there a lot of risks involved?"

"Can't be any worse than surfing in a hurricane," I said. She laughed. "That's a true fact, but I'm sure Braden had to have his parents' permission to take part in a drug study; that young daredevil today certainly didn't tell his folks. It would be just criminal if Braden had a reaction to the drug and it contributed to his death in some way. Could the medicine have made him dizzy so that he fell?"

"I suppose it's possible," I said, rinsing out my bowl and putting it in the drainer. "But don't forget that someone smothered him. If the fall was an accident, why would someone stalk him at the hospital and kill him? I'd been thinking that the murderer finished him off at the hospital because they were afraid he'd wake up and ID them."

"That makes sense," Mom said. She gazed at me over the lenses of her rimless glasses. "How much money would a pharmaceutical company have invested in a drug? If it's a lot—millions—and a test subject had a potentially fatal accident because of it, mightn't they want to cover it up?"

"With murder?" I laughed. "You've been watching too many thrillers, Mom. This isn't that Rachel Weisz movie where the evil pharmaceutical company tested drugs on innocent Africans. What was it called? Something about a gardener. Corporations don't run around killing people. Thanks for the soup. It hit the spot."

"It was just out of a can." Mom pursed her lips. "I still think you should follow up on the drug test thing. Maybe that boy who was here yesterday, Braden's friend, could tell you more about it."

"Mark Crenshaw." I'd already planned to talk to him. "Maybe I'll run over to the school and see if I can catch him before football practice. Then I'll come back here in time to help with the Locks of Love cuts."

"You should be resting." Mom put her hands on her hips.

"I got wet," I said, kissing her cheek. "It's not like I was in a car wreck or something. I don't need to rest."

"Hmmph. You got pretty beat up. Look at the bruises on your arm."

The sight of the bruises reminded me of what Rachel had said about Mark's dad maybe abusing him and I told my mom. "Should I tell someone?"

"I don't know how you can," she said, tapping a finger on her lower lip. "You heard it from Rachel who heard it from Lindsay who noticed some bruises on Mark. That's hardly proof of abuse. You don't want to start rumors based on such flimsy evidence."

"His mother had a bruise, too," I said. "I noticed it this morning."

"Well, if having a couple bruises is proof of parental or spousal abuse, anyone looking at you would toss me in jail quicker than I can say 'Jack Robinson.'"

"Good point," I said, eyeing my bruised and scraped arms. I hadn't relished going to the police or anyone with those accusations and I was relieved to hear Mom didn't think I should.

I gave her a hug. "Thanks for worrying about me."

"It's my job." She sounded severe, but I caught the twinkle in her eye. "But the pay stinks and the hours are lousy."

ARRIVING BACK AT THE HIGH SCHOOL, I HEADED around back to the practice field. Unless things had changed since I went there, the football team practiced last period and then for an additional hour or so after school. I hoped to intercept Mark Crenshaw before practice kicked off. Coach Peet, I knew, was unlikely to let me distract his players once practice got underway. The field, goal posts at either end, stretched greenly away from the back of the high school. A single section of rickety bleachers—once white, now a silvery gray where the sun and humidity had chewed away the paint—marked the fifty-yard line. A girl sat midway up, holding her long hair back with one hand and pressing the pages of a textbook open with the other.

I expected to see a steady stream of football players trickling from the exterior gym door onto the field; instead, two players in practice jerseys tossed a football back and forth in the middle of the field. Coach Peet was nowhere in sight. I crossed the field, behind the players, my low-heeled pumps sinking into the grass. I noticed "Crenshaw" stenciled on the back of one of the kids' jerseys. The other player suddenly cut across the field, then zigzagged toward the middle. Mark brought his arm back and launched the ball in a tight spiral. The receiver snagged it with his fingertips and raced for the end zone.

"Mark?"

He turned, startled. "What? Oh, hi, Miss Terhune." His eyes slid to his teammate down the field. He caught the football as the receiver lobbed it back to him.

"Do you have a moment to talk?" I asked. "About Braden?"

"I've got lots of moments," he said. "No practice today because of the hurricane. Too many people have evacuated. Give me ten, okay, Josh?" he called to his teammate. "Then we'll run some more patterns."

Josh gave him a thumbs-up and joined the girl on the bleachers. I felt awkward standing in the middle of the field, but the bleachers were too small to allow for private conversation.

"My car's just over there," Mark said with a nod toward

a blue Mustang parked outside the fence. "We could sit there if you want, out of the wind."

"Sounds good."

As we headed toward the car, he asked, "What happened to your face?" His hand brushed the air around his own cheek.

"Swimming accident." I didn't want to go into it. "How are you holding up? Everyone says you and Braden were best friends."

"It's hard," Mark said. Pulling off his helmet, he tossed his hair out of his eyes with a flip of his head. "I just can't believe he's gone. At practice yesterday, Lonnie would run the pattern and turn, waiting for me to throw to him, but it just wasn't the same. Every time I hit Lonnie with a pass, it reminded me that Braden's gone. Dead. It was like finding out he's dead over and over again, you know? Before, I was really pumped about this season, looking forward to the playoffs. Now . . ." He shrugged. "I'm just kinda going through the motions. I'm thinking about quitting."

He beeped open the car's locks and we climbed in. The interior was immaculate and smelled vaguely of pine. A sleeve on the visor held a selection of CDs; other than that, the car looked like it had just come off the showroom floor. "She was a present from my folks," Mark said self-consciously, smoothing a hand along the dashboard. "When I got my appointment to the Naval Academy."

Whatever happened to giving a kid a suitcase for a graduation present? "What's Coach Peet think? About you leaving the team?"

"That I should stick with it. My backup's just a freshman. He's good, but Coach would rather go with a known quantity."

I felt for Mark, but I wasn't qualified to advise him on his football dilemma. "Look, Mark, a couple of people have told me Braden was participating in some sort of drug study. Do you know anything about that?"

"The Relamin study? What about it?" He looked startled, then uneasy, bringing his thumb to his mouth to chew on his cuticle.

"What is it? When did he start with the study?"

Mark turned his head away to stare out the window. "It's a new antidepressant. It's supposed to work differently—better than the serotonin re-uptake inhibitors—but I don't really understand the chemistry behind it."

Sero-what? I quickly decided I didn't need to understand how it worked, either. "Did you see any changes in Mark after he started the study?"

He thought for a moment. "Nah. Not really. He hadn't been through a major depressive episode in quite a while, at least not that I knew about. And I don't think I would've missed it. We spent a lot of time together. He could have been receiving the placebo anyway, in which case—obviously—he wouldn't have side effects."

It wasn't obvious to me. "What do you mean?"

"In drug studies, there's always a control group that receives a placebo instead of the new medication. You don't know which group you're in, so you might be getting the new drug, or you might just be getting a sugar pill." His brows twitched together with a hint of suspicion. "Why are you asking about Relamin? Do you know something about it? Have you heard something?"

"Nothing. I was wondering about possible side effects, that's all."

He seemed to lose interest. "Dr. Solomon would know.

But she probably won't tell you. These drug studies are very hush-hush; at least, that's what Braden said."

"Dr. Solomon?"

"Yeah. She's the one running the study. You met her— she was at the ghost hunt."

The short woman with the widow's peak. A chill trickled down my spine. Was it mere coincidence that she was at Rothmere the night Braden fell? I bit my lip. I was letting Mom's theory color my thinking; of course it was coincidence. I changed the subject, sensing that Mark was about to bail on me by the way his hand rested on the door handle. "Look, can you think of anyone who hated Braden or who might've wanted to hurt him?"

Mark was shaking his head before I finished. "No. Everyone liked Braden."

"Even Lonnie?"

He paused and began gnawing on his cuticle again. "Oh, Lonnie's okay. He was pissed at Braden after his brother got sent to juvie, but he's okay with Braden now."

Hm. Clearly, Mark wasn't going to rat out a teammate, or probably anyone else. The culture of "don't tattle" was alive and well in high school, even with a murderer on the loose. I tried to squelch my irritation; it must be incredibly hard to believe that someone you knew, someone who kind of *was* you—a high school senior looking forward to graduation and maybe college, who played ball and struggled with calculus tests—could kill someone. "He told Rachel that there was some situation he was dealing with, or aware of, and he was debating whether or not to 'intervene.' That's the word he used. Do you know what he was talking about?"

Mark's eyes widened. "He said that? To Rachel?"

I couldn't tell if he was more puzzled about what Braden

might have meant or about his talking it over with Rachel. "Uh-huh."

"I don't know—He didn't say—" His teeth worried at the cuticle and a fleck of blood appeared.

His mother was right—Mark was wound way too tight. I put a hand on his arm, but before I could say anything, the door on my side swung open, letting in a gust of sea-scented wind. A strong pair of hands grabbed my upper arm and yanked. I tumbled out of the seat, my feet getting caught somehow. My shoulder thudded against the door and then I was on the ground. Ow.

"You bitch! What the hell do you—"

"Lindsay!" Mark's horrified voice cut through his girl-friend's tirade.

"Oh my God! Miss Terhune! I'm so sorry. I thought you were—Are you okay?" Lindsay hovered over me, contrition on her face.

From my upside-down position on the ground, she looked like a young Amazon warrior with a really good haircut. Thank God she wasn't carrying a spear. The driver's door slammed as Mark scrambled out and came around to our side.

Pushing to a sitting position, I freed my foot, grateful I wasn't wearing a skirt. I felt undignified enough as it was without my lavender Jockey hipsters on display. I massaged my twisted ankle for a moment, then stood, dusting off my slacks. Adrenaline still surged through me and my voice was tight as I said, "You attacked me."

Wearing skinny jeans that made her look even taller than she was, Lindsay looked like she was going to cry. "I'm so sorry. I thought you were . . . were putting the moves on Mark."

"You what?" Incredulity and anger flooded me and I felt

my face flush. I was pretty sure I'd never "put the moves" on anyone, and I couldn't imagine being interested in an eighteen-year-old. The idea made me faintly nauseated.

"Not you. I didn't mean—I mean, I thought you were a girl, like, you know, a student here, and that you—she—was hitting on my boyfriend."

I followed her disjointed sentence with difficulty. "Is that how you react whenever Mark talks to another student?"

"Of course not." Mark jumped in to defend Lindsay. He put an arm around her shoulders and she leaned into him. "She misinterpreted the situation, that's all."

"That's all?" Pulling a twig from my hair, I gave the pair a level look. "You reacted like a kindergartner. At your age, I'd expect a little more impulse control."

"I'm really sorry," Lindsay whispered again. "You won't tell, will you?"

Tell who? The police? Her folks? I could just see that conversation: "Hello, Mrs. Tandy? I'm calling to let you know your daughter pulled me out of a car—no, it wasn't moving at the time—because she thought I was getting cozy with her boyfriend. Well, yes, I was alone in the car with him, but there was nothing going on. I was just grilling him about his best friend's murder." Not a conversation I wanted to have.

"I can't afford detention," Lindsay said. "Coach Adkins won't let someone play for a week if they get detention."

Ah, she was worried I'd tell Principal Kornhiser. Merle. Suddenly, I felt too weary to bother with this conversation anymore. I was tired from fighting the sea this morning, and being bounced onto the ground by Lindsay had awakened all the aches that two painkillers had put to sleep. "I'm going home," I said grumpily. "If you think of anything else, Mark, or have thoughts about what Braden meant when he talked about 'intervening,' give me a call at Violetta's."

The kids exchanged a look I didn't know how to interpret but said nothing. When the silence had stretched to thirty seconds, I turned and started toward Mom's. Mark's belated, "Will do," and Lindsay's, "Sorry," floated after me.

# Chapter Fourteen

I ARRIVED BACK AT MOM'S TO FIND FRED WILKERSON, Mom's handyman, nailing plywood over the salon windows. Mom was starting to take Horatio seriously.

"Hi, Fred," I greeted him.

"Gonna be a big blow," he said, shaking his grizzled head. At least seventy, he wore denim overalls and work boots. A patch of stubbly white whiskers sprouted from his jaw where his razor had missed a spot. "I saw this morning that most of the boats have moved out of the marina."

Leaving him to his work—*whack, whack, whack* went the hammer—I entered the salon. With some of the windows boarded up, it felt like a dim cave. "Are we closed?" I asked Mom, who was rearranging the bottles and tubes of Althea's Organic Skin Care Solutions. The weather repo... played without sound on the television behind her. ... swirly mass of clouds had moved closer to Georgia.

"No."

"But we might as well be," Althea said, emerging from the bathroom, "for all the business we've had this morning. You might want Fred to have a look at the toilet while he's here, Vi; I had to jiggle the handle again. Why are you limping?" She stared at my foot.

"Didn't Mom tell you about my adventure this morning?" I didn't want to talk about the Lindsay incident, so it was easier to let her think I'd twisted my ankle in the sea.

"Yes, she did, and let me tell you, baby-girl, that was the stupidest damn thing you've ever done. And also one of the bravest." Concern and pride warred on her handsome cocoa face. "Why, you don't swim much better than a cat."

"Thanks," I said drily, helping myself to a diet A&W from the mini fridge.

"Facts is facts," she observed. "I've never been one to mince words."

Mom and I laughed.

"What?" Althea gave us a mock glare.

The door swung open and I glanced over, thinking it was Fred, but a stranger stood on the threshold. Almost six feet tall, she had glossy black hair that draped from a side part, almost obscuring one eye, and fell to mid-back. Pale skin, pale blue eyes, and lush lips made a dramatic contrast with her hair. Designer jeans and boots emphasized long legs. She'd wrapped a spangly silver scarf twice around her neck and the ends dangled to her waist.

"Hello." Her voice was warm and throaty. "I'm looking for Grace Terhune."

"That's me," I said, setting my soda on the counter.

"That's Avaline," Althea suddenly said. "Avaline van ̄el."

"̄ho?"

Mom and I looked from Althea to the newcomer. She clapped her hands together and I saw she was wearing at least one ring on every finger. Blue, red, and green stones—surely they couldn't be real gems?—twinkled even in the low light. "That's right. How lovely of you to recognize me. Are you a fan of the show?"

"What show?" Mom asked.

"She's the spirit whisperer," Althea said. "And, no," she answered the woman's question. "I wouldn't say I'm a fan. I don't believe in that nonsense . . . talking to spirits and all." She jutted her chin out in her characteristic way. "Dead is dead, is what I say. Until the Second Coming."

"A nonbeliever." A small smile curved the corner of Avaline's mouth. "That's okay. The world is filled with disbelief, but still I carry on with my mission."

"What mission?" I asked. "And why are you looking for me?"

"My mission is to communicate with the spirits," she said, "especially ones tied to the earth by profound emotion—usually anger or sorrow—experienced at their deaths."

I had a feeling I knew where this was going and wished I'd gone straight home from the high school.

"I understand you were present when the ghost of Cyril Rothmere pushed a local boy down a staircase. I want to interview you about that for my television show."

The three of us looked at her with varying degrees of mistrust and discomfort. I didn't know which part of her statement to disagree with first, so I asked, "Who gave you my name?"

"A Dr. Lucy Mortimer at Rothmere. She also gave me the name of the high school teacher who sponsored the trip, but he's teaching and I can't get hold of him." She smiled winningly. "So I decided to start with you."

I was going to kill Lucy. "Well, I appreciate your think-ing of me," I lied, "but I don't want to be on your show."

"Really?" She looked puzzled. "We have a viewership of almost twelve million. Friday nights at eight o'clock."

"Twelve million? Really?" Althea sounded flabber-gasted. "And I thought you had lame plans for your week-end nights, baby-girl. Can you believe there are twelve million people in this country with a sorrier love life than yours?"

"Leave her alone, Althea," Mom commanded.

"I like my Friday nights the way they are," I said loftily, "and besides—" I stopped short of telling them I was going out with Agent Dillon this Friday. Turning back to Avaline, I said, "I'm not interested. And anyway, I didn't see the ac-cident, but whoever pushed Braden wasn't a ghost."

"Well, we'll let Cyril tell us about that," Avaline said with a throaty laugh.

"Come again?" Mom said.

"That's what she does," Althea explained. "She talks to spirits. Or so she says."

Avaline didn't seem offended by Althea's blatant skepti-cism. "That's right. And I've got a feeling Cyril's got a lot to tell our audience. From what Dr. Mortimer told me, he was murdered—maybe by a family member—and has haunted his old home ever since. Well, maybe once he gets a chance to tell his story on national TV, he'll be free."

Mom and I exchanged looks. Even if I believed in ghosts—which I didn't—I had a hard time thinking they were hanging around in the ether, waiting their chance to appear on a talk show like the desperate, dysfunctional peo-ple who squabbled about family issues on *Jerry Springer*.

"Well, good luck with it," I said. "Sorry I can't help."

Avaline didn't take the hint. Running the spangled scarf

through her hand, she said, "Dr. Mortimer told me you have some documents that might shed some light on Cyril's case. I'd like to use them—"

"There wasn't anything interesting in them," I said, determined not to let this woman get her hands on Clarissa's letters. For some reason, it seemed like a gross violation of her privacy.

"Oh, you must let me be the judge of that," Avaline said, narrowing her eyes. "Given the right spin, any historic document can be fascinating."

I didn't want her "spinning" Clarissa's life. "Well, I'll look for them," I said with a false I'll-get-right-on-it air. "Where are you staying?"

"Can't you find them now?" she said, pointing to the ceiling.

"I don't live here."

"Oh." Momentarily stymied, she said, "Well, the sooner the better. We were hoping to film this week and get out of here ahead of the hurricane. Normally, we'd take longer on a project, but we've had legal issues with one of the episodes we thought was in the can and we need a replacement. I'm at the Magnolia House if you want to drop off the documents, and here's my cell phone number." She handed me a card.

Magnolia House! That was Vonda's B&B.

Tossing one end of the scarf over her shoulder, Avaline headed for the door. "Let me know if you change your mind about being on the show," she said. "My producer can be very persuasive." She rubbed her thumb and first two fingers together in the age-old sign for money. "He's already secured permission to film at the mansion." Her long hair fluttering in the breeze that sifted in as she opened door. Avaline made her exit.

I had to admit that she was a beautiful woman, not at all what I would have expected a ghost hunter to look like. If asked, I'd have pictured a short, middle-aged woman with a squeaky voice, a lot like the frizzy-haired actress in the original *Poltergeist* movie.

"Why didn't you want to give her the Rothmere documents?" Althea asked.

"I'm not done with them," I said shortly, embarrassed to explain my real reason.

Mom seemed to sense something because she pulled Althea away by saying, "Let's run over to the Piggly Wiggly and get some bottled water and ice before the girls come in to do Locks of Love."

"I'll stay here in case they're early," I said, giving Mom a grateful look.

I PAID FRED WHEN HE FINISHED PUTTING UP THE plywood and then brought a couple of lamps down from the bedrooms to brighten up the salon. It was light enough, I decided, stepping back to survey my efforts, but lightbulbs just don't have the same quality as sunlight. I called Vonda to gab about Avaline and the film crew, but her ex-husband, Ricky, who still co-owns the B&B with her, answered and said she was at the hardware store. After a moment, I dialed Marty's number, but got his voice mail again. Was he in Phoenix or Houston today? Was it significant that I didn't know?

Feeling unsettled—it was probably the weather—I wandered out onto the veranda, leaving the door open to get a ▪le fresh air and sunlight into the salon. I leaned my fore- ▪ against the rail and stared off in the direction of the sea. ▪dn't see it, but I could smell it. I took a deep breath, holding the air in my lungs for a moment, and blew it out. Birds chirruped and tweeted from the azaleas and oleanders growing against the side of the house, and a pair of squirrels chased each other around the magnolia's trunk. I knew the storm wasn't imminent; the animals would disappear and the yard would get eerily quiet as the hurricane drew near.

Noticing the hammock, I descended the steps to take it down, figuring it wouldn't fare well in the hurricane. As I unwrapped the nylon cord from the magnolia's trunk, a police car pulled up at the curb and Hank got out.

"Need some help?" he asked. Without waiting for an answer, he got started on untying the other end of the rope.

"Thanks," I said. "The criminals must've all evacuated if the SEPD's got time to help citizens with their hurricane prep."

He smiled but then his face turned serious. Balling up his end of the hammock, he thrust the unwieldy mass into my arms. "I came to tell you something I think you should know." He puffed his chest out self-importantly. "It's about that Spaatz fellow you're so keen on."

I didn't bother telling Hank I wasn't "keen on" Glen Spaatz. The hammock was heavy in my arms and the raspy nylon dug into my skin, but I didn't want to take it inside to stow it and risk Hank following me. He wasn't much good at taking hints . . . witness all the hints in our marriage vows about "forsaking all others" that he'd completely missed. "What about him?"

"He had a run-in with the law in Los Angeles," he said. His eyes gleamed with that "I was right, you were wrong" look he'd perfected when we were married and used right up until the day we signed the divorced papers.

His news startled me but I didn't want to show it. "Wh a traffic ticket?"

"Worse than that." He paused, looking at me to gauge my reaction.

I refused to play his game and merely waited for him to speak, even though curiosity pricked at me.

"The ATF stormed his house," Hank announced.

Ye gods. I wouldn't have expected something like that. Maybe a little pot or something, but not a SWAT-unit-breaks-down-your-door type of offense. "What were they after?" I couldn't resist asking.

He kicked at a fire ant hill, rousing the inhabitants to fury as they swarmed over the toe of his boot. "I dunno," he admitted. "The file is sealed, but a buddy of mine was on patrol the night it went down."

"So, Glen wasn't arrested and didn't end up in court or anything?"

"Just because we don't have access to the details doesn't mean something criminal didn't go down," Hank said hotly. "Damn it, Grace, can't you see that the guy is no good? If the cops didn't have something on him, why'd he leave LA and come here? Damn it!" The last exclamation was directed at the fire ants, not me, as Hank hopped around, slapping at his ankle.

"Who wouldn't want to leave LA, given an option?" I asked.

Althea's old LTD pulled up before Hank could answer, and she and my mom got out. "Hank Parker, if that's your idea of a rain dance, I think you'll find it's unnecessary," Althea said as Hank almost tumbled over trying to stop an ant that had apparently climbed up his shin.

"Fire ants," I explained.

"These fu—These buggers sting," he hollered.

I bit back a smile at the sight of him dancing around in

his uniform, trying to simultaneously peel his sock down and smack the ants.

Althea shook her head. "That boy was born and raised here—you'd think he'd know better than to go stirring up a fire ant nest, which I'll bet my last dollar he did."

"I'll get some calamine," Mom said, disappearing around the corner of the house.

Hank had smushed the last ant and was sitting on the curb by his patrol car, one pant leg hiked above his knee, displaying large red welts on his hairy calf, when Mom returned with the calamine bottle.

"You could kiss 'em and make 'em all better, sugar," he said to me with a smirk.

Eew.

"You want I should call the EMTs, have them come check you out, Hank?" Althea asked with spurious concern. "Doesn't that look like an allergic reaction to you, Vi?"

The bites were red and painful looking, but I didn't think Hank was in any danger of anaphylactic shock. Althea was just threatening to embarrass him in front of his cop buddies if he didn't behave. Ant bites didn't rank with a bullet hole when telling wounded-in-the-line-of-duty stories at the bar.

"Just give me the lotion," he mumbled, holding out his hand. After using a cotton ball to dab pink dots of calamine on the bites, he rolled down his pant leg, muttered, "Thanks, Vi," and got back in his patrol car.

"What was he doing here, anyway?" Mom asked as we watched him drive down the street.

I told them what Hank had said about Glen Spaatz. Mom pursed her lips and looked thoughtful. "I don't suppose there's any way Braden could have known something

about Mr. Spaatz that he wouldn't want spread around the
school? That might even have cost him his job?" she asked.

Althea and I stared at her. I liked Glen and didn't want
to visualize him pushing Braden or pressing down on his
face with a pillow, but what Mom said made sense. Except,
how could Braden have learned something about Glen that
Hank, a cop, couldn't dig up? The whole thing made my
head hurt.

RACHEL BROUGHT ANOTHER SEVEN LOCKS OF LOVE
girls to the salon after school let out. I cut and styled on
autopilot, thinking through what I'd learned about Braden's
death. It saddened me to think that there would be so many
suspects in the murder of a high schooler. Lonnie could
have done it, either as revenge for Braden testifying against
his brother or to become the starting wide receiver. It was
almost incomprehensible to me that someone would kill
for such a reason, but I'd seen reports of people killing
for high-end tennis shoes or because someone walked on
their lawn, so I knew it was possible. If Mark's dad was an
abuser, would he kill to keep that abuse a secret? Could that
be what Braden had meant when he talked about needing
to "intervene"? Very possibly. I could see where a sensitive
kid like Braden would want to intervene to protect his
friend. And then there was Dr. Solomon. What if Braden
knew something about the Relamin study that would cost
the doctor or the pharmaceutical company money? Or their
reputation? And how could he "intervene" in such a case?
Maybe he'd confronted the doctor, or threatened to go to
the media.

"It's really short, isn't it?"

The girl in my chair, a plump sophomore with auburn

hair, recalled me from my thoughts. She peered at her reflection unhappily. Per her request, I'd kept her hair as long as possible, but it still barely grazed the bottom of her ears after I'd taken the ten inches required by Locks of Love.

"It's for a great cause," I reminded her. "Look, how about if we part it on the side, like this"—I made a deep part on the left—"and sweep the bangs across."

"That's better," she said, tilting her head this way and that to see the effect. "But it's still really short."

"It'll grow back," I promised. "Think how much easier it'll be to take care of. You can sleep an extra twenty minutes every morning instead of getting up to use the curling iron." I hated it when clients weren't happy with their hair.

Her freckled face brightened. "That's true. And it was worth it." She sat still while I blew hair off the cape with the dryer and then she bounded away like a prisoner being paroled.

Mom was determined to keep the salon open until the normal closing time, despite the lack of customers, but she told me to go ahead when I said I wanted to track down Lonnie Farber.

"I'll go with you," Althea said, surprising me. When I looked a question at her, she added, "I know that boy's aunt Loretta—she's raising him—and that trailer park they live in is in a rough area. You don't want to go there on your own, baby-girl." She tucked her purse under her arm and said, "I'll drive."

I shot Mom a look—Althea drove like a moonshiner evading the law—but she just smiled and shrugged. Reluctantly, I followed Althea to her LTD. Once maroon, it had faded to an ugly pink. Getting in, I buckled my seat belt as Althea reversed out of the narrow driveway at Mach speed.

She headed to the south side of St. Elizabeth, past the new housing development where quite a few navy families lived, and turned onto a sand and gravel driveway where a rickety sign proclaimed "Green Acres." I didn't know if it was a joke about the TV show or not, but I had trouble picturing Eva Gabor living in one of the dilapidated trailers that came into view as we rounded a corner. Although Arnold the pig would have felt right at home.

Twelve or so trailer homes in gray, white, and tan were planted higgledy-piggledy around the clearing, with one hot pink trailer standing out like a wedding guest at a wake. I guessed there wasn't much in the way of HOA restrictions. Rusty old beaters squatted in front of a couple of the mobile homes. Several of the trailers looked deserted—not surprising with a hurricane bearing down. Hurricanes sometimes spawned tornados, which seemed to have a special affinity for trailer parks. Live oak trees created an almost solid canopy overhead, even at this time of year, and dripped with Spanish moss. A layer of browned leaves and acorns almost obscured the scraggly grass. Getting out of the car, I avoided a shallow, muddy ditch where tiny crabs scuttled for cover.

"Over there." Althea pointed to a trailer that wasn't quite as rundown as some of the others. Clay pots filled with bronzy mums stood on either side of the metal steps leading to the front door, and cheery red and white curtains hung in the windows. A new red pickup with jazzy hubcaps and a tool box fastened in the bed didn't seem to fit with the rundown surroundings.

Althea frowned at the truck. "That's not Loretta's."

As we walked to the front door and Althea knocked, I got a tingly feeling between my shoulder blades. I glanced round. The blinds of the trailer behind us flickered and I knew some*one* was watching us. Suddenly, I was glad Althea had elected to come with me.

The door swung open and a black woman in yellow medical scrubs printed with teddy bears stared at us. A silver nametag said, "Loretta Farber, RN." She might have been pretty, but a sallow cast to her skin testified to exhaustion, and a world-weary look in her eyes made me think not much would surprise her. She could've been anywhere between thirty-five and fifty-five. She kept her face impassive as she gazed through the screen at us. "Yes?"

"You going to invite us in, Loretta?" Althea asked.

Loretta's face brightened with recognition, taking ten years off her age, and she pushed the screen door open. "Althea Jenkins! What in the world are you doing here?" She gave me a curious look.

We stepped into a kitchen with a small dinette and two chairs and cabinets painted red to match the curtains. A faint odor of bacon lingered in the air. Althea introduced us, adding, "We just want to talk to Lonnie. Is he here?"

"Now, why would you be wanting my Lonnie, Althea?" Loretta asked, crossing her arms over her chest. Wariness settled again on her features.

"I wanted to talk to him about what he might have seen at Rothmere," I said. "The night Braden McCullers got hurt."

"He didn't see anything," she said flatly.

"We're not here to get Lonnie in trouble," Althea said. "But since he was there that night, we thought—"

"Well, you thought wrong. Lonnie's not above playing a prank or two—the cops told me about the fireworks and I grounded him for that—but he wouldn't deliberately hurt someone. Deep down, he's a good kid. He's had a tough time of it since his dad ran off—my brother Leroy always was about as useless as teats on a boar hog—but he's getting good grades now and might have a shot at a football scholarship that would get him a college education. He could get away from—" She gestured to the trailer and its surroundings.

"He'll be the starting wide receiver now that Braden's gone, won't he? That will get him more visibility with the college scouts."

I was mostly thinking aloud, but I knew I'd said the wrong thing when Loretta leaned toward me and poked a finger at my chest. "Don't go there, girl. You do not want to imply that my nephew killed Braden McCullers so he could have his spot on the football team. I have a half a mind—"

A scraping noise, followed by a thud, cut her off. The trailer shifted slightly. Loretta looked down the narrow hall and then stepped to the window as an engine roared to life. Althea and I joined her at the window, craning our necks to look over her shoulders in time to see the red pickup peel out of the lot, kicking up a rooster tail of sand, gravel, and leaves. It took me half a second to realize Lonnie had exited through a window and taken off rather than talk to us. Not the way we do hospitality in the South.

"C'mon." Althea grabbed my hand and dragged me out the door. "Good to see you, Loretta," she called over her shoulder as we piled into the car.

"You're not planning to—" I began as she gunned the old LTD and took off with my door still open. I slammed it shut and groped for my seat belt, shutting my eyes as we rocketed down the narrow lane.

"Which way did he go?" she asked as we approached the T intersection.

I looked both ways and spotted a red blur just about out of sight. "Right." Bracing myself, I said a quick prayer when it became apparent Althea wasn't even going to stop at the intersection. The force of the turn threw me against the door and the LTD's rear end swung halfway across the center line, but no one hit us as she stomped on the accelerator.

"No one bugs out like that unless he's got something to hide," Althea said. "And I aim to find out what it is."

# Chapter Fifteen

"WE COULD'VE ASKED FOR HIS CELL PHONE NUMBER," I said, flinching as we passed a bicyclist and sent him wavering onto the shoulder. He gave us the finger and I couldn't blame him. I watched as the speedometer topped sixty and headed for seventy. We were on a two-lane road with a speed limit of forty-five, and I couldn't decide whether to close my eyes and let disaster take me by surprise, or keep them open and see it coming.

"There he is!" Althea pointed, and the car swerved into the path of a semitruck in the oncoming lane.

"Both hands on the wheel!" I yelped, gripping the dashboard.

She slewed the car into our lane at the last second and shot me an amused look. "I've been driving since before you were born, Grace Ann, and nothing terrible's happened yet. Have faith."

Althea's guardian angel must be nearly dead from exhaustion if it'd been keeping her out of accidents for almost fifty years. I hoped mine would pick up the slack. After a couple of minutes, it looked like we were gaining on Lonnie, mainly because he didn't seem to know we were following him and was tooling along at a reasonable—safe—pace, unlike us. The old LTD might not have been much to look at, but the engine purred like a satisfied tiger as we cruised along at eighty, Althea hunched over the wheel. I loosed my fingers from their grip on the dash and let the blood tingle back into them.

"What are you going to do when we catch up to him?" I asked. "We can't just run him off the road."

Big mistake. Althea was incapable of talking without looking at the person she's conversing with. She swiveled her head now to say, "Why not?" The car drifted right and bumped along the shoulder for a moment before she swung it back onto the asphalt.

"His truck's bigger than this dinosaur," I said, patting the LTD's dash.

"Hm. You might be right about that. I wouldn't want my baby to get dinged up." She pursed her lips thoughtfully. "You can write him a note and we'll hold it up to the window. There's a notepad and a pen—or maybe you'll have to use a lipstick—in my handbag."

She started to rifle through her purse, but I stopped her with a screech as the car aimed itself at a telephone pole. "Watch the road. I'll get it." With trembling fingers, I found the notepad and a black pen and wrote "PLEASE PULL OVER." Looking at it, I felt fairly stupid and wondered what the heck we were doing out here, chasing down a

teenager in a pickup truck who might or might not know
anything about Braden's death. As Dillon would surely tell
me, this was the police's job. Maybe, I thought with a glimmer of hope, Dillon wouldn't have to know.

Lonnie's truck, now only a quarter mile ahead of us,
seemed to slow. "Is he—? Yes," I said, "he's turning left."

"I've got eyes in my head, don't I?" Althea said, clicking
on the blinker. She braked and waited for an RV to trundle
by in the oncoming lane, slowed by the Ski-Doos on a
trailer behind it.

"Uh-oh." Lonnie's truck had not only slowed, it had
come to a stop beside a green metal mailbox, facing back
the way we'd come. And Lonnie had gotten out. All six
foot four, two hundred pounds of him. He stood with feet
spread wide, leather jacket flapping open, looking like a
pillar of muscle in jeans that outlined his quads and with
the wind flattening his tee shirt against ridged abs. For a
moment, I thought he should abandon the whole football
thing and consider trying to make it as a *Men's Health*
model. He'd have to work on his expression, though; sultry
sold more magazines than surly. Or was that fear on his
face? Before I could make up my mind, I saw the gun. It
was big and silver and he gripped it in his right hand, half
hidden behind his thigh.

"Go, go, go," I yelled at Althea. "He's got a gun." Reaching my left foot over, I pressed down on her foot where it
was letting off the accelerator.

"Wha—?" Althea's head whipped to the left. I leaned
over to grab the wheel as the tires spun and we lurched toward Lonnie. His eyes widened and he stumbled back
when it looked like we were going to plow into him. Then,
I cut the wheel and steered us back into our own lane, los-

ing sight of Lonnie as I concentrated on getting us out of there.

Half a mile down the road, Althea recovered enough to push me aside and take over the driving. "I cannot believe Loretta Farber lets that boy have a gun," she said. "I'm going to have to give her a piece of my mind."

I doubted Lonnie had consulted his aunt on the gun purchase. "I think we need to have a word with the police," I said.

We rode in silence, working our way west on rural roads until we reached I-95 and Althea merged onto the northbound ramp so we could return to St. Elizabeth without having to cross paths with Lonnie Farber again. The sight of Lonnie with a gun had jolted me so badly that riding on the freeway with Althea at the wheel didn't even faze me now. When the St. Elizabeth exit came into view, Althea said airily, "I don't think we need to mention any of this to Vi, do you?"

The thought of my mom's reaction to our car chase and almost confrontation with a gun-wielding teenager made me shudder. "Absolutely not!"

ALTHEA DROPPED ME AT MY APARTMENT, BOTH OF US tacitly agreeing that it might be best to avoid Mom until we'd had a chance to calm down a bit. I watched Althea speed away before tottering into my apartment. I put off calling Dillon while I made myself an early dinner—grilled cheese sandwich—and drank a big glass of milk at my dinette. Hoping to distract myself from the image of Lonnie on the roadside holding a gun, I pulled some papers from the Rothmere box and scanned them, careful not to drip cheese on the brittle pages.

*20 October 1831*

*Dear Quentin,*

*Oh, my love, I wish you were here. I am prey to such fears! I have had conversation with Matilda, the maid who found my father, and I am afraid he did not die of natural causes. Matilda spoke of vomit on the landing. I will tell you all when next I see you, but I am afraid that my brother, so burdened with his debts, may have had a hand in my father's death. How it pains me to write such words! And I must admit that I have even had doubts about my mother. Mr. Angus Carlisle has been much about the plantation, visiting with my mother and helping her with estate issues, she says. I cannot like the way he looks at her, nor, if I am honest, the way she looks at him. Come soon, my dearest Quentin. I long for you more with each day that passes.*

*Your perturbed Clarissa*

I checked the date and saw that this letter preceded the one from Quentin I'd read earlier. I was dying to know what Matilda had told Clarissa that convinced her her father was murdered. For the briefest of seconds, I thought that if Avaline van Tassel really had a link to the spirits, she could get Cyril to tell us what happened. I brushed the foolish thought away as the phone rang. I grabbed it up.

"Hey, sweetheart, what's this I hear about you playing lifeguard in the Atlantic in the middle of a hurricane? I couldn't believe the story when it came across the wire."

Marty. I smiled involuntarily. "How did you—" I re

membered the reporter. "Just a little morning swim," I said. "Swimming is excellent exercise, you know."

"Hm." The words "venti" and "cappuccino" filtered through the phone. "I was worried about you."

"I'm fine," I said. Silence fell. "So, where are you— Timbuktu? Kiev?"

"Nothing so exotic." He laughed. "Albuquerque. I'm probably stuck here for the next two or three days, though. My source needs some coaxing. You could evacuate here . . . I can pretty well guarantee the hurricane won't reach Santa Fe. It's so brown here I'm convinced they haven't had rain since Nixon resigned."

"I wish I could," I said wistfully. "But I can't desert Mom. And this thing with Braden—"

"How's that going?" Marty asked. The chink of coins reached me and Marty said, "Thanks," in a muffled voice, presumably to the barista.

I filled him in. "It's not your fault, you know," he said when I finished.

His comment surprised me. "What?"

"You're trying to ID the killer because you think you were somehow responsible for the kid getting killed. He died in the hospital, Grace, with dozens of medical professionals around. You're—"

"If I hadn't let him get pushed down the stairs, he wouldn't have been in the hospital," I said, my voice near tears. No one else had guessed how much I blamed myself for Braden's death, not even Mom or Vonda. "I should have—"

"You were one of four adults responsible for—What? Twenty, twenty-two kids spread across a mansion the size of Mount Vernon? And—"

"It's not that big. And that's not the point."

"It is," Marty insisted. I could hear him more clearly and thought he might have moved outside. For a moment I let myself imagine the stark blue of the New Mexico sky, un-muddied by clouds and humidity. "It's—Oh, damn. There's the senator. Look, Grace, I'll call you tonight, tomorrow at the latest."

I didn't know if he heard my "Thank you," as he hung up. I was truly grateful to him for trying to absolve me, even thought I couldn't accept the absolution.

My hand was still on the phone when it rang again. It was Lucy Mortimer, demanding the return of the box of documents so that Avaline van Tassel could use them for her TV project. "She's in my office right now," Lucy said, "and has agreed to review the documents right here since I was reluctant to have her keep them in a hotel room. So, if you could bring them by—."

"I'll have them there within the hour." I hung up, scooped up the box, and headed to a copy center on the far side of Bedford Square from Violetta's. I might have to give up the box, but I wasn't willing to let go of my "rela-tionship" with Clarissa, so I tamped down the guilty feel-ing that told me Lucy would have a conniption fit if she knew I was making copies, and told the clerk what I needed. He gave me the fob for a machine and a quick tutorial. There was no way I could copy everything, and the ledgers and old sales receipts held little interest for me, so I fished out anything that looked like a letter and pressed it gently on the platen to copy it. In all, I had only fifteen pages when I finished, including the letters I'd already read. The thin stack seemed a pitiful legacy of the family's life, and I wondered if other correspondence existed elsewhere.

Arriving at Rothmere, I was astonished by the number of cars in the parking lot. With Hurricane Horatio off the coast, I'd figured the tourists would be sight-seeing in places where they were less likely to get drenched . . . say, South Dakota. But at least six cars and a couple of mini-vans sat in the small lot when I pulled up. The reason for the crowd became apparent when I pushed through the oak doors, box under one arm, and nearly tripped over a thick cable snaking through the foyer and up the stairs. A thin man with receding hair and glasses looked up at a burlier man on the landing with a large camera on his shoulder. "I don't like the angle," the cameraman complained. "That chandelier spoils the shot."

They must be filming *The Spirit Whisperer*. Avaline wasted no time, I'd give her that. The two men ignored me completely as I stepped over their cables and wound my way back to Lucy's office. Inside, I found not only Lucy and Avaline, but also Agent John Dillon. He leaned against the wall, arms crossed over his chest, a watchful look on his face. A slanting sunbeam touched his profile and turned his eyes marine blue. My gaze dropped to his firm mouth as Lucy bustled forward and took the box, saying huffily, "Finally!"

"Thank you, Grace," Avaline said, sending a gracious smile my way. "I was just telling John here how excited I am to be interviewing Cyril. I expect he'll have a fascinating story to tell."

John? I raised my brows at him. He smiled but kept his eyes on Avaline, who was leaning forward in such a way that he couldn't avoid the view of her robust cleavage offered by the white blouse unbuttoned to approximately her navel. Okay, only the top two buttons were undone, but they were enough.

"And I can't wait to get John on camera. I'm sure he'll e very photogenic. Just look at his bone structure!"

We all stared at Dillon and I thought he flushed under our scrutiny.

"You weren't even here when Braden fell," I said, sounding more accusatory than I wanted.

"I'm not doing an interview," Dillon said, and I felt a rush of relief. I remembered his hostility toward the press from an earlier case and thought Avaline van Tassel might not find it so easy to get him on camera.

"I'm trying to persuade him to give us background on the investigation," Avaline said. "The fact that the police can't pinpoint a suspect makes it that much more likely that Cyril pushed Braden."

"So you think Cyril dressed up like a werewolf and smothered Braden at the hospital when pushing him off the landing didn't do the trick?"

Avaline was unperturbed by the hint of skepticism in my tone. "Spirits have been known to travel some distance from where they died, especially when the emotional impetus is significant enough. I interviewed a spirit—a woman—in Montana who journeyed more than a hundred miles in 1912 to be with her daughter who had gotten trapped in a well. And perhaps the nurse, startled by Cyril's presence, was . . . less than accurate in her description of what she saw in that hospital room. I'm interviewing her, too."

Dillon pushed off the desk he was leaning against and said, "Look, I've got a couple of questions for Dr. Mortimer so if you could excuse us . . ."

His firm tone dislodged even the smug Avaline from her perch on Lucy's desk. Lucy looked startled and a bit nervous but said, "Of course, Agent Dillon. Not that I saw what happened, but I'll be happy to answer your questions." Her hands fluttered to the cameo at her throat and she blinked rapidly.

Dillon's gaze settled on me, and he said, "If you could wait until I'm done here, Miss Terhune, I've got a couple of questions for you, too."

I couldn't tell from his tone if he'd heard about Althea's and my car chase so I said, "Sure," as casually as I could and followed Avaline into the hall. A short man wearing horn-rimmed glasses and highlighted hair gelled into short points hurried up to her. A Vandyke beard quivered as he talked. "Ava, darling, what do you think about doing the show live?"

"Live?" She sounded doubtful.

"Live," he affirmed, nodding quickly. He spread his hands expansively and a diamond ring sparked on his pinkie. "We'll have the spirit and the hurricane, just like in 1831 when Cyril moved on. And we can hire reenactors to play his wife and the party guests."

"But, Les, you know the spirits don't always respond to my overtures immediately," Avaline said with a sidelong glance at me.

Studying a portrait on the wall, I pretended not to be listening. Despite myself, I was marginally interested. I'd never thought about it, but I supposed you couldn't whistle for a ghost like you could for a dog. Could you lure it with . . . what? A ghost wouldn't have much use for food or money or a complete set of Ginsu steak knives. Maybe ghosts could be tempted with promises of fame or a desire to accuse their murderers.

"Not a problem," Les said. "We can pad the show if we have to, or maybe make it a two-parter. You know the ratings need a boost, darling, and doing it live—"

They moved toward the front entryway, out of earshot, and I wondered if Les was the show's producer, who could make problems disappear by applying a little cash. I didn't envy them trying to film the show during a hurricane and wondered if they had any idea how *loud* a hurricane was. When Dillon hadn't appeared after a couple of minutes, I made my way back to the foyer—Avaline and Les were nowhere in sight—and stepped over cables to climb the stairs. The cameraman was gone from the landing and I headed down the hall toward the portrait gallery. Stopping in front of the painting Lucy had shown the high schoolers, I studied Clarissa Rothmere's painted likeness. She looked happy in this picture, one arm around the waist of a taller, plumper girl seated beside her—an older sister, surely— and the other stroking the head of a spaniel with its paws on her knee. She gazed out at me without a shadow of self-consciousness or worry, and I wondered what had happened to turn this carefree girl into the anxious, sickly writer whose seemingly privileged life was a veneer over the rot of murder, adultery, and greed, just like some of the South's historic mansions were no more than wooden shells hollowed by termites, weather, and Union bullets.

"Friends of yours?"

Dillon's voice came from behind me and I turned with a half smile. He stood a couple of paces away, hands crossed over his chest, gaze fixed on the painting. "Sort of." I explained about my interest in Clarissa.

Dillon moved closer to study the painting and his shoulder brushed mine. "She looks like a nice kid," he observed. "This guy, though"—he pointed to a blond young man with a narrow face—"looks like a weasel."

I laughed. "Maybe that's the brother who was in debt, the one Clarissa is afraid killed their father."

"My money's on the wife," Dillon said. "She's got that unsatisfied look that means trouble. Ever looked at a portrait of Henry the Eighth? Or Marie Antoinette? They had the same look. You can probably find it in cave paintings, too, for all I know. The 'I want more' look you see on the faces of shoppers at the mall."

"Wow, you're almost as good as Ms. Van Tassel," I said. "Maybe you could get your own show—*The Portrait Whisperer*."

"TV's not for me," he said shortly.

"Why not?"

He eyed me for a long moment and then said, "I don't trust reporters."

"Why not?"

"Because getting the story first is more important to most of 'em than getting the facts straight or keeping a murderer behind bars."

"That doesn't sound like a hypothetical situation."

"It's not. It wasn't." Before I could probe for more details, he took a step forward, and he gently touched the abraded spot on my cheekbone. "Should I be asking what the other guy looks like?"

His touch confused me and I didn't want to talk about my dip in the Atlantic. Resisting the impulse to turn my face into his palm, I stepped back and his hand fell to his side. "Grace, zero. Ocean, one," I said lightly. At his questioning frown, I gave him an abbreviated version of my morning's swim. His brows arched toward his hairline, but I distracted him by recounting the story of Althea's and my trip to the trailer park and our almost run-in with Lonnie. I downplayed the car chase, making it sound like nothing more than a Sunday drive down a shady lane, but he was still frowning by the time I got to the gun.

"Lonnie pulled a gun on you?" Anger and something else vibrated in his voice.

"Well, I'm not sure he knew it was Althea and me," I

said, "and he didn't point it at us or anything. In fact"—I
visualized the scene in my head—"he seemed scared.
Frightened of something. And I don't know why Althea or
I would frighten him." The more I thought about it, the
more I became convinced that Lonnie hadn't realized who
was trailing him.

Dillon flipped open his cell phone and issued an order to
someone to pick up Alonso Farber for questioning. "He's
armed," he said into the phone. "Let me know when you've
got him." He hung up and concentrated on me again.
"You've had a busy day." His tone didn't lead me to think it
was a compliment. "Anything else I should know?"

"Well . . ." I relayed what Hank had said about Glen
Spaatz and what Mark had said about Braden's involve-
ment with the Relamin study.

Dillon received the news impassively and I couldn't tell
what he thought.

"Could Braden have been a threat to the pharmaceutical
company somehow?" I asked.

"I think you've been watching too many whistle-blower
movies," he said.

"I guess I'd rather have Braden's killer be a faceless cor-
poration than some kid that Rachel goes to school with," I
said. I hadn't realized it before, but it was true.

"That's understandable."

I hesitated for a moment, on the brink of mentioning my
concern about Mark Crenshaw, but drew back.

"What?" Dillon asked, clearly sensing my indecision.
"You'd better tell me."

I shook my head, my hair whisking against my cheek.
"No. It's nothing." I couldn't justify siccing the police on
Mark's father with no more than an easily explained bruise
and vague suspicions to go on. Maybe I could find an op-

portunity to talk with Captain Crenshaw myself and get a feel for the man. Or maybe I should approach Mrs. Crenshaw. To distract Dillon, who was looking at me with one brow quirked, I asked, "Where do you send Groucho when there's a hurricane?" Groucho was his horse, a big black brute I'd only seen in photos.

"A woman I know owns a boarding farm a couple hours northwest of here," he said. "I had Groucho taken up there a couple days ago."

Conjuring an image of a svelte blonde in jodhpurs and riding boots, I suppressed a completely unreasonable sting of jealousy at the phrase "a woman I know." "That's good," I said lamely. "I suppose he's not used to hurricanes."

"Nope. They're few and far between in Wisconsin."

I was suddenly overwhelmed with a desire to hear all about his life in Wisconsin, his life before he arrived in Georgia. I realized I didn't know if he had been married before, if he had siblings or children, or what he liked to do in his off time, other than hang out with Groucho. "What—" I started.

Dillon's phone rang. He answered it, raising one finger in a "hold that thought" gesture. "I'm on my way," he said into the phone. "I've got to go," he told me as he ended the call. "We're still on for Friday?"

"Barring hurricane intervention."

He grinned and strode away. I listened to his steps as he ran down the stairs and started thinking about what to wear Friday night. Maybe my halter-top dress with the leaf design. But that wouldn't work if it was chilly in the aftermath of the hurricane. Possibly the blue . . .

A creaking sound, like someone stepping on a loose floorboard, pulled me out of my thoughts. Looking over my shoulder, I saw no one, just Clarissa and Cyril and the

rest of the Rothmere family gazing at me from the oil painting. Was there a new urgency in Clarissa's expression? I
leaned closer to the painting and touched a finger to the
painted fabric of Clarissa's yellow gown, almost expecting
the feel of silk under my fingertip. But the hundred-and-
fifty-year-old paint was rough and dry. Too much talk of
ghosts and spirit whisperers was getting to me. Or maybe it
was the falling barometer making me feel so strange. Another almost creak—more a sigh of air compressed between two boards—goosed me out of the portrait gallery
and closer to the stairs. Old houses make noises, I told myself, looking over my shoulder toward the shadowy pas-
sage that led out of the gallery in the other direction. And
this house was full of people—cameramen and other people involved in Avaline's show. Creaks and squeaks were
nothing to worry about.

I breathed a sigh of relief as I reached the stairs and began descending them. Sunlight, muted by clouds, streamed
into the foyer from the open door. It felt welcoming after
the stingy light in the upstairs hall. At the bottom of the
stairs, under the magnificent chandelier, Avaline stood talking to a woman who looked vaguely familiar. She turned as
I stepped into the marbled entryway and I recognized the
other chaperone from the field trip, Dr. Solomon. Dark
brows arched toward the widow's peak, and she looked as
startled to see me as I was to see her.

The lines in her brow smoothed out as I approached.
"Grace, right?" she said, extending her hand. "I guess
you're here for an interview about that night, too."

I shook her hand, noting the somewhat stubby fingers
with their bare nails filed short. The rest of her look was
equally no-nonsense: smooth, olive-toned skin free of
makeup; hair pulled back into a low ponytail like on Satur-

day; deep-set brown eyes and a wide mouth that pulled down
a tad at the corners. I could definitely envision her in a white
lab coat rather than the navy slacks and pinstriped oxford
blouse she wore with a cardigan knotted around her neck.

"We haven't talked her into it yet," Avaline said, tossing
back her mane of black hair. "Maybe you can convince her
it won't be painful, Tasha." She laughed, and with a glance
at her watch, excused herself, disappearing down the hall
toward Lucy's office.

"I'd guess it will be more painful for you than it would
be for me," I said, taking the opening Avaline had unwit-
tingly supplied. "I mean, you knew Braden so much better
than I did."

Tasha Solomon drew in a fast breath, nostrils flaring
wide. "What do you mean?"

"Well, you worked with him in that drug study, didn't
you?" I said innocently. "I'd only met him a couple of
times with Rachel."

A technician walked past us, unwinding cable from a
big spool and I stepped aside. Tasha Solomon didn't move.

"Ah." She seemed to be thinking. "Who told you about
the drug study?" Her eyes, hooded under heavy lids,
watched me closely. "Not that I can confirm whether or not
Braden McCullers was taking part."

"I heard it from one of his friends," I said, deliberately
vague. "I guess there was some talk that maybe the drug
made him light-headed or dizzy."

"That's bullshit," she said, thrusting her face forward
pugnaciously. "Relamin is a miracle drug. It's going to
make a huge difference in the lives of thousands of people
trying to cope with depression. It's—" She cut herself off.
"Why am I explaining this to you?" She hefted her purse
higher on her shoulder, preparing to leave.

"I didn't mean to offend you," I said, a little startled by the severity of her reaction.

"No, I'm sorry for blowing up at you," she said. Some of the tension eased out of her shoulders. "This whole thing with Braden has made me a little edgy. He was a good kid and it's just awful to think that someone would want to kill him. Ari—my daughter—spent a whole day in bed when she heard. Look, I've got an appointment."

"I've played over that night so often in my head," I said, falling into step with her as she moved through the door and out onto the steps. "I keep thinking that I might have seen or heard something useful, but if I did, I don't know what it was. Did you see anything?"

"I was in the museum most of the evening, with Ari and Rudy."

"So you were all together the whole evening? Even when the fireworks started?" I hadn't seen her when I wandered into the museum.

Her tongue poked a tent in her cheek as we crunched across the gravel parking lot to her car, a white Volvo sedan. "Well, I guess each of us went to the bathroom at some point. And the kids went to check in with some of their friends. You know how kids are!" She laughed and fitted a key into the Volvo's lock. "I don't think any of them took the ghost-hunting thing too seriously. And who can blame them?" She arched her brows, inviting me to share her amusement at such an unscientific assignment.

"Not me," I agreed. I dragged the conversation back to the drug study as she slid onto the front seat. "Can you give me a ballpark figure for how much a drug like Relamin would be worth if it gets on the market?"

She scowled. "I don't have anything to do with marketing or accounting."

"What's your best guess?"

Turning the key in the ignition, she said, "Five hundred, maybe?"

I felt let down. Half a million wouldn't be worth killing Braden, not for a pharmaceutical company.

"Maybe even three-quarters of a billion," Dr. Solomon continued, "depending. And it *will* get approved." She started the car forward, almost clipping me with the still-open door before she pulled it shut.

Five hundred *million*, not thousand. That was real money. I stood in the small lot for a moment, the wind whipping at my hair, and speculated about what kind of money Dr. Solomon got for ensuring the drug made it through the FDA wickets. I'd bet last week's tips that it was enough to murder for. It crossed my mind that Dr. Solomon didn't have much of an alibi for Saturday night—although she'd freely admitted that, so maybe she was innocent?— and I wondered where she'd been on Sunday night when a werewolf-costumed murderer smothered Braden. Her daughter had hosted a Halloween party for her friends. Had Dr. Solomon been there, chaperoning again? Or had she played least in sight, trusting her daughter and her friends, or giving herself an opportunity to drive to Brunswick with no one the wiser?

# Chapter Sixteen

I HAD JUST STARTED TOWARD MY CAR WHEN THE sound of an approaching motor brought my head around. Glen Spaatz's Corvette cornered into the lot and came to a stop in front of me, blocking my path. Looking impossibly handsome, Glen grinned from the driver's seat, all white teeth and crisp dark hair against a red Henley shirt. His tanned hands flexed on the leather steering wheel cover. "You're here to find fame and fortune in Hollywood, right?" he asked through the open window.

"Not hardly." I was getting tired of people assuming I wanted to grab fifteen minutes of fame by letting Avaline van Tassel interview me for her show.

"Good," he said, surprising me. "You wouldn't like it. You're much too real to fit in with the Hollywood crowd."

"Thank you, I think."

He laughed. "It was a compliment. You know I tried that

scene and it wasn't for me, either. It's the capital of fakery. Fake boobs, fake friends, fake bling, fake emotion." A hint of bitterness colored his voice. "More fake stuff than you'd find at a drag queen contest."

The idea surprised a laugh out of me and his grin broadened. "Hop in," he said, pushing open the passenger side door.

"What?"

"The St. Elizabeth Sabertooths' volleyball team has a game in Kingsland tonight. I like to go to school sports events—wrestling, soccer, baseball, you name it—to support my students when I can. Since my other option for tonight is grading the pop quiz I gave today, I'm rarin' to go to the volleyball game."

"But aren't you here to do an interview for *The Spirit Whisperer*?" I asked. As the words left my mouth, I realized I was making the same assumption about him that had annoyed me when he made it about me.

"Nope. I'm here to find you. Your mom told me you were here."

"Me? Why?"

"Because you're beautiful and fun and I enjoy your company."

"Oh." His flattery and the look in his eyes took me aback.

"Coming?"

"My car—"

"I'll drop you back here to pick it up when we get back from the game," he promised.

Why not? I moved around the front of the Vette and climbed in.

\* \* \*

THE CROWD IN THE CAMDEN COUNTY HIGH SCHOOL
gym in Kingsland was sparse, maybe because of Horatio
and maybe because women's volleyball wasn't on a par
with men's basketball when it came to filling the bleachers.
The first game had already started when we arrived and
cries of "Mine!" mingled with the thud of the ball, the
ref's whistle, and cheers and groans from parents and a
handful of students. Glen and I found a spot halfway up on
the right-most section of risers and sat. The ridged metal
was cold and I shifted to get comfortable, accidentally
bumping Glen's thigh with my leg. Principal Kornhiser sat
just behind the volleyball team's bench, wearing a yellow
shirt printed with purple palm trees. He caught my eye and
waved.

"Now, he'd fit right in in Hollyweird," Glen whispered
into my ear, returning Kornhiser's wave.

"Are you saying he's a fake?" I asked.

"And how," Glen said. "He's all 'good karma' and 'I've
got your back' to your face, but he'll throw you to the
wolves to preserve his and the school's reputation."

Protecting the school's reputation didn't sound so hideous to me, and I wondered if Glen was getting some back-
lash about the ghost-hunting fiasco.

I spotted Lindsay Tandy on the court immediately; she
was half a head taller than all but one of her teammates.
She waited for the serve, arms extended, knees bent, a look
of fierce concentration on her face. The ball sailed over the
net with terrific force and a blond girl got the dig, going
down on her padded knees to do it. The ball popped up and
another player moved into position to set it with her fingertips, floating it high and just a foot inside the net. Lindsay
bounded up and smacked the ball down into the opponents'
court, palm rigid and feet four inches off the floor.

"Way to go, Linds!" The blonde high-fived her.

"She's really good," I said as play continued.

"The best we've ever had at St. Elizabeth, according to Coach Adkins," Glen said. "And she's a damn good student, too. Stanford recruited her, but she opted to sign with Maryland because Mark Crenshaw's going to the Naval Academy."

"I heard that," I said. "It's too bad." I scanned the bleachers and found Mark seated alone at the far end, his eyes fixed on Lindsay as she caromed around the court.

Glen looked a question at me as the Wildcats coach waved a finger in the ref's face over a line call.

"It's too bad she's letting the whole boyfriend-girlfriend thing dictate her decisions," I explained. "Chances are, their relationship will come to nothing, but she'll be stuck with the results of the education choices she makes now for the rest of her life." As I was. What choices would I have made differently if I hadn't been set on marrying Hank? Ye gods. A BA would've done me a lot more good in the long run than my temporary MRS.

"It's not like Maryland is a diploma mill or something," Glen observed mildly.

"You're right. I'm sure it'll work out. Where did you go to college?"

"UC Santa Barbara. It's a big-time party school, but I managed to get my degree."

"And how did a biology major end up as an actor?" The second game had started—the Sabertooths took the first one—and I kept half an eye on it as we talked. Someone behind us was munching on a candy bar and the smell of chocolate made my tummy gurgle.

"I was 'discovered,'" he said with air quotes.

"Really?" I didn't know that happened in the real world.

He nodded. "I was working at Sea World the summer after I graduated, doing the show with the walruses and sea lions, when an agent came up to me and said she could get me work in commercials. I did a deodorant ad and a spot for Home Depot and then I landed a movie."

"Quite the fairy tale," I said.

"More like a black comedy," he said ruefully. "A couple of my movies went straight to DVD and one was never released because something got screwed up with the distribution deal, and—But you don't want to hear about all that." He waved a hand. "Teaching is a much more stable career," he said, eyes tracking the volleyball as a Sabertooth served it, "and I get a lot of satisfaction out of helping the kids achieve their goals, whatever they are."

"Why Georgia?" I asked, mindful of Hank's cautionary story about Glen. "Why not stay in California?"

His eyes narrowed slightly, and I wondered if something in my voice let him know my question wasn't as casual as it seemed. After a moment, he said with a forced laugh, "Ever seen the traffic in LA?"

I laughed with him, but I noted that he hadn't really answered my question.


GLEN DROPPED ME BACK IN THE ROTHMERE PARKING lot—now empty except for my Fiesta—a little before seven. The Sabertooths had won the match and we mostly talked high school sports on our way back to St. Elizabeth.

"Don't bother getting out," I said as he cut the motor.

Ignoring me, he came around to my door and opened it. I stepped out and found my face only inches from his as stood. "I'd take you to dinner," he said, "but I've got to on with the grading." He leaned forward as if to kiss but I reared back, bumping my back painfully against the door frame.

"Why did you kiss me the other day? In front of Hank?"

It was almost pitch-black out here with only a couple of small spotlights casting fantastical shadows from a topiary stag and unicorn, and I found it hard to read Glen's face. His eyes seemed to hold a speculative look as he studied me. "Can't a guy kiss an attractive woman without getting the third degree about it?"

"You just made up that bit about me inviting you in."

"Guilty." He backed away from the door and I stepped around it. He closed it behind me with a *thunk*. "Let's just say cops aren't my favorite breed and he was obviously so jealous that I couldn't help myself. It wasn't fair of me to put you in an awkward position—did I?—and I'm sorry."

Honest contrition sounded in his voice and I found myself confused by him. He was handsome and fun, but he was pushing things too quickly, and even though he'd now apologized, his using me to needle Hank was off-putting. "Where were you Sunday night?" I asked.

"So, now I'm a suspect because I don't like cops?" His voice hovered between irritation and amusement and I wished I could read his face better in the darkness.

"No, you're a suspect because you were at Rothmere when Braden was pushed."

"I was home—alone—grading papers. What about you?"

"Home—alone—watching a DVD," I admitted. "I enjoyed the game." I offered my hand. "Thanks for asking me."

He shook my hand with mock solemnity, but there was a glint in his eyes. "You're welcome. Maybe next time we can go to a Jaguars game, if you like football."

"I like football." Smiling noncommittally, I crunched across the gravel to my Fiesta and unlocked it. A bat zipped by, no more than a foot over my head. Glen waited until I was in the car with the door locked before beeping his horn in farewell and taking off.

LIGHTS WERE ON IN MRS. JONES'S HOUSE WHEN I pulled up to the curb, and I debated going in to see how she was doing. I was tired, though—maybe from my early morning swim—and I elected to skip the socializing in favor of some scrambled eggs and toast. I couldn't remember when I last ate, and I felt light-headed as I approached my door. A glimmer of white attracted my attention and I moved faster when I realized someone had left a note on my door. As I stepped onto the stoop, something squished underfoot.

I looked down to see a squirrel carcass, its flattened form a grotesque doormat. "Ye gods!" I breathed, almost falling backward off the stoop in my haste to get away. I frantically wiped my foot in the grass for at least two minutes before returning to the stoop, stepping carefully around the dead squirrel, to snatch the note from the door. It was only taped up and came away easily when I tugged on it.

"Stop asking questions. Or you will end up like this squirrel."

The ugliness of the words hit me and I dropped the note, catching it before it fluttered to the ground. I read it again. The words were printed in a generic font on a plain sheet of bond paper. No signature. Duh. I started to call the police but thought better of it. I wasn't in immediate danger; there was nothing the police could do. Instead, I dialed my mom's number. No answer. Maybe she was out with Althe or Walter Highsmith. Wandering away from the stoop ward the comforting light streaming from Mrs. Jones's windows, I called Vonda.

"Ick," she said when I explained what had happened. "I'll be right over. Ricky can man the fort here."

While I waited for her to arrive, I stepped over the squirrel again, repressing a shudder, and entered the apartment. Grabbing a trash bag, rubber gloves, and barbecue tongs, I returned to the stoop and gingerly tweezed up the squirrel, depositing it into the bag and pulling the ties tight just as Vonda drove up in the old station wagon with a "Magnolia House" logo magneted to the door.

"Is that it?" she asked, nodding toward the bag.

"Yes." Vonda followed me as I carried the bag to the rear of Mrs. Jones's house, where two covered rubbish bins sat, and plopped it in.

"Maybe we should have given it a decent burial?" Vonda suggested.

"Vonda!"

She held her hands up in apology. "You're right. Sorry. I brought a little pick-me-up." She pulled a bottle of Jeremiah Weed, a bourbon liqueur, out of her purse. "Remember?"

I had to laugh. The first drink either of us had ever had was Jeremiah Weed liberally mixed with 7Up. We'd been on a church-sponsored retreat and one of the youth leaders had supplied the bottle, along with a case of beer. We'd both gotten royally sick and thrown up in the church van, as had a couple of the boys chugging beer. The youth leader had plenty of time to regret his stupidity as he hosed out the van. I don't think we ever told on him.

"This may be the same bottle," Vonda said, examining ˙, "I found it in the back of the pantry when I was setting mouse traps last week and I've been meaning to bring it over."

As she talked, we walked toward my apartment. "I don't see any blood," Vonda said, scanning the cement stoop. "I guess it wasn't killed here, which is a good thing You don't want someone performing animal sacrifices at your front door." Light from my living room illuminated her hair, which was back to the bright red she'd had me dye it a couple of weeks back. No more vampire black. Her bangs were long and swept to one side, emphasizing her big brown eyes.

"I think it was road kill," I said, stepping over the spot where the squirrel had lain, even though nothing remained to mark where it had been. I'd examined the poor critter when I bent to pick it up, and it seemed to have a greasy tire track pressed into its fur.

"I guess that's better," Vonda said doubtfully. "Why do kids get up to such sick pranks every Halloween?"

"I don't think it had anything to do with Halloween." I led her through the apartment and into the kitchen where I poured liberal measures of Jeremiah Weed into orange juice glasses. Then I caught her up on events and showed her the note. "Thanks for coming over," I added.

She gave me a hug and handed back the note. "Succinct," she said. "Are you going to tell the police?"

"I might drop it by tomorrow. It's not like they're going to open up a major investigation. They don't have time to follow up on penny-ante stuff like this."

"Hank would give it special attention," Vonda said archly.

"Another reason not to take it in."

She laughed.

We headed for the small living room and I sat in my recliner while Vonda settled onto the love seat. Vonda took a
long swallow of the amber liquid and held her glass up to
the light. "Liquor doesn't go bad, does it?"

"It gets better—and more expensive—with age." The
liquor warmed my throat and opened my nasal passages as
I held a small mouthful for a moment. Swallowing, I leaned
back in the puffy chair. My muscles ached, my scrapes
burned, and I felt about as energetic as an overcooked spa-
ghetti noodle. I was glad Vonda was here.

"Any idea who left it?"

"Not really." I tried to focus my tired brain. "Lonnie?
Seems a step down from pulling a gun on me and Althea.
Glen, because I'm asking about what happened in
LA? Doesn't seem like his style, and besides, he'd hardly
have had time to put it there before I got home. Coach Peet?
Dr. Solomon, because I'm asking about the drug study?
One of the students? Could be any of the kids who were at
the ghost hunt." I sighed and took another sip of the liquor.

"Maybe you should drop the whole thing," Vonda suggested. "Let the police find out who killed Braden."

"But I feel responsible," I said, blinking back tears. "I
was there. I was supposed to be keeping those kids safe.
And I didn't."

"Making the murderer nervous by asking questions all
over town won't bring Braden back."

I shrugged, not convinced. I didn't have the energy to
argue with her. "What's new with you?" I asked to distract her.

"The only thing going on in my week is a gaggle of Hollywood people staying with us."

"Coraline Spirit Whisperer and friends."

She stared at me, her eyes round. "Are you psychic? How did you know?"

I explained about Avaline's offer to interview me for the TV show.

"Lucky you," Vonda said. "Will they have a real Hollywood makeup artist do your makeup? Do you think you could work in a mention of Magnolia House? Do—"

"I'm not doing it." I poured a little more bourbon. It was making me feel pleasantly woozy.

"I'd do it," Vonda said enviously. She ran a hand through her short hair. "Anyway, things have been hectic with the B and B. Lots of hurricane prep to do, you know. Ricky wanted to shut the place up and evacuate, but then *The Spirit Whisperer* people showed up and rented every room in the place, and we decided to ride it out."

I knew Vonda and Ricky were barely breaking even with the B&B since business had slowed during the recession, so I was glad to hear they were making some money off Avaline and her crew. "Has the spirit summoner communicated with any phantoms at Magnolia House?" I asked.

A grin split Vonda's pixie-ish face. "No. She looked like she was going to give it a go last evening—started to look all trancey and mystical—but I started vacuuming the living room and she went up to her room. Ricky's always thought being able to say the house was haunted would bring more clients, but I can't imagine that people would want to *stay* in a house infested with ghosts. Visit one, maybe, but not stay. Speaking of which"—she set her empty glass down with a clink—"I've got to go. RJ's running a little fever and I promised I'd be home to read his bedtime story. He's really into the Percy Jackson books–the ones with the kid who's half god, half mortal. I tell y reading them with him has helped me brush up on my Greek mythology."

"Ever useful," I said, rising to give her a hug.

"Show the cops that note in the morning," she said.

"I will," I promised.

# Chapter Seventeen

✂

[Wednesday]

SLIGHTLY HUNGOVER THE NEXT MORNING, I DRAGGED myself to the police station before showing up at the salon. The officer on duty took the note and jotted a couple of lines about what happened but didn't promise anything would come of it. "Likely just a prank, miss," he said. "Do you have teenagers? Sometimes kids leave weird notes and stuff for each other."

I left, depressed that the officer thought I looked old enough to have teenagers. I was barely thirty. Maybe the cop was working from data that said teen pregnancies had increased in Georgia in recent years. Yeah, that must be it. We'd had a woman in the salon just last week who bragged about being a grandma at thirty-two. Ye gods. I crossed Bedford Square, noting that fewer cars than usual we_ parked at the meters and only a couple of Doralynn's ta_ were full when I peered in the café's window. St. Eli_ was turning into a ghost town, at least temporarily. At Mom's, I clumped up the stairs to the veranda before noticing the "Closed" sign on the door. Not really surprised after the dearth of business yesterday and how empty the town looked with so many people having evacuated. I traipsed around the side of the house to the kitchen door.

Mom and Althea looked up as the screen door banged shut behind me. "Hi, dear," Mom said, giving me a hug and a kiss. She was in the blue cotton robe that hugged her rounded figure and made her periwinkle blue eyes look even bluer. "Tea?"

"Thanks." I dropped into a chair at the table, catching my reflection in the copper pots that hung from a rack overhead. I hoped my complexion wasn't really that green.

"You look like something the cat yakked up," Althea said.

"I can always count on my friends to make me feel better." I added honey to the mug Mom handed me. She disappeared into the walk-in pantry.

"Just saying," Althea said with a shrug. She pursed her lips to blow on her coffee. "Since we're not making anyone beautiful today, I thought maybe I'd experiment with a new hand cream I've been thinking about for Althea's Organic Skincare Solutions. Glycerin, maybe some sandalwood oil and ginger to give it a more exotic scent . . ." She made a note on a lined pad.

"Did you hear from Loretta yesterday?" I asked Althea casually, aware of my mother shifting cans in the pantry.

Althea's eyes slanted toward the pantry door. "That boy never came home last night," she said in a low voice. "Loretta's worried sick about him."

wondered if I should mention that Dillon had wanted police to bring Lonnie in. Maybe he hadn't shown up at home because he was in jail? No, if that were the case, someone would have let his aunt know.

"Said several folks had been by asking for him and Loretta didn't like the looks of any of them."

"Did you mention the—" I made a gun with my hand.

Althea nodded heavily. "I thought she should know. If she gets a chance, maybe she can talk some sense into him."

"Into who?" Mom asked, emerging from the pantry with a can of crushed pineapple in her hand. Not waiting for an answer, she said, "I thought I'd make some pineapple upside-down cake. Just in case we lose power tomorrow, it'll be good to have something special to eat."

"Good idea." I finished my tea, feeling much better, and stood. "I'm going to find Rachel and see how she's doing."

"She'll be at school, dear," Mom pointed out.

"Oh." I'd forgotten. "Well, then I'm going to read through the rest of my Rothmere letters and maybe talk to Lucy to see what she's knows about Clarissa's fate. Can I come back for dinner?"

"Of course. Spend the night, too, if you want. The forecasters say Horatio should make landfall late tonight. You'd rather be here, wouldn't you, than in that dinky old carriage house?"

"Absolutely. We can play Crazy Eights and Spades if the electricity goes out."

"Yippee," Althea said with a marked lack of enthusiasm.

Mom and I laughed. I kissed them both and headed out, feeling strangely at loose ends.

The copies of the Rothmere letters were still in my car, so I walked home, the wind nudging me from behind. A big clump of pampas grass planted beside the Rivington driveway, taunted by the wind, reached out to slap me its long blades as I passed. Retrieving the pages from my Fiesta, I shut myself into my apartment and sorted out the ones I'd already read. The next one that came to hand was from Clarissa to her friend Felicity.

*Christmas Day 1831*

*Dear Felicity,*

*It is a labor to be truly joyous on this most holy day when my heart aches for my father. With my mother and my brothers and sisters, saving only Sophia, staying with us for the holidays, I should be able to put aside my grief. But in truth, the press of people in the house makes me nervous. I hear whisperings outside my door at night and footsteps in the empty gallery. I do not share these imaginings with my family since they already look askance at me and say I have been unbalanced by Father's death. Only the knowledge that I am to marry my dear Quentin next month makes it possible to bear with my family at this time. Do you think me unfeeling? I am ready to shed Rothmere like a snake sheds its skin and join Quentin at Oakdale Manor as Mrs. Dodd. If I did not know I could leave so soon, I think I must, indeed, go mad. I do so look forward to your arrival, my dearest friend, and trust that I will be feeling more the thing by then. My stomach ailments had subsided somewhat near Thanksgiving, but I'm feeling bilious again these past few days. Perhaps it is due to the stress of dealing with brother Geoffrey and his wife, who have embraced their roles as lord and lady of the manor with too much enthusiasm, even though Mama is still in residence! It seems disrespectful*

*to me. I must hasten to get this in today's post, so I bid*
*you adieu for now.*

*With deepest friendship,*
*Clarissa*

Clarissa's illness was beginning to worry me. Maybe
she had ulcers. Or a mid-nineteenth century version of
IBS. Another thought occurred to me and I smoothed a
hand down the copied page, irritated by its textureless
modernity, wanting the rougher, richer paper that Clarissa had written on. Could Clarissa's symptoms be explained by a poison of some kind? Hadn't ladies used
lead in their makeup in those days? I couldn't remember.
Could she have been exposed to some household toxin
that was making her ill?

I stood, then sat again, feeling foolish that I'd thought I
could do something about Clarissa's illness. She'd been
dead of one cause or another—old age, I hoped—for well
over a century. Still, it might be interesting to do some Internet research on household poisons of that era and see if
I could match anything with Clarissa's symptoms. I'd use
the computer at the salon next time I was there and search
the Internet.

Better yet . . . I dug through my purse for the card Stuart
Varnet had given me. I didn't know if he'd be back at work
yet after his near drowning, but it was worth a phone call. I
ran my finger over the embossed agency name as I dialed:
"Agency for Toxic Substances and Disease Registry."

"Varnet," he answered the phone.

"Hi," I said, feeling awkward. "This is Grace Terhune
I—"

I was spared the embarrassment of explaining w

was. "Grace!" He sounded genuinely pleased to hear from me. "Are you in Atlanta? I'm clearing my schedule right now so I can take you to Bacchanalia. It's my favorite restaurant in the city."

"No." I laughed. "I'm still in St. Elizabeth, waiting for the hurricane. But I have a question."

"Shoot."

"Does your job have anything to do with poisons directly? Do you know anything about them?"

"'Poison' is my middle name," he said cheerily. "Shall I tell you about my organic chemistry degrees and my dissertation on industrial poisons?"

Dissertation. He must have a PhD. He didn't trumpet his degree on his business card and that modesty made me more comfortable. "If you have a moment, I'd like to ask you something." I told him about Clarissa's letters, about her father's death, and her illness. He didn't interrupt and I finished with, "So, I was wondering if there might have been a poison in the eighteen hundreds that would have those effects."

"Plenty," Stuart said. "Mercury, lead, arsenic. And that's just for starters. I don't suppose your Clarissa and her father were metal workers?"

"No," I said. "They owned a plantation."

"Almost as good," Stuart said. "Arsenic was widely used for rodent control and, of course, upper-class women used lead in their makeup. And arsenic was actually used as a medicine. Any chance this Cyril Rothmere had syphilis?"

I stored that thought away to ponder later. Hadn't Lucy Mortimer said Cyril had a reputation as a philanderer?

"Doesn't arsenic kill quickly?" I asked, vague memo-
s of a high school production of *Arsenic and Old Lace*
ing through my mind. The old men had keeled over

pretty quickly after drinking the poisoned tea, if I remembered correctly.

"It depends on the dose," he said. "Small doses can actually build up a tolerance, but they would produce the tummy problems you mentioned. It's too bad you don't have a hair sample."

"Hair? Why?"

"In people exposed to arsenic over a long period, traces appear in the hair. Or fingernails would also work if you've got some nail clippings?"

"Afraid not."

"Even a single strand would do it," he said, clearly enthused by the subject. "A little synchrotron radiation based X-ray fluorescence spectroscopy or microparticle-induced X-ray emission and we could nail it. Without a sample, though, I can't narrow it down much for you."

"That's okay," I said. "At least you've been able to tell me they might have been poisoned." Although that didn't go a long way toward helping me figure out if it was accidental or deliberate.

"Sorry I couldn't help more," Stuart said. "Let me know if you come up with a sample."

"Sure." Fat chance of that, I thought, hanging up.

As I pulled the next letter from the box, my phone rang.

"Glad I caught you," said a vaguely familiar voice on the other end of the line. "This is Merle."

Merle? My mind raced, trying to place the caller. "Yes?" I said cautiously.

"I was wondering if it might be possible for you to come by the school this afternoon to shave the heads of the folks who 'won' the fund-raiser. I'm afraid I'm one of them." He laughed.

Principal Kornhiser. Of course. I pictured him sit

cross-legged on his orange pillow, the phone tucked between his chin and shoulder. He kept talking before I could
jump in.

"The school board has decided to close the school tomorrow and Friday—they have to take snow days in New
York and Minnesota; we have to factor in hurricane days
here!—and so we're moving up our pep rally to this afternoon. I know it's an inconvenience—"

"It's no problem," I said. "I'm happy to do it.

"Good, good. Two o'clock?"

I agreed and hung up. It was actually kind of nice to
have something on my schedule for today. I wasn't used to
being at loose ends. I looked at the stack of documents
again, but I was feeling too antsy to sit and read any longer.
I had the feeling that something more than the hurricane
was coming to a head. The events of the past few days
sifted through my brain, images of Rothmere, Cyril, the
high schoolers—especially Rachel so upset about the vi-
cious rumors that she'd pushed Braden—and the other
people I'd talked to this week. My mind went back to the
conversation with Rachel where she'd told me Braden was
wrestling with a dilemma of some sort, wondering whether
he should intervene. Somehow, that seemed like the crux of
the matter to me, the motivation for his murder. He hadn't
told Rachel what his quandary was, and he hadn't told his
best friend Mark, so who else might know?

His therapist, assuming he had one. But no therapist
would talk about a patient's confidences. His family. I focused on the image of Mr. and Mrs. McCullers as I'd last
seen them in the hospital waiting room, confused and worried. They'd gone out of town, someone had said, but
maybe they were back? I headed for my bedroom. It would
appropriate to visit them to express my condolences, I

told myself, shrugging out of my tee shirt and reaching into my closet for a less casual white blouse with a small ruffle on the front. I could take them some flowers. Slipping on a dark green denim skirt that fell to mid calf, I wound my hair into a knot and secured it with an enameled chopstick Vonda had given me two birthdays ago. Satisfied that I looked suitably somber, I looked up their address in the phone book and headed for my car.

Stopping by the Piggly Wiggly to pick up some flowers—I decided on a potted African violet and a tray of cookies—I drove to the two-story stucco home on a street of similar houses where the McCullerses lived. Nothing about the home shouted "tragedy." The lawn was neatly mowed and raked clean of leaves, begonias added a note of cheerful color in pots at the door, the cement driveway was free of pine needles and old newspapers, and a mixed flock of sparrows, mockingbirds, and finches squabbled over the seed in a house-shaped birdfeeder.

The birds gave me hope that someone was in residence. Birds could deplete a feeder in a matter of hours; the fact that this one was full told me someone had filled it recently, maybe even this morning. Holding the violet in one hand and the cookies in the other, I walked to the door, suddenly beset with qualms. Southern society put a premium on graciousness and manners, and what I was doing was pretty suspect. On the face of it, I was bringing food to a recently bereaved family—an approved, even encouraged gesture— but I was really hoping to grill them about their deceased son—an underhanded, insensitive thing no one with the least pretension to Southern good manners would consider. I had made it to the covered porch when conscience overcame me. I couldn't do this. I bent to leave the cookies and flowerpot on the welcome mat.

As I straightened up, the door swung open. Startled, I stumbled back a step as a girl of maybe nineteen, wearing a long-sleeved coral tee, shorts, and high-end running shoes, flapped a dust cloth over me.

I sneezed.

"Ohmigod, I'm so sorry," the girl said. "I didn't see— Who are you?" She pulled ear buds out of her ears and let them dangle around her neck, merging with thick, taffy colored hair.

"Grace Terhune," I said. I indicated the offerings on the mat. "I was just leaving these for the McCullerses."

"They're not here," the girl said. She stooped to pick up the cookie tray, loosening the plastic wrap to examine the contents. "These look great. Come on in. I was due for a break, anyway. I told my folks it wasn't fair to stick me with the cleaning, but they both went to the hardware store, anyway, since Mom finally convinced Dad that the hurricane is really coming. Won't it be exciting?"

Without waiting for an answer, she started down a hallway, leaving the door open behind her. Hesitantly, I entered the foyer, a ceramic-tiled space with a coat closet on one side and a staircase marching upward six feet away. The girl called, "In the kitchen," and I started down the hallway that led off to the right, wondering who she was. I'd originally thought she might be a cleaning lady, but her assault on the cookies suggested she was more than a hired worker.

I emerged into the kitchen, a large room with an eating nook decorated in the country style that made me claustrophobic: lots of natural oak, dusty blue and rose pink for colors, flat cushions tied to the chairs with perky bows, ruffled curtains, a toaster cover shaped like a rooster, and a tea cozy in the form of a hen. The girl—lean, athletic, and modern—seemed out of place in the fussy kitchen.

"Awful, isn't it?" she said, glancing around the room. She wrinkled a slightly snub nose dusted with freckles. "But Aunt Darla just loves it. I gave her that for Christmas." She nodded at a wreath of dried flowers and herbs hanging between the stove and a refrigerator plastered with photos. "You couldn't pay me to hang that in my dorm room, but it's so her."

"So . . . you were Braden's cousin?" I asked.

"Sorry!" She offered a hand. "I'm Catelyn Allen. My folks and I are staying here to help . . . to take care of the place while Aunt Darla and Uncle Ed are . . . away."

"Oh." I took a cookie from the tray when she pushed it at me. "So you're not from around here?"

"Nah. We're in Virginia. Actually, I'm a sophomore at UVA, but I got an okay from my professors to take a couple of weeks off after what happened to Braden. It was so awful. Why would anyone want to hurt a really nice kid like him? I mean, Braden's just about the nicest person I know, even if he is my cousin."

"I'm very sorry for your loss," I said, noticing that she was still using the present tense when she talked about Braden. Poor girl. The past tense must seem so final.

"Thank you. It's just awful." Catelyn sniffed and fumbled with the tray, and I reached out to steady it.

"I should go," I said. "I just stopped by to give the McCullerses my condolences."

"You don't need to go," Catelyn said, clearly happy to have company. "At least finish your cookie. And I'll go get the list of people who've come by so you can put your name on it. I'm trying to keep track for Aunt Darla and Uncle Ed. Everyone's been so kind. One lady brought a coffee cake yesterday that was absolutely scrumptious. Cream cheese crumbles and cherries."

Before I could say anything, she whisked out of the kitchen. Left alone, I nibbled on the cookie and examined the photos on the fridge. Braden's senior portrait was front and center. Clad in his letter jacket, he smiled straight at me, making me want to smile back. I swallowed a lump in my throat and looked at photos of what I assumed were assorted relatives and friends. A young couple in wedding garb kissed in one photo, kids splashed in the surf in another—it didn't look like the Georgia coastline—a baby posed in a Santa hat on a Christmas postcard, and a younger Braden, his arm around a buddy's neck, stared from a snapshot. The boys looked to be twelve or thirteen and wore matching tee shirts with a name and a logo printed on them, like summer campers. I was peering at the last photo, wondering if the second kid could really be Mark Crenshaw—hadn't his family only moved here two or three years ago?—when Catelyn came back with a clipboard.

"That's my sister Jessica," she said, wrongly assuming I was looking at the bride. "I was her maid of honor in August. I wore a strapless dress in a heavenly shade of blue and danced all night with the best man. Alexander. We really hit it off, but he's a Husky, so we haven't seen each other since, although we talk every night and text *all* the time. I'm trying to find a summer job in the Seattle area for next year, maybe at a camp or a resort."

I let her words drift past me. "What about this photo?" I asked. "Isn't that Mark Crenshaw with Braden?"

"Oh, yeah, they've been best friends ever since they met at whatever that place was called. It was in South Carolina."

The camp's name didn't interest me and I arched my rows, inviting her to continue. "Braden was over the moon en it turned out Mark's dad was getting stationed down here, Aunt Darla said. Mark came with them when they visited us—well, they were really visiting historic sites in Virginia—last summer, and he seemed nice enough, even though all they talked about was football, football, football. Bor-ing." She rolled her eyes.

Knitting my brows, I wondered if this bit of information changed anything, I couldn't see how it made any difference. Catelyn thrust the clipboard at me and I wrote my name at the end of a long list of names, mostly women, who had dropped off meals, cards, and flowers for the bereaved family. "I'd really like to know when the funeral is," I said, sliding the clipboard onto the counter.

Catelyn bit her lip. "I don't know when . . . but, absolutely. A funeral . . . Isn't it just awful?"

"Yes," I agreed, starting for the door.

"You don't have to go yet, do you?" she asked, trailing after me. Some of the bounce had gone from her voice and I wondered how uncomfortable it must feel to be alone in a relatively strange house when a cousin even younger than you had been murdered. He hadn't died in the house, but still. His room was probably right down the hall, chock-full of books he'd never read and sports equipment he'd never use and clothes he'd never wear. I hoped her parents got back soon. "It was nice meeting you," I said at the door.

"Likewise." She peered over my shoulder. "Oh, here's Mom and Dad now." A blue SUV was slowing to make the turn into the driveway. The garage door rumbled up.

Feeling better that I wasn't leaving her alone, I waved to the couple looking at me through the SUV's windows and climbed into my Fiesta as they pulled into the garage. I needed to step on it, or I was going to be late for the head shaving at the high school.

# Chapter Eighteen

THE HIGH SCHOOL HALLS DIDN'T SEEM AS CROWDED as usual when I walked in, and I realized a fair number of kids must have evacuated with their parents. It was just as well the school board had called off classes for Thursday and Friday—the place was going to be a ghost town. Still, the kids who remained chattered with excitement as they filed into the auditorium, eager to see some of their friends get shaved bald in order to help finance the Winter Ball. I poked my head into the office where Merle was talking with the secretary. He shot me a thumbs-up when he caught sight of me. "Ready?"

"Sure." I'd stopped at the salon to pick up some tools on the way. I raised them now so Merle could see.

"Super. Let's get going." He gestured me out of the office and walked me to a side hall that gave access to the auditorium's backstage area.

I waited in the wings, inhaling the scent of sawdust and fabric freshener from the heavy red curtain on my right while Merle bounded onto the stage with a microphone. It was bare except for a wooden stool set in the middle. "Are we ready for some fun, Sabertooths?" he called out.

The auditorium erupted with cheers and catcalls. "As you know . . ." He talked about the Winter Ball and how the votes had been tallied, and announced with a mimed drum roll that they'd raised six hundred fifty-two dollars. That sounded like a lot to me. Who pays that kind of money to watch their buddies have their heads shaved? A lot of kids, apparently.

"Since we only had three days of voting, we only have three 'winners.' And they are Josh Washington, Mark Crenshaw, and yours truly." He bowed and pulled the elastic off his ponytail, shaking his hair free so it settled on the shoulders of his orange and chartreuse shirt. The kids hollered and pounded their feet rhythmically on the floor of the auditorium. I couldn't help smiling as I tried to imagine Principal Iselin from my day getting that kind of response. He'd been as charismatic as dishwater. Merle might be a bit off the beaten path, but the teens responded to him.

I'd missed part of what he was saying, but tuned back in in time to hear my name.

". . . Grace Terhune of Violetta's salon."

I crossed the stage toward him, embarrassed by the attention. I'd never been much of one for the limelight, and the kids' stares unnerved me. "Who's my first victim—I mean customer?" I asked when I got to where Merle stood. I held up the razor and let it buzz. A chuckle ran through the audience and I immediately felt more comfortable. I scanned the faces in the audience and spotted Rachel, looking less animated than usual, and Glen Spaatz, leaning against a wall toward the back with a couple of other teachers, arms crossed over his chest. Was it my imagination, or was he glaring at me? His handsome face was set, his lips thinned, his brows drawn together.

I didn't have time to worry about it as Josh Washington, a short black teen with a six-inch Afro, bounced onto the stage, mugging for his buddies. He finally settled on the stool. "Be gentle," he said loud enough for the microphone to pick up. "It's my first time."

The audience howled when I picked up my shears and cut a big chunk out of the middle of Josh's Afro. By the time I revved the razor, the crowd was chanting, "Take it off! Take it all off!" They applauded when Josh rose after I finished, ran a hand over his smooth pate, and showed a shocked face. He gave me a big hug, surprising me, before rejoining his friends in the audience.

Mark Crenshaw came up next and settled onto the stool vacated by Josh. Merle handed the mike off to a student stagehand before ceremoniously helping Mark off with his letter jacket and draping a towel around his neck.

"If you ever get tired of the principal thing, we could use you at the salon," I told him.

"I may come see you about a summer job," he returned with a laugh.

Merle was growing on me. I smiled at him and turned my attention to Mark, who looked at me under his brows with a shade of apprehension, clearly recalling the end of our last meeting. What—was he worried I'd take revenge by shaving off his ear or something? He must hang out with the wrong people.

"It'll grow back," I whispered, in case his apprehension was really a reluctance to go bald. His hair was already so short that shaving it took only a few minutes. "Now, you can skip the haircut when you report to the Naval Academy," I said to him, smiling when I finished.

"Something else to look forward to," he muttered, his tone an odd mix of anger and resignation. "Rules about hair, rules about uniforms, rules about walking and talking and eating and crapping. Frickin' rules."

I flicked a glance at Merle to see if he'd heard, but apparently not. I didn't know how to respond and merely whisked the towel off Mark's shoulders as the crowd hooted. The Sabertooth mascot, a student in a moth-eaten costume with one fang hanging crooked, gamboled around the stage and escorted Mark off.

The pep band played something brassy and the cheer-leaders bounced forward for a quick routine as Merle folded down his collar and took his place on the stool, making a show of dusting it off before he sat. The high schoolers went wild, launching into their "Take it all off" chant when I picked up my scissors. I felt him wince as the blades bit into a section of hair I held taught between my fingers.

"Did I hurt you?"

"Just my image. There it goes," he said, watching the long, gingery strands flutter to the stage.

"I think the kids know there's more to you than just hair," I said.

He gave me a grateful smile. "Take it all off."


MERLE'S KNOBBY, BALD HEAD WAS A HUGE HIT WITH the crowd. He dismissed the pep rally and school with admonitions to be safe during the hurricane and with a couple of words about keeping Braden's family in their thoughts. The fund established with the money they had raised would be called the Braden McCullers Memorial

Fund, he announced to a now sober audience. Before I could escape, hoping to catch Rachel and take her for an ice cream and a chat, he touched my shoulder and asked if I'd stay for a yearbook photograph. I agreed, catching sight of Rachel's back as she exited the auditorium with the stream of students. A serious-looking young woman with trendy blue glasses and braces took several photos of me with Merle, Mark, and Josh. A disembodied voice paged Merle over the PA system and he left with a warm handshake and a "Thank you."

Left alone, I descended the stairs to the right of the stage and headed up the aisle toward the hall. Pushing through the swinging doors, I caught a faint whiff of bubble gum before it was overpowered by the scent of pine cleaner coming from the mop a janitor wielded energetically outside the restrooms. A hand clamped around my upper arm and startled me.

"I've got something to say to you," Glen Spaatz said, his voice hard.

"What is your problem?" I asked, twisting my arm free. "I don't know what—"

Shooting a glance at the janitor, now propping himself up with the mop and watching us avidly, he said, "In my classroom." He started down the hall.

After a moment's hesitation, I followed. I didn't like his attitude, but I was curious. I couldn't think of anything I'd done to piss him off, so I was at a loss to explain his current mood. He turned down a side hall and then into a classroom. Entering it, I was swept back to my science classes, to the stink of chemicals and burned stuff and the "ew" factor of dissecting rubbery fetal pigs and frogs. I'd tried to get Mom to write a note excusing me from amphibian mutilation, but she'd refused. Two sinks with high arched faucets gleamed at the back of the room, and stacks of glassware occupied a long table. Largely forgotten chemical symbols decorated the blackboard. From the rotten-egg odor in the room, I'd guess today's lesson had had something to do with sulfur.

Glen ignored his surroundings and turned to face me as I hovered near the closed door. "I think it's pretty low of you to get your ex-husband to check me out," he said.

My lower jaw literally dropped and I stared at him, open-mouthed. Before I could respond, he added, "The Gestapo tactics didn't work in California and they're not going to work here." Thinning his mouth until his lips disappeared, he crossed his arms over his chest.

"You are out of your frickin' mind," I said, taking a step forward in my anger. My fists clenched at my sides, my nails digging into my palms. "I didn't put Hank up to anything. If you must know, you pissed him off so badly with that kissing stunt that he took it upon himself to look into your background. I had nothing to do with it. But from your reaction, I'd say his instincts were dead-on."

"You didn't—" The merest hint of uncertainty sounded in his voice, but his whole body stayed rigid.

"No, I didn't. I didn't and I wouldn't. I hardly know you!" And I'd sure as heck lost any desire to get to know him better after his accusations. "There's a murder investigation going on, in case you hadn't noticed, and the police are checking into everyone who was at Rothmere Saturday night."

"When Agent Dillon came to interview me, he said—"

"I don't believe he said anything about me!"

"No. He mentioned that he was following up on information that had come to the attention of the SEPD. I put two and two together and—"

"And came up with a big, fat goose egg." I made a zero with my thumb and forefinger. "Good thing you teach science and not math."

He snorted what might have been a laugh and gave me a rueful smile. "I'm sorry?"

"Not enough." I spun on my heel, the green denim skirt belling slightly around my calves, and was reaching for the doorknob when his voice stopped me.

"Please. Let me tell you what I told Agent Dillon."

"Not interested." I tried to make myself go through the door but curiosity stopped me. Okay, I *was* interested, not in Glen, but in what had happened in California.

Scraping forward a chair, he sat with his arms draped over its back, facing me, and gestured for me to take another chair. I did, scooting it away from him first.

"Your ex might have mentioned that the ATF and the police busted down my door one day, searching for a shipment of automatic weapons an informant had told them was in my condo."

His eyes scanned my face, but I kept my expression noncommittal.

"They had a search warrant and everything. Only thing was, they had the wrong address. Some moron had transposed two numbers—the gun runner they were looking for lived in the next building over." He ran a hand through his hair and drew it across his cheek, smudging his mouth.

"Good heavens! They must have scared you to death." The thought of armed strangers busting into my house made me grip the chair seat.

"You can say that again."

"But I don't understand why it's such a big secret." Cocking my head, I said, "What's the big deal? It was a mistake, right? They apologize and fix your door, you go back to learning lines or fixing dinner, and—"

"I wasn't alone."

I couldn't see why that mattered, but I motioned for him to continue.

"When the ATF broke in, I was—engaged, shall we say?—with a woman. A woman whose name is synonymous with 'blockbuster' and 'Oscar nomination.'" He paused. "A married woman."

"Oh." Ignoring an irrational ping of jealousy, I asked, "They recognized her?"

"Of course they recognized her. Any male between the ages of four and a hundred-and-four would recognize her. She was deathly afraid it would get into the media, that her husband would find out, that it would trash her career. So I made a deal with the ATF and the LAPD. I wouldn't sue the pants off of them for invading my home and pointing guns at me, damn near giving me cardiac arrest, and they'd make sure no one talked to the media. We signed all sorts of legal documents, nondisclosure agreements, so that's why I don't go around explaining why I really left California." He hunched forward, resting his chin on the chair back and looking up at me from beneath his brows. "It's not such a horrible secret after all, is it?"

Not horrible enough to kill for, I wouldn't think. For the actress, maybe, but not for Glen. And I didn't see how Braden could possibly have known about it. "Not really, no."

"So, we're okay?" There was something quizzical in the look he gave me, as if he could read my withdrawal but couldn't figure out the reason for it. "I *am* sorry for jumping all over you like that."

"Apology accepted." I left it at that. If his unjustified

attack on me hadn't squashed any interest I had in him, the revelation that he slept with married women was the final nail in the coffin. I stood.

He walked me to the door and pulled it open. "Avaline and her crew are filming this evening. Are you going to watch?"

"I don't think so. You?"

He nodded. "I suppose so. I'm going to wallow in melancholy and mourn my lost acting career." He said it with enough self-deprecating humor that I laughed, but I wondered, walking through the empty halls, if there weren't more than a kernel of truth in it.

When I walked out the door, the wind flung a plastic grocery bag at me. I noticed Rachel waiting for me near the slot where her pink scooter was parked. "I thought you were, like, never coming out," she said.

"I'm glad you waited." I hugged her. "Want to get some ice cream?"

"Mom wants me to pick up some ice and fill our coolers. You know, in case we lose power tomorrow."

"I'll drive you."

"I was hoping you'd say that. I didn't know how I was going to balance, like, forty pounds of ice on my scooter."

I laughed and drove her to a convenience store. Only one soggy bag of ice lay in the bottom of the silver insulated hut outside the store. We bought it and moved on to the Winn-Dixie, where they were completely out of ice.

"People buy up ice before a hurricane," the helpful clerk explained the obvious, "for if the power goes out. Otherwise, you've got to throw out a lot of spoilt food if Georgia Power don't get the electricity back up quick enough. I lost a shitload of venison steaks last time."

Barely pausing to commiserate with the clerk, who seemed inclined to list every food item he'd lost after the last hurricane, we hustled back to the parking lot. "I've got an idea," I told Rachel, and pointed the car toward Magnolia House, Vonda's B&B. They had a commercial ice making machine and I was sure she'd give us enough ice to fill Rachel's cooler.

"Have you found anything out?" Rachel asked diffidently as we waited at a red light. "About Braden's murderer, I mean?"

Keeping my eyes on the traffic even though it was abnormally light, I told her about some of the conversations I'd had.

"I've met Braden's cousin," Rachel volunteered when I told her about finding Catelyn at the McCullerses' house. "She's really nice. She's majoring in psychology because she wants to help teens with depression and addiction problems. She got all interested in that when she visited Braden at Sandy Point."

"Sandy Point? Is that—?"

"It's the place he went to for depression counseling and stuff when he was, like, thirteen. He said it saved his life. He met with doctors and therapists and had 'group' and did a lot of stuff outdoors like hiking and fishing in the lake. I guess he was there for three or four months."

I hit the brakes and the car behind me honked before swerving around the Fiesta. I stared at Rachel. "Sandy Point is a hospital sort of place? It's not a summer camp?"

She shook her head. "No. Sandy Point Residential Intervention Center. It's a place for kids and teens with depression or addictions or eating disorders and stuff. Braden told me it cost his folks over a hundred thousand a month to keep him there."

The unbelievable number startled me, but I let it go. I was more interested in figuring out why Mark Crenshaw had been wearing a Sandy Point tee shirt and looking very much at home on what had to be the Sandy Point campus in the photo on the McCullerses' refrigerator.

# Chapter Nineteen

MY BRAIN BUZZING, I DROPPED RACHEL OFF AT HER scooter after we heisted some ice from Vonda and loaded it into coolers at Rachel's house. Still parked in the high school lot, I dialed Agent Dillon's number and told him that Mark Crenshaw had been in a mental health facility with Braden McCullers.

"That's potentially interesting," he said when I finished. "How do you know this?"

I explained, and asked, "Can you find out if Mark was really there? And what he went there for?"

"Maybe," Dillon said. "Health records—especially mental health records—are notoriously hard to get. And I don't know that we have probable cause to persuade a judge to issue a subpoena for the records. We don't know, after all, that there's any tie between the Crenshaw kid's stay at Sandy Point and Braden McCullers' murder."

"That's true," I admitted, feeling a bit deflated, "but it seems strange he wouldn't have mentioned it."

"No, it doesn't. It may be cool for adults to talk about being in therapy and paying their therapists a hundred bucks an hour to 'analyze' them, but I'm darned sure a high schooler would think it was as uncool as a pocket protector and a Barbie lunchbox."

"I had one of those." I'd taken the lunchbox to school every day in first and second grade, gazing at Barbie in her pink ruffled evening gown as I ate my PB&J and drank the milk Mom always put in the little thermos that came with the lunchbox.

"Mine was Batman."

"Of course it was."

"What's that supposed to mean?" Dillon's voice was half suspicious, half amused.

"You just seem like a superhero kind of guy," I said.

"Just as long as you don't think I hang by my heels from the ceiling and go hunting at nightfall."

I laughed and hung up after he thanked me for the information and told me he'd follow up. Feeling pretty darn good about having discovered something that might actually help the police, I headed for home. My good feeling evaporated on the way as I realized that the information might implicate Mark in Braden's death.

I noticed a pickup truck in Mrs. Jones's driveway as I pulled to the curb, but I didn't pay it much attention. My landlady had more relatives than your average rabbit—nieces and nephews and great-nieces and great-nephews and first- and second-removed whatevers—and I couldn't possibly keep track of their vehicles. Probably just someone helping her batten down the hatches before Horatio hit.

Someone moved on her veranda and I waved as I swung the car door shut.

As I started toward my carriage house, heavy footsteps sounded on the stairs leading down from Mrs. Jones's veranda. I turned, ready to smile and exchange greetings, to see Lonnie Farber hurrying toward me, leather jacket open over a black tee shirt and distressed blue jeans. I stood still, unable to decide if it would be smarter to try and make it into my apartment or confront him out here. I doubted I could unlock the apartment, get inside, and rebolt it before he caught me up, so I stood my ground, looking around to see if any neighbors were working in their yards or pushing strollers down the walk. I couldn't spot a single soul on the entire block.

"Miss Terhune. I've been waiting for you. Don't you live there?" He nodded at Mrs. Jones's house, puzzlement creasing his smooth brow. He stopped about a yard from me, feet planted a bit more than hip width, big receiver's hands hanging at his sides. I didn't see a gun. "You don't gotta worry about me," he said, correctly interpreting my look. "I'm not carrying."

"What do you want?"

I couldn't read his face as he stared down at the foot he was scuffing in a dry patch on the lawn. The black and silver training shoes he wore probably cost more than my monthly groceries. "My aunt Retta says I need to apologize to you and Miss Althea, for scaring you the other day. Even though you scared the crap outta me."

His version of an apology sounded like my four-year-old nephew's: "I'm sorry, but it was your fault." Still, he didn't look threatening and I felt the tension ease out of my shoulders.

"We didn't mean to scare you," I said. "We just wanted to talk to you about Braden and that night at Rothmere. Why did you take off like that?"

"I thought you were someone else," he mumbled. "Someone I been doin' some business with."

"Hm. I guess you haven't been out selling Girl Scout cookies."

"I haven't been selling anything," Lonnie said swiftly.

Ye gods. Did he think I'd just accused him of dealing drugs? Once the thought lodged in my brain, it refused to go away. I hoped for Loretta's sake, and Lonnie's, that he wasn't mixed up with drug dealers. "So, that night at Rothmere, what was the bit with the ghost costume all about?"

Lonnie flashed a grin. "It wasn't *about* nothing. It was just for kicks. You're pretty fast for an old chick. You almost caught me before I went out the window."

His praise left me underwhelmed. "And the fireworks? Were those meant as a distraction so that someone could push Braden McCullers down the stairs?"

"Shit, no!" Lonnie's wide nostrils flared with alarm. "Braden was my man. I wouldn't set him up."

"Really? I heard you were pissed at him for testifying against your brother."

"We worked that out," Lonnie said, but his eyes didn't meet mine.

"You beat him up, you mean."

"Shit, lady, he gave as good as he got." Lonnie scowled. "We were cool."

"So you're okay with Braden getting your brother thrown in prison."

"Juvie. Look, Randall's got his issues, you know?"

I didn't want to hear about Randall's issues and Lonnie's insistence that he wasn't mad at Braden rang true. "So what about the fireworks?"

"The fireworks were just for fun, for livening up the party. Sittin' around all night waiting for a ghost to show up didn't sound like much of a party, you know? So me and some of the others made plans, if you know what I mean."

"Who else? What kind of plans?"

Lonnie shrugged. "Well, someone mighta brought some beer, and maybe there was some weed—but I don't touch that shit—and a coupla other kids brought sheets, although they chickened out of doing their Cyril impressions, I guess."

My heartbeat quickened and I took half a step toward him. "Who did, Lonnie? Who else had a ghost costume?"

He shrugged. "Ari Solomon and Crenshaw did, for sure, and maybe some others. It was s'posed to be a contest—see who could get the biggest reaction, scare the most people. But the way we was all split up, it was hard to get an audience together, you know? But Tyler and me, we got you all going, didn't we?" He smiled, clearly pleased with himself.

I bit down on my lip to keep from gasping at the news that Mark had taken a sheet with him to Rothmere. "How did you smuggle in all this beer and stuff?" I asked.

"Backpacks," Lonnie said, looking at me like I was a moron. A black sedan cruised past and Lonnie shot it a glance. He shuffled his big feet. "Look, I gotta be hitting the road."

"Are you evacuating?"

A funny look came over his face. "You could say that. I'm evacuating permanently."

"You're leaving town?"

"Yeah. Aunt Retta thinks it's smarter for me to move on, to

get away from my . . . associates." Fear flickered across his face at the mere thought of his business partners. "I'm going to live with my Aunt Cora. She's a parole officer in Portland. Aunt Retta says that the path I'm taking, I'm gonna have me a parole officer before long, so I might as well live with one."

"What about football?" I asked. "Your scholarship chances?"

He shrugged strongly muscled shoulders. "Aunt Retta says it wouldn't hurt me none to repeat my junior year, so I'll have two years to play in Portland. The scouts'll find me. Maybe I'll play for Oregon, instead of Georgia." His faith in his football prowess was so complete that he took it as a given he'd get recruited by an NCAA Division I program. I didn't think I'd ever had that much confidence in any of my abilities.

"I hope it works out for you," I said, offering my hand.

After a moment's hesitation, he shook it, swallowing it in his callused hand. "Can you tell Miss Althea I'm sorry?" The hint of nervousness in his eyes told me he found Althea almost as intimidating as the people he was leaving town to avoid.

"Sure thing."

"And your neighbor, for the pumpkin?" He nodded toward Mrs. Jones's veranda. "I thought you lived there."

"And you thought I'd enjoy pumpkin guts exploded all over?"

A shadow of the cocky smile appeared on his face. "My homeys thought you were too nosy, you know? Talkin' 'bout the cops, an' all. And that trick with the toilet bowl cleaner and tinfoil is *bitchin'*."

"You almost gave her a heart attack."

Lonnie had apparently exhausted his supply of apologies. "You'll let Aunt Retta know I came by?"

I nodded. "Good luck, Lonnie."

His long, athletic stride carried him to the red pickup in just a few steps. Gunning the engine, he reversed down the driveway and sped west toward I-95. He had a long road in front of him, and I wasn't just thinking about the interstate.

Even before the pickup was out of sight, my mind was sorting out what Lonnie had told me. Mark Crenshaw had taken a ghost costume to Rothmere. On the face of it, it looked like Braden's best friend had pushed him down the stairs. But why? And how? Lindsay said she and Mark had been together the entire evening. It took only a nanosecond for me to realize that Lindsay would lie for Mark. Okay, so that left why. Of course, Ari Solomon had a sheet with her, too, and there might've been others Lonnie didn't know about. I hadn't come across any hint of motive for Ari to want to kill Braden. Her mother, however . . . Could Tasha have taken Ari's ghost costume, snuck from the kitchen to the main house, and pushed Braden? Would Ari lie to the police for her mom? Very possibly. Teen girls would either lie for their moms or try to frame them, depending on how their hormones were acting up. I'd felt both ways about my mom at various times between twelve and sixteen. But how would Dr. Solomon have worked the timing, showing up on the landing just as Rachel left Braden alone? I growled with frustration.

The wind rattled the trash cans behind Mrs. Jones's house and I walked in that direction as I thought, planning to stow them in the garage before Horatio hit. Hurricane winds could fling garbage cans around like pebbles, hurling them through windows or bowling them down streets to damage cars. Grabbing their handles, I dragged them toward the garage. Mrs. Jones didn't have a car anymore—she'd quit driving a couple of years back, much to the relief of

pedestrians who'd thought they'd be safe on the sidewalk—
and the garage housed only a mower, some tools, and plastic tubs full of stuff Mrs. Jones couldn't bring herself to
give away or trash. Stowing the cans, I wondered if Braden
had suspected Mark's dad was abusing him and his mother.
Maybe he'd even witnessed a punch or a beating.

Excitement pounded through me. It made sense. Braden
had told Rachel he was trying to figure out whether or not
to intervene in some situation. Well, if he suspected abuse,
he might have wrestled with whether or not to tell someone. I'd been mulling it over myself, and I didn't know
Mark or his family half as well as Braden did. Was Mark
trying to protect his family by pushing Braden? Closing the
garage door behind me, I hurried to my apartment. Whether
my reasoning was right or wrong, I definitely had to let
Agent Dillon know about Mark and the sheet.

WHEN I PHONED HIM, AGENT DILLON SAID HE WAS AT
Rothmere and I agreed to meet him there. I parked in the
graveled lot fifteen minutes later, reflecting that I'd spent
more time at Rothmere in the last few months than I had
in the last twenty years. Until I attended a fund-raising
ball there in May, I hadn't been near the place since I left
elementary school. I found Dillon in the detached kitchen,
staring at a roughly drawn map of some kind as he surveyed
the brick walls and gaping mouth of the original fireplace.
The wind huffed down the chimney, sending a whiff of
grilled meat into the room, perhaps from some long-dead
ox or pig.

The door squealed when I closed it, and Dillon looked
up. The marine blue of his eyes warmed as his gaze rested
on me. His suit and tie looked ludicrously out of place in

the rough kitchen with its scarred wooden table and iron pots stacked on shelves.

"What's that?" I asked, nodding at the page he held.

"Spaatz's version of where everyone was—or was supposed to be—on Saturday night," he said. "I compared it with yours."

"Useful," I commented, studying the page over his shoulder. Neatly labeled with last names, Xs showed where each pair of students had set up their ghost observation points. I could feel Dillon's warmth through his jacket and see a tiny scar curving down from the corner of his mouth that I hadn't noticed before. Discombobulated by his closeness, I stepped back a pace.

"Not as useful as one would hope," Dillon said, "since almost no one stayed put."

"Speaking of which . . ." I told him about my conversation with Lonnie and Lonnie's assertion that Mark Crenshaw had come to Rothmere with a sheet stuffed in his backpack. "So did Ari Solomon and maybe some others."

"Interesting," he said when I finished. Moving toward the door, he held it open for me. "I'm visiting each of these sites," he said, shaking the paper, "to see what was or wasn't visible from each room."

I followed him across the acorn-strewn lawn, through the front hall—with cables still stretched across the floor, but empty of people—and into the huge ballroom with its French doors looking out to the garden and the cemetery beyond. I remembered it as a peaceful view, but today the wind tore at the trees and angry clouds blocked the sky's blue. "Those doors were open when I came in here Saturday night," I said, gesturing to the French doors. "I felt a draft, but then the Lonnie and Tyler ghost show started and I forgot about them."

"So anyone could've gone in or out without cutting through the hall and being seen," Dillon said, strolling from one end of the room to the other.

I didn't know what he was looking for, but I stayed silent while he made notes. Finally, he rattled one of the doorknobs and turned to me.

"So you think Mark pushed his best friend," he said. "Any thoughts on why?"

"As a matter of fact, I do," I said, nettled by his tone. As I gave him my theory about Mark's father abusing him and Braden feeling he had to intervene, Dillon kept his gaze fixed on my face.

His expression was grave by the time I finished, and he rubbed his forefinger against his slightly crooked nose. "That sounds almost plausible, Grace," he said. "But I don't know how we prove it. The Tandy girl has already said Mark was with her the whole evening, and I can't see getting his mother to swear out an abuse complaint. She never has before, and if she does so now, she gives her son a motive for murder."

"No mother would do that," I murmured.

"Exactly."

"What about Sunday night when Braden was . . . Was Lindsay at Ari's party?"

"Supposedly. Only a couple of the kids who were here Saturday have solid alibis. Almost all of them were at the Solomon girl's party, so no one really kept track of who was there or not, or for how long they stayed. Anyone could've ducked out, driven to the hospital, smothered Mc-Cullers, and slipped back into the party, all within an hour." He crumpled the map in his fist. "It really gets my goat to think that a high schooler pulled this off and may get away with it."

As he spoke, he gave the ballroom a final glance and headed toward the door. We walked in silence down the hall, but he grabbed my arm to steady me when I tripped over a black cable left by the TV crew. "You know," I said when I regained my balance, "I've got an idea for how to get some proof." Dillon's hand slid down my arm to my hand and squeezed it, generating tingles that made me stutter. "B-but we're going to need some help."

# Chapter Twenty

"YOU WANT MY HELP? I'M FLATTERED," AVALINE VAN Tassel said half an hour later when Dillon and I cornered her in the Magnolia House parlor. She lounged against the back of a rose-colored settee, her black hair and another white blouse striking against the rose velvet. A mischievous smile played at the corner of her lush mouth.

Was it my imagination, or was Dillon focused too intently on her lips?

Sitting near the window, I shifted uncomfortably on the upholstered chair with the brass studs that dug into the back of my thighs. My hand went to the fringed tassel on the drape tieback, and I let the silky strands sift through my fingers as Dillon talked. We'd agreed while still at Rothmere that Avaline would be more receptive to the idea if it were an official GBI request.

"But I don't know that I can use my gift to trick our

viewing audience," Avaline continued. She took a sip of the iced tea supplied by Vonda, Avaline's throat working as she swallowed.

"We're not asking you to use your gift," Dillon clarified.

I gave him points for not stumbling over the word "gift," since I strongly suspected he didn't believe in Avaline's—or anyone's—ability to chat with ghosts.

"We need you to *pretend* to contact Cyril and pretend that he's revealing the name of the person who pushed Braden McCullers. You'd be helping to bring a murderer to justice," he added when Avaline hesitated. "You'll invite all the people who were present last Saturday to attend the filming—some of them have evacuated, but most of the main suspects are still in town—and tell them that Cyril has let you know he has something important to reveal. Curiosity should get them all there."

"And you won't really air this episode," I put in, "so you won't be tricking anyone except the murderer."

Tapping a ruby red nail against her iced tea glass, Avaline looked from Dillon to me. "We were going to tape the program tonight," she said. "I don't see how we'd have time to put on a bogus production for you and get the show done. On top of which, spirits are sensitive. Cyril might not choose to communicate with me if there are hordes of people clomping around the house, disturbing the atmosphere. And then where would I be? I can't risk disappointing my fans."

Dillon made a frustrated noise in the back of his throat and leaned toward Avaline. "Miss Van Tassel, I can't compel you to cooperate—"

"No," she said sweetly, "you can't. But you'll have a better chance of persuading me if you call me Avaline."

The sultry glance she sent Dillon made me want to gag.

With a quick "Excuse me," I left the room, intending to track down Vonda in the kitchen. Dillon would have a better chance of talking the Spirit Whisperer into doing her civic duty if I wasn't there. Crossing the wide entry hall with beveled glass on either side of the oak door and the grand staircase sweeping up to the second floor, I almost bumped into a man who blasted out of the dining room carrying a plate piled high with little meatballs, undoubtedly from the hors d'oeuvres spread Vonda and Ricky put out every afternoon for happy hour.

Two meatballs fell and rolled toward the front door when the man jolted to a stop. "Sorry!" he said. "Damn." He tried bending to retrieve the meatballs but wasn't going to be able to do it without spilling his plate or the drink in his other hand. As he looked around for somewhere to set the plate, I tweaked a toothpick from his plate and speared the meatballs.

"Thanks," the man said, taking the toothpick from me with the fingers wrapped around the stem of his martini glass. "Ten-second rule." He popped the meatballs into his mouth and chewed, his Vandyke beard bobbing up and down.

Yuck.

"Want one?" He held the plate out to me, and the diamond on his pinkie sparkled. His gelled hair had lost a bit of its spikiness and the points drooped slightly. Georgia humidity will do that.

"No, thanks," I said. "Aren't you the producer for *The Spirit Whisperer*?"

"Guilty as charged. Les Spaulding," he said. "I'd shake, but—" He indicated the glass in his left hand and the plate in his right. "Didn't I see you at the mansion?" He studied me from behind his gold-rimmed glasses. "You had something to do with the kid dying."

"I wouldn't put it that way," I said, appalled.

He waved the martini dismissively. "Whatever. We're filming the show tonight. Would you like to come watch? I can make that happen." He put his plate on a stair behind him and patted his jacket pocket for a card.

"Actually," I said, seizing the opening, "the police were hoping you'd help them catch a murderer."

"Really? A murderer?" His eyes sparked with interest.

As succinctly as possible, I pitched him on the plan.

"I like it," he said, stabbing at me with the martini. A drop of gin splashed my blouse. "It's got 'big' written all over it. I think we could see a ten-point jump in the ratings with the right promo. Ava!" He shouted up the stairs.

"She's in there," I said, pointing to the parlor. I trailed him, standing back a couple of feet to avoid being christened with more martini.

Avaline shot me a poisonous glance as Spaulding told Dillon he wanted in on trapping the murderer. I tried not to feel smug and triumphant but didn't succeed too well.

"I was just discussing that with John," she said, an edge undercutting the sweetness of her voice.

"Great!" Spaulding said. "It's settled. Let's—"

"I think we ought to at least get John to agree to an interview in return for our help," Avaline interrupted. She pushed to her feet, gaining a height advantage over Spaulding, who couldn't have been taller than five-four. "Quid pro quo. Our show won't be complete without the official Georgia Bureau of Investigation point of view."

"I don't—" Dillon started.

"No interview, no deal." She bared her teeth in what would have passed for a smile if her eyes hadn't been so cold.

Dillon's jaw worked. After a long moment, he held out

his hand to Avaline. "Deal." His eyes were as stony as hers and I could tell he didn't like being blackmailed.

"Lovely," she said, holding on to his hand longer than necessary. "I'll look forward to getting to know you better. Much better." The tip of her tongue flicked out to moisten her lower lip. "Friday night work for you?"

Dillon's gaze flicked to me. "I've got plans—"

"I'm afraid it has to be Friday evening," Avaline said, her eyes narrowing. "Since we'll be helping you out tonight"— she put a delicate stress on the words—"we'll have to film the real show tomorrow night and I've got other interviews scheduled all day Friday. And I'm on a plane out of Jacksonville first thing Saturday morning. So, Friday night it is," she said as if it were settled. "Let's say six thirty."

Dillon looked at me again and I gave an infinitesimal shrug. We could always reschedule our date. Catching Braden's killer was more important. I don't know if he got all that from my expression, but he sighed. "Okay, Friday."


AGENT DILLON LEFT MAGNOLIA HOUSE ALMOST immediately to organize his team and get someone started on notifying everyone who'd been at Rothmere that the ghost of Cyril Rothmere had told Avaline van Tassel he would name Braden's assailant later that evening. Everyone was invited to watch the taping of the show. Spaulding, Avaline, and their crew left immediately after Dillon to finish setting up at Rothmere. Vonda caught me before I could leave and dragged me into the kitchen. The Magnolia House kitchen was disconcertingly modern, featuring stainless steel appliances and restaurant-caliber range and ovens. When she and Ricky bought the B&B, Vonda had stated in no uncertain terms that while period furnishings were a plus in the bedrooms and common areas, under no circumstances was she cooking in an antiquated kitchen.

"Can I come?" Vonda asked when I told her about the plan.

From my seat at the island, I watched her mix up blueberry muffins for the morning. "I don't see why not," I said, swiping a finger inside the lip of the mixing bowl to snag some batter. "There's going to be a cast of thousands as it is." I sucked the batter off my finger. Yum.

"Do you think I'll end up on TV?" She tucked a strand of red hair behind her ear, leaving a smear of batter on her cheek.

"Who knows?"

Vonda pushed the mixing bowl across the counter to me. "Here. Pour the batter into those muffin tins and pop them into the oven for twenty minutes. I've got to put my face on."

"But they're not starting until eight. That's four hours from now," I protested. The only response I got was a view of her backside disappearing through the swinging door. I filched a fat blueberry from the batter and popped it into my mouth.

I GOT AN ALMOST IDENTICAL RESPONSE FROM MOM and Althea when I had taken the muffins out of Vonda's oven and driven to Mom's. Mom was filling the upstairs bathtub with water when I arrived, so we'd have fresh drinking water and water to flush the toilets with if Horatio—God forbid—disrupted the water supply. Althea perched on the closed toilet seat, reading a styling magazine.

"Can we come to the taping?" Mom asked. "It'd be like watching a show from the inside out." Turning off the tap, she dried her hands on a towel. Fog coated her lenses, but I could see the interest in her eyes.

"It'll be more fun than sitting around here waiting for Horatio to hit," Althea agreed. "There's nothing on the TV except weather updates." She rolled up the magazine and whapped a fly with it. "Got 'im," she said with satisfaction.

"What's the latest?" I asked as we trooped out of the small bathroom and headed back downstairs.

"Cat one, maybe cat two," Althea said. "Storm surge of ten to twelve feet."

"Not too bad, then," I said, relieved. Hurricane Katrina's storm surge had been somewhere in the neighborhood of twenty-eight feet. "When's it supposed to make landfall?"

"Before midnight."

With any luck, we'd have the murderer behind bars and everyone home before Horatio hit the coast.

BY THE TIME I ARRIVED AT ROTHMERE, THE LITTLE lot was crammed full of cars and I had to park in the circular drive fronting the house, where coachmen would have pulled up their horses so their masters and mistresses could alight for a dinner party or ball. The windows glowed with light—electric, not candles—and it spilled out the open door, as I imagined it would have for those long-ago parties, but at least I wasn't trapped in a hoop skirt. Still wearing the green denim skirt and white blouse I'd donned for my "condolence" call on the McCullerses, I had freshened my makeup—Vonda's influence—and French-braided my hair to keep it out of the way.

Stepping out of the car, I sensed a change. Not able to pinpoint it immediately, I turned in a slow circle, noting how the wind made the topiary unicorn bow its head, and the startling whiteness of the mansion against the solid expanse of gray clouds forming a barricade to the east. I stared in awe at the dark mass foreshortening the horizon, creating a wall that cut us off from the Atlantic and from everything east of us. Lightning flickered in the depths of the angry gray and suddenly I knew what was different. No birds chirped and fluttered in the hedges, no squirrels chased each other across the broad lawn. All the creatures had fled, seeking shelter in nests or hollows, leaving a disquieting stillness. Horatio was almost here, I realized. It wasn't waiting for midnight. If we didn't hurry, it might strike during our staged "Interview with a Ghost."

Stepping into the hall, I entered into a scene of controlled chaos. At least, I hoped someone had control. Huge lights blazed atop thin metal legs, looking like one-eyed insect aliens. Boom mikes hung suspended over the landing. Two large cameras, the kind I'd seen only in "The Making of . . ." extras on DVDs, squatted on tripods. Technicians scurried here and there, occasionally calling out to unseen persons down the hall. Some high schoolers, along with Glen Spaatz, Coach Peet, and what looked like a handful of parents, watched wide-eyed from the parlor to the right of the hall. So did Lucy Mortimer, dressed in full Amelia regalia. No cops in sight. If Cyril was a shy ghost, I thought wryly, trying to count the crowd, Avaline's show was doomed before it got started.

Mom, Althea, and Vonda waved at me from the far corner of the room. Before I could make my way to them, voices sounded behind me and I turned to see Mark Crenshaw and both his parents mounting the steps.

"This is just ludicrous," his mother said as they pushed into the hall. "Ghosts don't talk. And even if they did, it's got nothing to do with Mark."

Mark, bald head gleaming in the glare of the studio lights, edged away from her toward Lindsay Tandy, who emerged from the salon to clutch his arm. She cast a nervous look up at him and he smiled reassuringly into her eyes. I wondered if she was nervous because of the impending revelations—did she suspect her boyfriend of pushing his best friend?—or whether it was proximity to his parents that made her jumpy.

"It's no big deal, Joy," said Captain Crenshaw, looking very military despite wearing jeans and a long-sleeved tan golf shirt. "It's not like we were doing anything else tonight."

"We should have evacuated days ago," she muttered.

"Well, we didn't," he said shortly.

Dr. Solomon and Ari entered in their wake, Dr. Solomon holding fast to her daughter's forearm. "I'll be with my friends," Ari said, pulling away from her mother. Flipping her hair, she hurried toward the clump of high schoolers gathered near the parlor door. Dr. Solomon, worry in her eyes, looked like she would call her daughter back.

Before she could speak, a huge man in jeans and a *Spirit Whisperer* tee shirt stepped into the middle of the hall and clapped his hands. "If I could have your attention! My name's Bruno and I'm the stage manager."

With the competence of someone who had done this many times, he explained that Avaline would be on the landing, ready to talk to Cyril if he appeared. The audience—Bruno gestured to all of us—would be standing in the foyer. He pointed to taped Xs on the floor. We were not to make noise of any kind or leave during the taping for any reason.

"If I hear a cell phone during the taping, I will personally shoot the owner," he said.

I wondered if he and the rest of the crew knew this taping was fake. Everyone scrabbled in their purses or pockets
to silence their phones.

A grin split Bruno's face, showing a gold canine tooth.
"Just kidding."

Relieved laughter filtered through the group and everyone cooperated as crewmembers positioned them on the
taped Xs. I ended up near the front, directly under the chandelier, with Rachel to my left and Mark Crenshaw to my
right, with Lindsay still clinging to his arm. Dillon came in
from a side corridor and positioned himself near the foot of
the stairs. We locked eyes for a moment and then he looked
away, scanning the room. I didn't see any other cops, but I
figured they were there somewhere.

"What's he doing here?" Lindsay whispered to Mark.
She made a tiny motion with her head toward Dillon.

He shrugged. "I guess to haul away the murderer if the
ghost points a finger." He laughed, but there was no humor
in it.

"Quiet on set," Bruno bellowed, and silence fell over the
group.

The lights dimmed until it was difficult to make out the
features even of the people standing closest to me. Red
lights glowed atop the cameras. We stood uneasily, listening to the increasing anger of the wind as it slapped at the
old house and tore at the trees, producing eerie creaks and
groans. Raindrops rattled like bullets against the windows,
startling me. It sounded like Horatio might be arriving a bit
ahead of schedule.

Before I could start to worry about the hurricane, a
movement on the landing caught my attention. A bluish
light picked out the figure of Avaline van Tassel as she
glided to a spot just at the top of the stairs. She must have

been waiting in one of the bedrooms, I figured. I had to admit she looked beautiful, with her black hair streaming down her back and wearing a simple gown—little more than a shift—of white or gray that made her look pretty ghost-like herself. Smoky makeup around her eyes and red lipstick on her mouth made her features stand out against her pale skin and the pale dress.

"Cyril Rothmere," she breathed. Her hands came up in a gesture of supplication and a gem winked darkly from one of her rings. "Cyril, will you join us?"

Nothing happened. Someone shifted, clothes rustling. I could hear each breath Rachel took through her nose and felt soft exhales against the back of my neck from whoever stood behind me. I resisted the impulse to turn and look.

"Cyril," Avaline implored. Her throaty voice was that of a woman pleading with her lover.

I shivered. The woman was good. I didn't believe she could hobnob with ghosts, but she was mesmerizing as a performer. All of a sudden, I felt a chill. From the sound of indrawn breaths, I knew others felt it as well. The cold seemed to pool at my feet and then move up, bathing my calves and then my thighs in chilled air. Simultaneously, a new light appeared on the landing, little more than a glimmer. It grew, expanding to the size of a tennis ball and then a basketball. The light was opalescent, shimmering with tones of green and blue and occasional flashes of yellow. It reflected off what seemed to be a creeping mist. A fog machine, I told myself, stifling a shiver. Special effects wizardry. I almost wished for one of those Mel 87-whatever gadgets to see if weird things were happening in the electromagnetic realm.

"Will you show yourself?" Avaline asked.

I looked around surreptitiously; as far as I could tell,

every eye in the place was glued to the landing, except Dillon's. I couldn't see his face, but he seemed to be facing the onlookers. When I glanced back at the landing, I almost gasped. A form was taking shape. The eerie whiteness gradually solidified into the shape of a man, a man wearing the waistcoat, breeches, and long hair of a plantation owner from the 1800s. His eyes and mouth seemed no more than dark holes. Special effects, special effects, special effects, I chanted to myself. I didn't believe in ghosts, I knew this whole thing was staged, and even so the man's appearance made me shiver.

"I am Cyril Rothmere," the wraith proclaimed in a deep but hollow voice. It sounded like he was speaking from the end of a long tunnel.

Nervous whispers sounded around me and I heard one low, "Oh my God." Rachel's hand crept into mine and gripped it hard. I gave her a reassuring smile, but I didn't know if she could see it in the dimness. Even with my back to the windows, I knew when lightning zigzagged behind me because it cast strange shadows on the walls. Thunder rumbled a few seconds later.

"You were the victim of a murderous hand almost two hundred years ago," Avaline said. "Is that what you've come to tell us about?"

The apparition shook its head slowly from side to side.

"Then what disturbs your peace? A more recent act of violence?"

Cyril nodded. "Yes." The sound was sibilant, accusatory.

"This is such bullshit," someone muttered from behind me. I thought it might have been Captain Crenshaw's voice.

"What did you witness on this landing?" Avaline asked,

taking a step toward the ghostly figure. Her arms spread wide to encompass the landing and stairs.

"I saw betrayal, a friend betrayed." Cyril didn't face Avaline; instead, he loomed forward, his torso leaning over the balustrade, and seemed to hover over those of us in the foyer below.

I felt Mark startle, his shoulder bumping mine.

"I saw death. Death before its time." Cyril's voice grew stronger.

"Braden didn't die here," Rachel whispered. I squeezed her hand to hush her.

"Did you see . . . murder?" Avaline's voice dropped into a lower register on the last word.

"They argued. And then I saw you push him." Cyril's arm extended from shoulder height, lace dripping from his wrist, and his rigid forefinger pointed directly at Mark Crenshaw. "You."

"I didn't!" Mark jumped back, knocking me off balance. It sent a ripple effect through the close-packed crowd. The winds cracked a tree branch against the side of the house.

"My son would never—" Joy's shrill voice sounded behind me.

"He didn't!" Lindsay sounded on the verge of hysteria. "He wouldn't hurt Braden. Not even when Braden said—"

"Shut up, Lindsay," Mark whispered harshly.

"*I* talked to Braden that night. But I didn't mean—"

Lightning exploded just outside the windows, illuminating the scared and confused faces in the room before thunder boomed. The lights flickered once, twice, and went out.

# Chapter Twenty-one

I COULDN'T REMEMBER EVER EXPERIENCING SUCH total darkness. With the flash from the lightning still burned onto my retinas, I couldn't see a thing. Even the red lights from the cameras were extinguished, as was the small spotlight that had lit up Avaline. The landing where Avaline and Cyril had stood moments ago was as pitch dark as the depths of a nightmare. Lightning must have hit the transformer, I realized, just as someone shoved me sideways.

I toppled toward Rachel, reaching out instinctively to break my fall. All around me people were pushing and swaying, grabbing at each other to maintain their balance. I fell in an ungainly heap, dragging Rachel down with me. Someone kicked my shin and I caught an elbow in the breast. Ow. Footsteps sounded and the front door creaked open, letting rain spit into the foyer.

"Wait!" It sounded like Mark.

A gust of wind ripped the door from someone's hand— Lindsay's?—and it slammed into the wall. Running footsteps pounded down the stairs, grated in the wet gravel, and then faded.

"Damn it!" That was Dillon. His radio crackled and he said, "Suspect fled through front door."

A metallic voice said, ". . . in pursuit."

I struggled to my feet and pulled Rachel up. "It was Lindsay?" she asked in a bewildered voice. "Why?"

I couldn't answer her. If she'd killed Braden, it had been to protect Mark. I could reason through it that far. But from what? If Braden had threatened to tell the authorities or a teacher that Mark's father was beating him, wouldn't that have made Lindsay glad? Wouldn't she be relieved to know he wasn't going to be his father's punching bag anymore?

A strong beam of light cut across my thoughts. Dillon swung the flashlight from side to side, illuminating startled, scared, and worried faces. I caught a quick glimpse of Mom and Althea before the beam moved past them. The light landed on Mark, following him as he leaped over people still tangled on the floor and headed for the open doorway. His mother's hand caught at his arm.

"Mark! Where do you think you're going? There's a hurricane out there." Joy's face looked haggard in the harsh halogen glare.

"I've got to find Lindsay." He wrenched away from his mother's hold. His face was set in lines of grim resolve, and with his bald head, he looked older than he had earlier in the week. His mother winced away from the look in his eyes.

He took another step toward the door, but then stopped and flung his forearm across his eyes as the lights came blazing on. Someone must have flicked the wall switch after the lights went out, because the chandelier and every light fixture in the room lit up. I blinked rapidly, trying to adjust my eyes to the glare.

"Got her," a satisfied voice said loudly.

Hank appeared in the opening, holding a wet and bedraggled Lindsay Tandy by one arm. She held her head defiantly, oblivious to the wet, brown strands clinging to her cheeks and the sodden jeans dripping water onto the foyer floor. She'd lost a shoe during her flight and stood squarely on one bare foot and one muddy sneaker. Her gaze met Mark's for one pleading second and then she flung her head back, wet hair smacking Hank in the face, and said, "You can't prove anything."

"Lindsay!" The word exploded out of Mark as if torn from his lungs and vocal cords by a superhuman force. "You didn't—"

"I only talked to him," Lindsay said. "About . . . you know. That's all. Just talked." Her eyes searched his and she strained against Hank's hold.

"I Mirandized her," Hank said, restraining her easily, despite her height and athleticism.

"In here." Dillon took charge and shepherded Hank and Lindsay and Mark and his parents into the small parlor. I slipped in just as he closed the door in the face of the astonished crowd who were being herded into another part of the mansion by two uniformed police officers, Hank's partner and another woman.

"We're going home right now," Joy Crenshaw announced, drawing her lips into a tight circle.

"After we've sorted through a few things," Dillon said amiably. He directed the Crenshaws to the horsehair sofa against the wall and nodded Lindsay toward a ladder-back chair with a needlepoint cushion. Hank released her at a nod from Dillon and she settled on the chair, ostentatiously rubbing her arm. I hovered near the door, hoping Dillon wouldn't order me to leave.

"You can't keep us here," Joy said angrily. "We haven't done anything."

"You and Captain Crenshaw are free to go, if you wish," Dillon said, still in a calm voice. "But I'm afraid Mark has to stay so we can question him about lying to a police officer and obstructing a murder investigation." Very deliberately, he spoke his name and the date and time into a small recorder, then pulled a card from his wallet and Mirandized Mark.

"You don't—You're not going to file charges?" Joy gasped. "He'll lose his appointment to the Naval Academy if you arrest him!"

"Good!" The surprising word came from Mark.

"You don't mean that," his mother said, slewing on the sofa to face him. "You wanted to follow in your father's footsteps. It's been your dream for—"

"It's been *your* dream," he said. "I don't want to go. I've been dreading it."

"You're just upset," Joy said, reaching out to pat his hand. "That's understandable, what with finding out that Lindsay—"

He yanked his hand away. "Leave Lindsay out of it. The thought of going up there—of all the pressure—was making me sick. Braden knew it." Mark stood and faced Dillon. "Arrest me." He held his wrists out as if expecting Dillon to slap handcuffs on him. "Arrest me, God damn it, and make sure to notify the Academy."

"But, Mark," Lindsay cried, "if you lose your appointment, how will we be together? I'm going to Maryland to be near you. If you're not there—"

"He'll be there," Joy said, standing. Her wiry body vibrated with emotion. "Although you've been a bad influence from the start, distracting him from his studies and from football." She eyed Lindsay with loathing.

"I'm not going, Mom," Mark said, turning to face the sputtering woman. "Even if this"—he gestured to the room at large—"turns out okay, I'm not going. I'm declining the appointment. I'll fax them the letter today."

"You *are* going." Joy's hand swung back, and before anyone could guess what she was doing, she slapped Mark across the face. The smack of flesh on flesh was shocking in the small room and no one moved as a dull red handprint surfaced on Mark's face, right on top of the bruise I'd noticed the other day. Joy drew her hand back again, but Mark caught her wrist as she swung at him again. Now I knew where her bruise had come from.

Ye gods. I'd had it all wrong. Mark's father wasn't abusing him. It was his mother.

Joy flailed at Mark with her other hand, landing ineffectual punches on his torso before Dillon stepped forward to haul her away. She batted at him, shrieking hysterically and almost incomprehensibly about "Your father . . . Do what I say . . . Ungrateful . . . You must!" Dillon nodded at Hank, who pulled her arms behind her back and cuffed them. Throughout, Captain Crenshaw stood as if turned to stone, his eyes never leaving his wife's frantic figure. Tears slid down Mark's face and I looked away, not wanting to intrude on his anguish.

"Have an officer take her to the station," Dillon said, and Hank nudged the woman forward. I leaped to open the door for him, and Hank gave me a wink as he propelled Joy Crenshaw through the opening.

She swiveled her head to look over her shoulder into the room. "Eric! Help me, Eric. Don't let them do this."

Eric Crenshaw swallowed, his Adam's apple working. "I'm staying with Mark," he said. "He needs me."

I closed the door on Joy's outraged face and shriek of anger.

Silence lingered in the room for thirty seconds, broken only by the creaks and moans of the house as the wind buffeted it, before Dillon cleared his throat. Pulling up a delicate, gilt-legged chair, he sat on it, facing Mark. He placed the recorder on the marble plant stand at Mark's elbow. "Now, Mark, why don't you tell me what really happened Saturday night."

"I don't know!" Mark looked at Lindsay, but she was staring into her lap.

"Okay. Tell me what you do know. You arrived here with the science class, accompanied Dr. Mortimer on a tour to hear about Cyril Rothmere, and then what?"

"We went to our station—in the master bedroom on the second floor," Mark said. "We took readings on the Mel 8704 and recorded them, just like we were supposed to."

"And then?" Dillon prompted when Mark showed no sign of continuing.

"Then . . . then we started, you know, kissing and stuff." A slight stain of red suffused his cheeks. I looked at Lindsay, but she didn't react beyond raising her head to watch Mark.

"How long did you fool around?" Dillon asked.

Mark scrunched his brows together. "I don't know . . . maybe half an hour? Until just before the fireworks started. Lindsay had to go to the bathroom." He leaned toward his girlfriend, apology in his eyes. Betrayal stiffened her face before she bit her lip and turned her head away.

"Why didn't you tell us this before?" Dillon asked sharply. "Why did you lie about being together the entire time?"

"It was a . . . a woman thing," Mark said in a strangled voice. "She had her, you know . . . and she didn't want me to say anything."

I looked at Lindsay with new respect and wondered how much of this she had preplanned. She'd found a surefire way of making sure Mark wouldn't say anything to the cops; no teenage boy can talk about menstrual periods.

"So . . . you waited for her in the bedroom?"

Mark shook his head. "No, I went out to watch the fireworks. Lindsay caught up with me."

Dillon searched his face. "You knew there were going to be fireworks?"

"Oh, yeah. Lonnie planned it. He said ghosts didn't know how to party, but he did." Mark half smiled before his face turned somber again. "Ten o'clock was party time, he said."

Two or three flashes of lightning lit up the yard outside the window like daylight. Thunder rumbled. The room was quiet for a moment, then Dillon asked, "Did you bring a sheet with you that night? A ghost costume?"

Mark was nodding before Dillon finished. "Yeah. We were going to have a competition to see who could be the scariest ghost, but—" He broke off. "Is that it? Did Lindsay—?"

For the first time, Lindsay broke in. "I went to the bathroom. I changed my tampon." She put a sneer into the word. "I met Mark by the fireworks. No one can prove differently." Her face was impassive, her voice steady. Only her hands betrayed her as her fingers twisted in the wet hem of her shirt.

Mark's gaze stayed on her face for a long moment. Then, he looked at Dillon, me, his father. "Braden was my best friend," he cried. "I wouldn't ever have hurt him. He knew how I felt about going to the Academy. He knew I was having trouble with depression again. He was afraid I'd . . . I'd hurt myself if I had to go to Annapolis. He said he was going to send the superintendent a letter, tell him about my time at Sandy Point, my suicide attempt. That would've been enough to deep-six the appointment. He was only trying to help me! I wish he'd done it weeks ago," Mark said savagely, "that he'd told them without even telling me! Then I would never have discussed it with—"

A loud crack from overhead drew our eyes to the ceiling. The hurricane had hurled a large tree branch against the roof, I figured. We all froze as if someone had hit the "pause" button until it became clear water wasn't going to start pouring through the ceiling.

"I think that's enough, Mark." Eric Crenshaw broke the silence, speaking for the first time. His voice was rough, like he'd gargled with glass. He leaned forward to put a hand on his stepson's shoulder. "Maybe you shouldn't say any more until we get a lawyer."

He was a little late with that advice, I thought. Mark let his chin droop to his chest and covered his eyes with one forearm as he sobbed. I felt sorry for him, caught between the expectations of an abusive mother and a crippling depression.

It seemed pretty clear that Braden, having met Mark at Sandy Point where he was apparently recovering from a suicide attempt, was better at reading Mark than his parents or girlfriend were. He saw Mark's increasing anxiety and depression—his mother saw it, too, I realized, but wrote it off as her son being a "worry wart"—and was going to take the only action he thought would save his friend. Talking to Mark's folks certainly wasn't going to do the trick, not with Joy Crenshaw so fixated on seeing her son follow in his father's footsteps. So, Braden was going to get Mark's appointment cancelled or rescinded or whatever they called it by telling the Academy about his mental health issues. No wonder he'd wrestled with whether or not to intervene! What a horrible choice for a teenager to have to make: destroy your best buddy's college plans or watch him fret himself into another suicide attempt.

Dillon looked at me where I stood by the door. I saw weariness and a certain level of satisfaction on his face. "Grace, would you ask one of the officers to come in here please?"

I nodded and slipped through the door into the foyer. The storm's noise was louder here, the rain drumming on the roof amplified by the open space, maybe. It felt like hours had passed, but in reality it had probably been only twenty minutes since we entered the parlor. Crewmembers from *The Spirit Whisperer* did things with cameras and lights. I glanced up at the landing but didn't see Avaline.

"Do you know where the police officers went?" I asked a man fiddling with a camera.

"They were taking statements in the ballroom," he said. "A lot of folks have left, though, so maybe they're done? You might try in that woman's office, the one who thinks she's the reincarnation of Scarlet O'Hara or something."

"Amelia Rothmere," I corrected him, heading down the hall to Lucy's office. The door was open and I heard voices as I approached. They were almost drowned out by the howling wind that rattled the old house like a terrier shaking a rat. I touched a hand to the wall, maybe to steady myself and maybe to assure myself it was sturdy. Pushing open the office door, I found Lucy, Mom, Althea, and Hank gathered around a small radio, listening to weather updates. Mom and Althea sat in chairs at the small dinette set that served as a conference table. Hank stood with his shoulders propped against the far wall, cleaning his fingernails with a pocketknife while Lucy stared at him with revulsion from the chair behind her desk.

"Join the party," Althea said when she spotted me. "Not that it's much of a party."

"Are you okay, honey?" Mom asked, looking at me with concern. "We waited for you."

"Thanks," I said, leaning down to give her a kiss. I straightened and looked across at my ex as he snapped the little knife closed. "Hank," I said, "Agent Dillon needs you to take the Crenshaws down to the station while they wait for a lawyer, or something."

"No can do, darlin'," he said, shaking his head. "Horatio has heated up out there. Radio says it's not safe to travel. It looks like we're stuck here for the duration. I put dibs on the master bedroom for you and me." He swaggered closer, thumbs tucked into his utility belt.

I rolled my eyes while Althea swatted him with a dried cattail she took from an arrangement on the table. It exploded into a cloud of fluffy seedlets, speckling Hank's uniform, the table, and the floor.

"Now look what you've done, Althea," he said, brushing at the tan flecks on his sleeve. They clung stubbornly.

"Maybe next time you'll think before you open your potty mouth," she said, pulling another cattail from the vase and waving it threateningly.

Mom hid a smile behind her hand as Hank stomped into

the hall. I followed him, anxious to get back to the parlor.
"There are worse things than being stuck together for the
night in an old plantation home, right?" Hank said. "Remember that B and B we stayed at, over near Vicksburg? It
was a lot like this place. We had ourselves a real good time
there." Hank waggled his eyebrows suggestively.

"We are not stuck 'together,'" I said, picking up my pace
so I was half a step ahead of him. "You are here in an official
capacity. I am here with my mom and Althea. Separate.
Apart." I pushed open the parlor door before he could reply.
It didn't look like anyone had moved or said anything in the
few minutes I'd been gone. Mark and his stepfather sat side
by side on the sofa, not looking at each other. Lindsay stared
at Mark as if willing him to look at her. Her telepathic pow-
ers weren't working because he kept his eyes fixed on the
floor as if memorizing the rug's pattern. Agent Dillon sat on
his tufted chair, flipping through the pages of the notebook
he had propped on one knee.

Hank explained the situation, concluding with, "No
one'll be able to leave until the eye passes over in another
hour or so."

Dillon nodded, accepting the inevitable. "All right. Find
a room for Mr. Crenshaw and his son. They want to call a
lawyer. Stay with them."

Hank nodded and made for the sofa as if to pull Mark to
his feet. Eric Crenshaw forestalled him, standing and helping Mark rise with a hand beneath his elbow. It wasn't until
they were halfway out the door that Lindsay cried, "Mark!"

He started to turn around, but his stepdad nudged him
forward and Hank closed the door.

"I don't have to say anything," Lindsay said belliger-
ently, crossing her arms over her chest.

"No, you don't," Dillon agreed. He turned back to his

notebook and crinkled his brow as if puzzling over something on its pages.

I drifted to the window and watched the rain slanting down, a solid silver sheet in the light from the windows. The wind ripped at the live oak tree closest to the window, flailing its branches and making it genuflect to the great god hurricane. Water puddled on the lawn, turning it into a shallow lake, and I wondered uneasily exactly how far Rothmere was from the river. The house stood on a rise, but the storm surge could push the water up the hill in a scarily short time.

"Look, all I did was talk to Braden." Lindsay's exasperated voice broke the silence.

She leaned forward and I noticed the upholstery around her was damp from her wet clothes and hair. She must be freezing. Dillon flipped a page in his notebook, not even looking up.

"You're not listening!" Lindsay's fist pounded the cushion beside her. "I was really going to the bathroom, but then I saw Rachel go in and I knew Braden was on his own. I thought it would be a good time to talk to him about what he was doing to Mark. He was going to tell the Naval Academy stuff he had no right to tell them. He was going to ruin Mark's life!"

Or save it, I thought.

"So I slipped on the sheet, thinking I could give him a scare, even if there was no one else around, and I glided onto the landing, making this sort of moaning sound." She demonstrated. It was a low, pain-filled sound, not at all like the yowling Lonnie and Tyler had used. "Braden came up the stairs and then, I don't know how, he tripped and fell."

"Really?" Dillon raised his brows in pretend puzzlement. "I thought you said you talked to him?"

"Well," she hesitated, looping a strand of hair around her forefinger and pulling on it. "I guess I might've said something about how he was wrecking Mark's life and he should just mind his own effing business."

"And then he just fell," Dillon said, nodding as if it were plausible.

Lindsay's eyes shifted from side to side, like she knew her story was weak, but she said strongly, "Right."

Anger at her callousness fizzed in me like a carbonated beverage shaken too long. "Then why didn't you get help?" I blurted.

Dillon shot me a "shut up" glare, but Lindsay answered. "I could see he was dead and I was scared. I didn't know what I was doing, so I just ran down the back way and out to where they were doing the fireworks."

"But he wasn't dead," Dillon said softly.

"I thought he was," she said. A self-satisfied smirk crept across her arrogant young face. "That's how it happened. I admit I lied to you at first, okay, because I was scared about how it would look. But it was an accident and you've got no one to say it wasn't."

Dillon looked her dead in the eyes. "Except Braden Mc-Cullers."

# Chapter Twenty-two

"YOU'RE LYING!" LINDSAY'S EYES WIDENED, AND ONE trembling hand pulled her hair again, squeezing drops of water from it.

Feeling like I'd been punched in the stomach, I looked at Dillon. His eyes were on me, not Lindsay, and he mouthed, "Sorry," before turning back to the girl.

Anger, shock, and relief warred within me. Suddenly, little things I hadn't understood made sense. Like Braden's family leaving town immediately after his death. Like no funeral or memorial services. Like Catelyn referring to Braden in the present tense. He was alive. He'd survived the attack and the police and his family had put out the word he'd been killed to forestall other attempts on his life. Was he still at the hospital in Brunswick, or had they moved him? Had he come out of his coma? A moment's thought told me that if he had, he didn't remember much about his encounter with Lindsay at Rothmere; if he did, Dillon would never have sanctioned the charade this evening.

"You failed at the hospital," Dillon said, leaning into Lindsay's space.

"I didn't!" she blurted. "The lines on the machines went flat. His—" She cut herself off as if suddenly realizing what she was admitting.

"The nurse revived him," Dillon said. "That's the only reason you were able to get away. By the time they had him stabilized and the nurse was able to describe you, you were long gone."

"I don't know what you're talking about," Lindsay said. Her hand clawed through her wet hair, and I thought she was going to yank a section out.

"We'll have a search warrant for your house as soon as I can get hold of a judge," Dillon said. "What do you want to bet we find a werewolf costume in your closet or under your bed? And it will have Braden McCullers' DNA on it."

"You won't," Lindsay said with a triumphant smile. "I've never had a werewolf costume. I went as a genie to Ari's party. Ask Mark. Or Ari or anyone."

Dillon didn't look perturbed, although I thought Lindsay's confidence meant she'd gotten rid of the costume, maybe in a Dumpster in Brunswick, even, where the cops would never find it.

"And if we don't find the costume, I suspect we'll find someone who remembers selling it to you." His voice was still conversational, his posture relaxed, but his gaze never left Lindsay's face. "You stand out—tall, beautiful, young—the clerk will remember you."

Lindsay looked suddenly less confident. Smothering Braden in the hospital had all been too last minute; I could read in her face that she hadn't thought to get the costume in Jacksonville or somewhere she wouldn't be noticed. "I love Mark," she said. "More than anything in this world." Her voice throbbed with passion and I believed her.

"And you tried to kill Braden because he was trying to split you up. He was going to make sure Mark didn't go to Annapolis."

"He had no right!" Lindsay burst out. "He said he was worried about Mark, worried the pressure would get to him and he'd try to kill himself. But I make Mark happy. I do! As long as we're together, he wouldn't—" A sob choked off her words and quickly turned to a crying jag that had tears and snot running down her face and her breath coming in gasps. I spied a box of tissues on an antique writing desk and handed them to her silently. She flung the box at me and wiped her nose defiantly on her sleeve as her sobs turned into hiccups. "I want—*hic*—a lawyer." *Hic. Hic.*

Agent Dillon nodded and made a show of turning off his recorder and slipping it back into his pocket. "That's your right. I'm afraid you won't be able to get one until the hurricane lets up a bit, though. C'mon."

He prodded Lindsay to her feet and guided her through the door I opened. We emerged into the foyer to see Ava line, still garbed in the white dress, talking to Cyril. Only now Cyril had mahogany-colored hair poking through a net that held it close to his scalp and his face was half natural looking as he rubbed off white makeup with a towelette of some kind. He still wore his mid-nineteenth-century clothes but had pulled off the boots and was padding around in navy argyle socks.

". . . a full size too small," he said, nodding at the discarded boots, which lay near the bottom of the stairs.

"Really, Bruce, it's not like we had a lot of time to do

wardrobe," Avaline said, dismissing his complaint with an airy wave of her hand. She swanned toward Dillon with a sultry smile. "Happy?"

He nodded briefly. "I think we got the outcome we were hoping for."

"We make a great team," Avaline said, leaning forward to plant a red kiss on his cheek. Laughing, she rubbed at it with her thumb.

I turned my back on the nauseating scene. "You were great," I told the actor. "I don't know how you did it on such short notice."

"Thanks." He beamed. "I always had a flair for improv. Scripts are just too confining."

"It was a trick?" Astonishment had startled Lindsay's hiccups out of her. "You're not really—?"

"A ghost?" Bruce laughed. "Not me, darling. Not for a good many more years, God willing." He knocked on the wooden banister.

If looks could kill, Lindsay's glare would have turned him into a ghost on the spot.

"I've got to tell Mom and Althea," I told Dillon, who had extricated himself from Avaline's clutches and was signaling to Officer Qualls to come take Lindsay off his hands. Residual anger bubbled up. "How could you?"

"Lie about McCullers being dead?"

"Yes! I blamed myself. I felt horribly guilty. And Rachel! How could you?"

"I'm not going to apologize for trying to save the kid's life, Grace. It was obvious the murderer was going to keep trying until she succeeded. We picked the easiest and most effective way of stopping her. His parents went along with it."

"You could have told me."

Dillon looked at me and slowly shook his head. "No. Not anyone."

I bit my lower lip. "I'm going to find Mom and Althea."

He nodded. "You can tell them Braden is at a specialized facility outside of Atlanta. He regained consciousness yesterday and the doctors are hopeful that there won't be any permanent damage."

Despite my anger and hurt, a bubble of light floated up inside me and I almost ran down the hall to Lucy's office, where I shared the wonderful news with my mom and Althea. Tears moistened Mom's eyes when I finished, and Althea said, "Well, thank the good Lord."

"We've got to tell Rachel," I said.

"Her folks picked her up just before the hurricane got nasty," Mom said. "Call her."

I did, using the land line on Lucy's desk when my cell wouldn't connect. Rachel gasped when I told her that Braden was still alive and asked me, "Are you sure?" three times before seeming to accept my news with tears and laughter. "I'm going to see him, like, now," she announced.

"Better wait until the hurricane peters out," I said as her mom's voice in the background said, "You're not going anywhere in this weather, young lady."

Hanging up, I sobered a bit as I related Lindsay's story to Mom, Althea, and Lucy. "She didn't exactly admit to trying to kill Braden," I finished, "but I think the cops will be able to dig up the evidence now that they know where to look. And, of course, there's always Braden's testimony."

"Hallelujah," Althea said. "C'mon, Vi. I'm hungry. Let's go see if those TV folk packed anything to eat. I know I saw a cooler." She dragged Mom into the hall, leaving me with Lucy.

"The important thing is that Cyril's been cleared," Lucy

said, folding her hands primly on her desk. "As if a Rothmere would be guilty of murder. Why, they're a family
that's always known the meaning of the word 'honorable.'"

"I wouldn't be too sure about that," I said. I told her
what Stuart Varnet had said about Cyril and maybe Clarissa
being victims of poisoning.

"That's ridiculous," Lucy said, affronted. "Everyone
knows Cyril died after falling down the stairs, and Clarissa
died in childbirth five years after she married Quentin
Dodd."

The news broke over me like one of the waves that had
smashed me to the sea floor earlier in the week. The air left
my lungs and a sharp stab of sadness felt like a sword in my
ribcage. I had so hoped that Clarissa had lived a long life
and died in her eighties or nineties, surrounded by children
and grandchildren. The news that she'd died so young almost brought tears to my eyes. I blinked rapidly.

Lucy watched me not unsympathetically. "You get attached sometimes," she said simply.

I just nodded, feeling foolish. Taking a deep breath, I
said, "Stuart says they would know for sure if they had a
hair or fingernail sample to work with."

Lucy hesitated, her lips working. Finally, she said in the
voice of one goaded beyond endurance. "We do. For Cyril
anyway. The funerary hair art, remember?"

"Would you—?" I hardly dared ask her to allow me to
send a sample to Stuart for testing.

"Not if they have to cut it up or dissolve it or—"

"He said he could run the test on one hair." I plucked a
single strand from my head and waved the delicate filament
at her. "One."

Calculation gleamed in her eyes. "I suppose it would be
okay . . . if you agree to be a docent."

"How often would I have to be here?"

"Maybe a couple days a month?" Lucy said. Her hand went to the cameo at her neck, and I wondered if she were regretting the offer.

I'd found reading the old letters and learning about Clarissa amazingly interesting. It might be fun to learn more about the history of this area and the Rothmeres. Mind you, I didn't want to turn into Lucy, half convinced I was a Rothmere, or even Mom's beau Walter Highsmith, who spent weekends reenacting Civil War battles, but it wouldn't hurt to become more familiar with the rhythms of plantation life that had shaped St. Elizabeth society and culture. Maybe I'd start by looking up Althea's great-whatever-granny Matilda.

"Deal," I said, surprising Lucy and myself.

I LEFT LUCY IN HER OFFICE AND WANDERED BACK TO the main hall. Laughter came from the dining room down the hall, and I figured Mom and Althea had hooked up with the television people. I didn't see Agent Dillon and I wondered where Hank had sequestered Mark and his father and where Hank's partner had taken Lindsay. The hurricane still raged outside, rain swishing against the weathered oak boards of the house, and wind ricocheting through the tree limbs, down the chimneys, and against the windows. Carefully avoiding the cables that still crisscrossed the foyer and trailed up the stairs, I mounted the staircase, drawn to the portrait of Cyril and his family.

Before I reached the landing, a shout came from above me. "She's gone! Agent Dillon, the Tandy girl escaped."

# Chapter Twenty-three

SUDDENLY DILLON WAS BESIDE ME AND WE CHARGED up the stairs. Up here, closer to the roof, the rain sounded louder, pounding like a million woodpeckers trying to drill through the slate. I followed Dillon as he ran down the hall toward the distraught officer. Medium height with strong biceps swelling the short sleeves of her blue uniform, Officer Ally Qualls had short dark hair and wore a guilt-ridden expression.

"She needed to go to the bathroom, sir," Officer Qualls said as Dillon slid to a halt. "I didn't think—It's a hurricane! She climbed out the window."

"Damn it," Dillon said forcefully. "She could die out there. Those slate tiles have got to be slicker than ice with all the rain, and the winds . . ."

"I know, sir. I'm sorry. I should have gone in with her."

The cop met Dillon's gaze for a moment, then let her head droop.

Dillon didn't waste time chewing her out. "Find Parker. Have him meet me outside. We'll scan the roof, see if we can find the girl. You call the fire department and see if they can get a ladder truck out here. If they're tied up with storm emergencies, call a tree-trimming company—anyone who might have a cherry picker we could use to retrieve the girl from the roof."

Officer Qualls was already contacting the dispatcher as Dillon wheeled and thudded down the stairs. His foot caught on one of the cables and he lurched forward, grabbing the handrail. I followed him, stepping into the foyer as he wrenched open the front door and wind gusted in. Our eyes met for a moment as he turned to heave the door closed, and I said, "Be careful." I couldn't tell if he heard me.

Knowing Officer Qualls was still upstairs, I ran from room to room calling for Hank until I found him in what must have been a music room, keeping watch over the Crenshaws. An antique piano held pride of place in the room, with a harp backed into a corner.

"Dillon needs you," I gasped. "Lindsay . . . roof."

Hank didn't hesitate and I had to admit he wasn't a coward. Directing a terse, "Stay put," at Mark and his dad, Hank strode from the room. I heard the door open and slam shut again and felt the draft from the wind, even thirty yards away from the entrance.

I turned to go, but Mark's hand on my arm stopped me. "What's happened?" he asked, his dark eyes searching mine. "What's happened to Lindsay?"

"She escaped," I said. "Out a second-story window."

"Oh my God," Eric Crenshaw said. He rose from the

chair he'd been sitting on and put an arm around Mark's shoulders. "She'll be okay, son."

Mark shot him an incredulous look. "There's a hurricane out there, in case you hadn't noticed. She will not be 'okay' unless we can get her down."

"There's nothing you can do," Crenshaw said. "Officer Parker told us to stay here."

"Screw that." Mark pushed past me and into the hall.

I caught up with him as he started up the stairs toward a startled Officer Qualls, who was still on the phone. "I know there's flooding," she was saying, "but this is a police emergency."

The response obviously angered her because she flipped the phone closed sharply and faced Mark with her holster unsnapped. "Back off."

Mark raised his hands to shoulder height, placatingly. "I just want to see where she went."

Officer Qualls exchanged a look with me and then shrugged. "The bathroom down here." She led the way past a couple of bedrooms to a small bathroom on the north side of the house. A toilet with a wooden seat and water tank above it, a sink with chipped porcelain, and a claw-footed tub sat surrounded by mildewed aqua tiles, someone's unfortunate remodeling job, which the Rothmere Trust hadn't been able to return to period authenticity yet. Although, I wasn't sure what "authentic" meant in terms of nineteenth-century toilets. An outhouse? A hole in a bench? When had flush toilets become a standard-issue item in upper-class houses?

Mark lunged toward the window and struggled to push the sash up, breaking my pointless train of thought. Wind drove rain at us and I gasped at the hurricane's fury in the confined space. Officer Qualls grabbed at Mark, her hand snagging in his belt, as if afraid he were going to follow Lindsay out the window. "I'm only looking," he said with an impatient glance over his shoulder.

Having learned her lesson, Officer Qualls kept her hold on him as he stuck his head and shoulders out the window, craning his neck first left and then right. He pulled his head back in, like a turtle ducking into its shell, and looked at us with worried eyes. Water dripped from his brows and eyelashes. "I don't see her. Do you think she fell?" Water slid off his bald head and spattered on the floor. I handed him a dingy towel from a ring by the sink and he swabbed it over his head and neck.

"They'd've found her if she fell," Officer Qualls said pragmatically.

"How could she be so stupid?" Mark cried, turning to stare out the window again. The lightning had moved past us and flickered from farther north, illuminating billowing clouds. The wind still blew with the force of the Atlantic behind it, and I didn't know how anyone could cling to the roof for a minute, never mind the ten or so minutes that Lindsay had now been out there.

A thought came to me. Lindsay wasn't stupid. Desperate, yes; stupid, no. Even if she'd clambered out the window impulsively, seizing the opportunity to escape without planning for it, mere seconds on the roof must have convinced her she couldn't make it to the ground. Not in this weather. Not with climbing handholds like gutters slicked with rain. She might have lodged herself someplace relatively secure, like against a chimney, and planned to ride out the storm, or . . .

I slipped out of the bathroom, unnoticed by Mark and Officer Qualls, and made my way down to the next room on the same side of the hall. A bedroom. Bare. Window closed. The next room down was the room where Glen and I had found Lindsay's sheet. I pushed the door and it yielded with a whine. Cautiously, I poked my head into the room. Nothing looked different. The bed with the rag doll sat undisturbed. The window was closed. The armoire was closed. I turned to leave, wondering if I'd guessed wrong, when something caught my eye. A footprint. A wet footprint in the middle of the rag rug by the bed. My gaze drifted to the armoire, the only hiding place in the room. Should I leave to summon Officer Qualls and risk having Lindsay escape to the roof again, or should I talk to the girl and convince her to turn herself in?

I compromised. Tiptoeing to the armoire, I leaned my back against it, bracing myself, and yelled, "Officer Qualls! Ally! She's in here."

The doors bucked, bruising my back and behind. Running footsteps pounded down the hall. "In here," I called as the doors banged against me with such force I went flying onto my hands and knees. Dang. I really needed to work out more. Looking over my shoulder, I saw that Lindsay had braced herself against the back of the armoire, drawn her knees to her chest, and exploded her legs against the doors. Now, she tumbled from the armoire, arms and legs sprawling, but quickly leaped to her feet. She turned toward the bedroom door, hesitated as the footsteps drew nearer, then lurched toward the window.

"Don't!" I shouted. Unable to get much purchase on the smooth wood floor, I flung myself sideways toward Lindsay, stretching an arm out as she threw up the window sash. My hand snagged around her ankle.

"Let me go!" She kicked out at me, like a mail carrier trying to detach a Rottweiler from her leg. Her foot connected with my jaw, and my teeth snapped together with a crunch that reverberated up through my temples and down my neck. I felt my hand slipping off her ankle and clutched desperately at the hem of her jeans.

"Let go. I will stomp you like that squirrel, you nosy bitch." She raised her foot and aimed at my face. I rolled but still caught a blow on my cheek that made me see stars.

The door burst open and suddenly a crowd of people— Mark, Officer Qualls, Dillon, Hank—surged into the room. Mark rushed to Lindsay and grabbed her around the waist. She strained against him for a moment, then collapsed into his arms, sobbing. I flopped onto my back, dazed and bruised, happy to lie still.

Dillon came and stood over me, smiling slightly. He was drenched and water sluiced off him, spattering me. He reached down a hand, but I ignored it for a moment, not up to moving.

"How'd you know?" I asked. "That she was up here?" I gazed up at him, liking his face with its crooked nose and strong jaw from this upside-down perspective.

"No body on the ground," he said succinctly. "So being the experienced detective that I am, I figured she snuck back into the house. C'mon."

He leaned over and hooked his hands under my armpits, hauling me to a sitting position. Our faces were close together and the look in his blue eyes, a mix of concern and appreciation, warmed me. I put a finger to a bruise blossoming on his forehead.

"Tree branch," he said.

Hank had hauled Lindsay away from Mark and was cuffing her hands behind her back. The clink of the metal cuffs sliding together brought my head up. It was quiet. Still. The wind had stopped. Rain no longer thrummed against the house. As if we all noticed it at the same time, we looked toward the window.

"It's the eye," Hank said.

The eye of a hurricane is a calm space in the middle of the storm with light winds and little precipitation. I didn't know what caused it, but Mom always said it was the storm taking a rest before socking you again with winds blowing from the opposite direction.

"Let's take advantage of it," Dillon said, helping me clamber to my feet. "We might have twenty or thirty minutes. Get Miss Tandy and the Crenshaws down to the station." Hank and his partner hustled the young pair out the door.

I stepped into the hall, intending to find Althea and Mom, but something drew me toward the opposite wing and the portrait.

The corridor grew dimmer as I left the landing and the huge chandelier behind. I didn't know where the light switches were in this part of the house—I guessed I'd find out when I did docent training—but it didn't matter. I didn't need to see the painting clearly. I stopped six inches in front of it, barely able to make out the figures, and closed my eyes. The rain had faded to a delicate plinking with no more force than tears. Weariness dragged at me. It had been a brutal week, emotionally and physically, and although I was thrilled that Braden was going to be okay, I was sad about Clarissa's untimely death and the knowledge that Lindsay's life—and maybe Mark's—was ruined by a moment's impulsive action. She probably hadn't planned to kill Braden, but when he refused to give in to her pleas, she'd snapped and pushed him, just like she'd snapped when she saw me in the car with Mark. And when she'd heard that he was being moved from ICU to a regular hospital room, she must have thought that meant he was coming out of the coma. Fear of what he might say when he recovered consciousness drove her to try to smother him, I figured. That was much harder to forgive or understand than the impulsive striking out on the landing. And the knowledge that his girlfriend had tried to kill his best friend wasn't going to ease Mark Crenshaw's depression, either. The whole thing was a mess. I sighed.

A slight sound alerted me to someone's presence. I froze, then recognized the familiar scent of soap, lime aftershave, and warm male. Relaxing, I breathed in deeply through my nose, trying not to be too obvious about it. I wondered if my sense of smell were more acute because it was so dark that I couldn't see much.

"I thought I might find you here," Dillon said. He stood close enough that I could feel the warmth of his body.

I could barely make out the distinctive line of his profile, and I felt rather than saw the strong expanse of shoulder and solid torso. "Just thinking," I said.

"Sometimes solving a case doesn't bring a whole lot of satisfaction."

"No." I didn't want to talk about the present and the wreck of several teenage lives. "I think Cyril was poisoned," I said, gesturing toward the painting.

"How do you figure?"

I told him about the letters and my deductions and the tests Stuart Varnet was going to run. "I don't think Cyril was pushed. I think someone was poisoning him and he fell, weakened or dizzied by the poison. That would account for the vomit the maid observed."

"That's fascinating," Dillon said with real interest.

"It is," I agreed. "But even if we prove conclusively that he was poisoned, we still won't know who killed him."

"Who the hell is Annabelle?" The voice drifted up from the main hall. After a moment, I identified it as Bruce, the actor impersonating Cyril Rothmere's ghost.

"The damn name keeps popping into my head, like a song I can't get rid of. Is anyone here named Annabelle?" Bruce sounded peevish.

I looked at Dillon, wide-eyed. "Do you think—?"

"That the spirit of Cyril possessed that actor and fed him the name of his murderer?"

I twisted my mouth sideways. "It sounds silly when you put it like that, but—"

"Anything is possible."

I felt his smile in the darkness.

"You'd better get going if you're going to make it home while it's calm." His warm hand on my shoulder turned me toward the landing and he moved with me to the top of the stairs. As I started down, less tired than I'd been only minutes before, he called after me, "Hey."

I looked back. His blue eyes glinted.

"I'm sorry about Friday night. Can I have a rain check?"

"Hurricane check." I smiled. "You know where to find me."

Reaching the bottom of the stairs, I almost bumped into Bruce, the actor. I stepped back as he muttered. "Annabelle, Annabelle, Annabelle. Jesus!"

# Chapter Twenty-four

✂

THURSDAY DAWNED BRIGHT AND SUNNY, AND YOU'D'VE never known Horatio had come through except for the detritus in the yards and streets, people sweeping water out of their garages, a live electric line sparking and whipping in the street like an angry cobra, and the huge magnolia limb that had smashed through the veranda roof and into Violetta's salon.

Mom and I surveyed the damage the next morning, me with a cream cheese–smeared bagel in one hand and Mom with a mug of coffee. Althea had gone home at first light to check on her bungalow after we listened to news updates that said no deaths had been reported during the storm and only minor flooding had occurred in low-lying areas near the river. Thank goodness! The wet grass was crisp and cool under my bare feet and the air smelled clean and fresh, all mugginess washed away. I knew it would return with a vengeance as rain-wetted items mildewed and rotted, and the sun steamed water from drenched foliage, but I enjoyed the freshness now. A crinkly sound from overhead brought my gaze up, and I noted plastic grocery bags flapping in the uppermost limbs of the trees in our yard and the neighbors' yards, pennants planted by Hurricane Horatio to claim the high ground.

Mom took a long swallow of coffee and sighed. "I suppose it could be worse."

The large branch had crushed the veranda roof and smashed one of the two plate glass windows that fronted the salon, despite its plywood covering. Glass glittered in the strong morning light. My styling chair lay knocked on its side, and I was sure rain had damaged the heart-of-pine floorboards. Still, insurance would cover most of the repairs and no one was hurt. The house would be livable once Fred nailed wood over the gaping hole so people couldn't come and go as they pleased. We'd spent the night upstairs—I'd dropped off much quicker than I thought I would—but I didn't want Mom sleeping here again until the house was looter-proof.

The magnolia tree had a gaping wound where the limb had been, and the sight saddened me. As a child, I'd spent many a day tucked into the crook where the limb met the trunk.

"Think it'll be okay?" I asked Mom, nodding at the tree.

She examined it, putting a hand against the blackened wood. That, plus the lingering odor of sulfur and campfire, convinced me lightning had severed the branch. "It's like it's been cauterized," she said. "I think it'll be fine. This is a tough old tree." She patted it.

"Not as tough as you are, Mom." I put an arm around her shoulders and squeezed.

She laughed. "Is that like calling me a tough old buzzard?"

"Not even close." I crept up to the veranda steps, careful to avoid the glass that lay like a skim of sparkly wax on the veranda and sidewalk, and peered into the salon's soggy interior. "I guess Violetta's is out of business for a week or two."

"Oh, I don't know about that," Mom said, joining me. "Maybe we can go back to cutting hair in the kitchen, like I did in the old days."

"That's a thought," I said doubtfully. Mom's clientele had expanded in the years since she and Althea did cuts and facials in the kitchen, and I couldn't see customers dangling their heads over the kitchen sink for a shampoo while others sat around the kitchen table.

Mom caught my expression and laughed. "Or maybe not. Finish that bagel, Grace Ann, and pick up a broom. We've got a lot of work to do today."

She moved toward the house, but I walked to my car where it sat at the curb, liberally plastered with wet oak leaves but luckily undamaged. Looking for the tennies I was sure I'd tossed in, I patted a hand across the nappy carpet in the foot well. A piece of paper under the passenger seat crackled when my hand brushed it. Extracting it, I smoothed a wrinkle from the photocopied page. My gaze fell to the familiar handwriting.

*14 October 1832*

*My dear Felicity,*

*As you predicted, I have been delivered of a boy, Quentin Cyril Dodd. My heart swells with love for him and I understand most clearly now how you dote on young Robert and my darling goddaughter Emily. Quentin is so pleased to have an heir that he has presented me with a string of lustrous pearls, which I cannot wait to show you. He is so generous to me and I do love him so.*

*When I look back over the past year, I almost feel like I'm leading a different life. In only twelve months I have travelled from the grief of my father's death to the comfort of my husband's home and the joy of birthing my son. In my new life, I don't mind so much that mother is now Mrs. Angus Carlisle. We rarely correspond these days, and although I miss Rothmere—South Carolina seems so far away—my life is here with Quentin and his people.*

*Congratulations to Andrew on his election to the state house. Mayhap I'll visit you in the governor's mansion one day.*

*Your dear friend,*
*Clarissa Dodd*

Laying the page carefully on the seat, I hooked two fingers into my tennies and started toward the house, comforted by Clarissa's happiness and her apparent recovery from her stomach problems. It had crossed my mind reading the earlier letters that Annabelle—if it was, indeed, Annabelle who poisoned her husband—was poisoning her own daughter because she was poking into her father's death. If so, marrying Quentin quickly had probably saved Clarissa's life. Killing a husband was one thing—by all accounts Cyril was no saint, not that his philandering justified murder—but poisoning a daughter! Lucy Mortimer might romanticize the Rothmeres, but Annabelle, at least, sounded like a real piece of work to me. Lucy's likely protest popped immediately into my mind: "But she was only a Rothmere *by marriage*." I smiled.

A clump of black and white caught my eye, and I bent to pick up a water-logged stuffed penguin from the lawn where it had blown from who-knows-where. Feeling its heaviness in my hand, I thought about the time and energy it takes to build a house or a relationship and how swiftly a hurricane or an infidelity can turn it to rubble. Or how geographical distance or ongoing slights and abuse can erode a relationship more slowly, like termites chewing at a home's foundation. But I believed almost anything could be rebuilt. Shoot, Georgians had rebuilt the entire state after Sherman razed it. And look how Cyril rebuilt Rothmere after it burned, how Braden had come back strong and compassionate after his bouts with depression (and would, hopefully, fully recover from his fall), how Mom and Althea had started Violetta's after their husbands' deaths.

Patching drywall and wood was the easiest form of rebuilding, I thought, padding around the side of the house to drag a trash can around front. Wounded souls and relationships, on the other hand . . .

My cell phone rang and an incautious step sent mud squishing coolly between my toes. I wiggled them. "Hello?"

"I'm in Atlanta and thought I'd drive down for the weekend," Marty said, a smile in his voice. "I heard a rumor about a hurricane down there. Need any help with cleanup?"

"I don't know." I pretended to hesitate. "Know anyone with a carpentry background and strong muscles for hauling tree limbs out of salons?"

"That's me. Hammer wielder and chainsaw operator extraordinaire. And I'm a good kisser, too."

Sunlight warmed my face. "Come on down."

Slipping the phone back in my pocket, I squeezed water out of the soggy penguin, letting it rinse the mud from between my toes. Clean felt good. I set the penguin on an unbroken section of veranda railing where he could supervise cleanup operations, and balanced on one foot at a time to lace up my shoes, sockless. Then I walked toward Mom, who was coming around the side of the house with a broom in one hand and a shovel in the other. Time to get to it.

# Althea's Top Ten
# Skincare Beauty Tips

1. Cleanse. Do not ever go to bed with your make-up on, girlfriend; it will age you beyond your years.
2. Moisturize. If you are over twelve years old, your skin needs moisture. Find a product made for your skin type—dry, oily, or combination—and use it daily.
3. Sunblock. Put it on in the morning before you ever leave the house. Slather it on your face, hands, neck, ears, arms—any exposed skin. If you're young enough, it'll help keep you from getting those ugly brown spots on your face and hands. Even if you baked yourself in your youth, before we knew what we know now about sun damage, using sunblock every day can help the skin repair itself.
4. Wear a hat.
5. Sleep. Yep. It may not come in a bottle with a fancy label, but eight hours of shut-eye does your skin more good than any ten products put together.
6. Use a night cream. While you're sleeping (and away from the sun) is the best time to use a skincare product to repair lines, spots, general sagginess, and loss of youthful color and texture.

7. See a dermatologist. Skin cancer (melanoma) can kill you. See a dermatologist annually if you're over forty, have a family history of skin cancer, or got lots of sun exposure young.
8. Did I mention sunblock?
9. Drink. Water, that is. Hydration is key to a dewy complexion.
10. Don't forget that Althea's Organic Skincare Solutions has a product for every need!

**For more about the Southern Beauty Shop Mysteries, visit www.liladare.com.**

# Cozy up with Berkley Prime Crime

## SUSAN WITTIG ALBERT
*Don't miss the national bestselling series featuring herbalist China Bayles.*

## LAURA CHILDS
*The Tea Shop Mysteries are the toast of Charleston, South Carolina.*

## KATE KINGSBURY
*The Pennyfoot Hotel Mystery series is a teatime delight.*

**For the armchair detective in you.**

penguin.com

M6G0708

# Searching for the perfect mystery?

Looking for a place to get the latest clues
and connect with fellow fans?

## "Like" The Crime Scene on Facebook!

- Participate in author chats
- Enter book giveaways
- Learn about the latest releases
- Get book recommendations
- Send mystery-themed gifts
  to friends and more!

**facebook.com/TheCrimeSceneBooks**

Obsidian

M884G0511